Team

Penny Priest is a mum, retired consultant clinical psychologist, singer, songwriter, Ironman, writer, and one of five members of the Midlands Psychology Group (midpsy.uk). This is her first novel.

Novels get to the parts that psychology textbooks cannot reach and there is no technical fix to human misery. Priest makes both points very well.

– David Pilgrim, Professor of Clinical Psychology

PENNY PRIEST

Team of One

Beware the latest fashion!
Penny Priest

EGALITARIAN PUBLISHING

EGALITARIAN PUBLISHING

Published by Egalitarian Publishing Ltd.
UK Company no. 12501497
Registered office: 7 Wagon Road, Lower Dolphinholme Lancaster, England, LA2 9AX

www.egalitarianpublishing.com

Copyright 2024 by Penny Priest
All rights reserved.

No part of this publication may be reproduced, distributed, or transmitted in any form or by any means, including photocopying, recording, or other electronic or mechanical methods, without the prior written permission of the publisher. For permission requests, please contact the publisher.

The story, all names, characters, and incidents portrayed in this production are fictitious. No identification with actual persons (living or deceased), places, buildings, and products is intended or should be inferred.

Typeset in Cormorant Garamond
Cover art by Penny Priest

Production Editor Ben Donner

Printed, bound and distributed by Bookvault (Copytech UK Ltd.)

British Library Cataloguing in Publication data
A catalogue record for this book is available on request from the British Library.

ISBN: 978-1-8380636-4-1

For Sheilagh Mary Cecilia Priest, former Catholic nun, English teacher, mother, gardener, tree-lover, would-be-novelist, socialist, feminist, rebel. Forever the wind at my back.
1932 – 2003

and

For David Smail, professor of clinical psychology, jazz drummer and coiner of outsight.
1938 -2014

Prologue

This is a story about what really happens in the psychological therapy industry. Many of the characters' experiences are based on real events. There really was a legal case where a therapy creator claimed trademark infringement. There really was a woman with cancer who got hooked on a reality TV show. There really was a little boy who was ashamed about his school lunch box. There really is a place where the sunset over the river takes your breath away. There really are mental health services where workers are hot-desking and sometimes can't find rooms to see patients in. There really are mental health group skills programmes where the members support each other but struggle to find the benefits of mindfulness practice. There really are hundreds of different psychological therapies. There really is a poor evidence base for many psychological therapies, but often therapists go along as if that was not the case. There really are people who believe that positive thinking can change reality. There really are people who experience violence and abuse every day, but instead of them being protected and the abuse being stopped, they are offered therapy. There really is a world where we are made to think that our problems are of our own making and that the solutions reside in ourselves.

I

We want to improve the current mental health services across Yewton and Ludfordshire and we need your help to do it right. Under our current system, people are referred to Community Mental Health Services but have to wait fifty-five months to be seen.

The brisk and confident tenor narrating the video spoke to the crowded meeting room. Frances imagined the voice belonged to a corporate type, in a suit, with perfectly groomed hair and expensive aftershave. In other contexts, there might have been open mouths and a collective gasp in response to the apparently shocking fifty-five months statistic, but it was old news to the team. Frances was aware from the quarterly returns that her own team's waiting times were more like three years rather than the four and a half claimed in the video. She was also well aware that this overstatement was a tactic to get people on board with how dire the current system was and why it therefore needed substantial improvement. Improvement that most of the people in the room seemed to be in agreement with, all apart from her.

'This is disingenuous!' Frances called out at the end of the video, which concluded by inviting people to take part in a consultation. 'It's already been decided that group work is going to be standard for all referrals to our service. Why pretend that we're involving people in the decision? Staff haven't even been involved in the decision! We're just copying what they're doing everywhere else in the country. This isn't going to help waiting times and it isn't going to help people feel any better. I won't be asking anyone I'm working with to get involved in this. I know you've heard it all before from me but I'm not going to stop saying it!'

'Frances, we really need to have everybody on board with this. We need the expertise of senior clinicians like yourself, especially with groups. We know it's not ideal but how else are we going to deal with our massive backlog?' Hayley, the team leader was generally very polite to Frances. It was probably in large part due to her youth in the face of Frances' advancing years. Hayley was seen as a bright young thing in the organisation, becoming team leader at the age of twenty-six, only three years after graduating as an occupational therapist. She had bags of energy and was very keen but, in Frances' opinion, hopelessly naïve and far too ready to toe the corporate line.

'Actually, Hayley, I beg to differ. I think moving to group work is a great thing,' Jason piped up. 'We've been getting fantastic results in our Zen Psyonics groups.' At forty-five, Jason was wiry, fit, pierced, tattooed and old enough to be Hayley's father, though not quite young enough to be Frances' son. He turned to her now. 'I was sceptical before moving people from individual work into a group but I swear there've been so many added benefits. All the things you've always talked about, Frances, like learning from each other, like the comfort of others and the power of the group.'

'So they don't need to be Zen Psyonics groups then, Jason. We could do gardening and writing and music and whatever anyone else suggests during the consultation', Frances came back.

'But we're a mental health service, Frances. We provide therapy, not leisure activities!'

'But you know very well, Jason, you just said yourself that the benefits come from being with other people. It doesn't matter what they do together.'

'I didn't say that, Frances. I was acknowledging the *added* benefits. But it's the Zen Psyonics which is fundamental to the therapeutic change. The evidence base is very strong. And I've been getting near enough a one hundred percent success rate with my patients.'

Frances took a long, slow breath in and fell silent. The fight was still within her but increasingly these days she noticed a feeling of futility engaging in these sorts of discussions, if they could be called that. Her husband, David, had told her time and again that she shouldn't be surprised and she should remember Brett Sanders, the American writer. Every time Frances arrived home claiming how much she despaired of the status quo, David would repeat Sanders's quote, 'It proves challenging to enlighten a person about a matter when their income relies on them remaining oblivious to it.' That observation could be applied to many people working in mental health services, including Jason, but in her experience, Jason was even worse than wanting to remain oblivious to hard facts. Not only did he have no time for anything Frances had to say, but he often actively sought to discredit her, telling others that her tendency for critique was because she was no good as a therapist and had no clue what she was doing when it came to the latest psychological therapies. Frances knew he said these things about her because he had recorded as much in clinical case notes, following conversations with patients who had been re-referred after seeing her. Far from seeming to care that Frances might come across some of these notes at some point, it was almost as if he *wanted* her to see them, so that she would know that both he, and some patients apparently, didn't rate her as being any good at her job.

Now that Frances had shut up, the team had quickly moved on and were ironing out the finer details about who would be running the new groups and when they would start. Frances couldn't be bothered to point out that the consultation with people referred to the service hadn't even started yet. What would happen if people were not in agreement with these new plans?

Frances knew from her own patients that many were well

aware the groups were going to be happening and that the consultation was just a tokenistic nod, in order to fulfil targets proving they had involved patients in the process. She also knew that whilst people she saw would often say they were willing to try anything that would help, they were also worried about what would happen if they didn't find the group work helpful. Many patients were quite savvy, as well as quite desperate to feel better. This often led them on trawls of the internet to find out what they needed to do to fix themselves and what sorts of treatment were recommended. Some would end up connecting with other patients through social media and reports would emerge about treatment in different parts of the country. There were horror stories about people being processed through mental health services as if they were on a production line, shunted into groups with facilitators who had no professional qualifications and given handbooks with sweeping statements like 'your brain doesn't work in the same way as other people's', with rules about attendance and homework and non-compliance being punished with discharge from the service. Still, Frances had relayed all this sort of thing to the team when they first started talking about how they would have to run groups. And it just floated out into the ether.

The discussion rumbled on and Frances had lost track of where they had got to, when someone poked their head around the door saying the room needed to be vacated for another team who had booked it. It was lunchtime, if that was even a thing in this workplace, and everyone trundled back to the main office, taking up positions at their workstations, those that had been lucky enough to find one for the day. Most people immediately got back to work on their laptops, responding to emails or writing notes. A few had impromptu catch-ups about particular patients, all within earshot of anyone nearby, though of course, confidentiality was assumed because they were all members of the same team.

Frances deliberately kept her laptop closed and got her sandwiches out, along with a flask of coffee. How lamentable that actually stopping work to have lunch now seemed to be an act of subversion. She found herself pondering Brett Sanders and his wisdom, when Margaret, her favourite nurse in the team, came by and settled into the chair at the adjacent workstation which, unusually, was free.

'What would I do without you, Fran?' Margaret pleaded. 'I know you get fed up saying the same old thing again and again but honestly, it makes me feel better even if you think it doesn't achieve anything. It's so important to keep saying it.'

'Thanks Margaret. I keep telling myself that it will all come out in the wash eventually but the longer time goes on, the crazier things get and I'll probably be dead before anyone significant wakes up and calls attention to the emperor's new clothes. But anyway,' Frances sighed heavily, 'it does help to know I'm not on my own.' She laid a hand on Margaret's arm. 'Have you been assigned to a group then?'

'Yes I have. But,' Margaret hushed her voice. 'I've told Hayley that I'm against the groups for all the same reasons as you and that I will be leaving if she insists on me being involved. I think she thinks it's just all talk but in actual fact, Fran,' Margaret scanned the nearby workstations to check nobody was listening in, 'I've got my resignation letter in my bag. I was speaking with Jim at the weekend. He knows I've been unhappy at work for the longest time, but especially since Hayley arrived. We can afford for me to leave. And I've been approached by the local GPs who want me to do some clinics at the surgery so hopefully that will be enough for us to keep ticking over until I can draw my pension.'

Frances smiled sadly at Margaret. 'You were just asking what you would do without me. What am *I* going to do without *you*, Margaret?'

'I know, Fran. I'm sorry. But I just can't do this anymore. It's sucking all the life out of me. I don't want to be carried out of here on a stretcher. I've still got some heart for this work and I want to use it, not wither away like a tired old neglected plant. That's what he makes me feel like, you know, Fran. Jason makes me feel like a dying, wilting thing and as if he's some splendid

5

bird of paradise flower in comparison!'

'Well, Margaret, it's a shame you're not a virulent form of bindweed, going to choke him out, clearing the space for me to reach the sun before you escape.'

Margaret laughed. 'But you don't need any bindweed, Fran. You're a beautiful, tall tree, touching the light!'

Now it was Frances's turn to laugh. 'Don't get carried away, Margaret. If I am a tree, I'm a gnarled, knobbly runt of a thing!'

'But you know as well as I do, Fran. The strongest tree in the forest is the one that has had to struggle for its existence.'

'Enough, Margaret! Motivational quotes stray way too close to Zen Psyonics for my liking! It's crazy that Jason has that effect on us both. We're highly experienced, highly qualified clinicians and we do a great job, especially protecting our patients from all this nonsense. I guess he makes us feel bad because we know that he thinks we're behind the times and don't know anything much about the wonders of modern therapies. That's what's irritating. Because it's actually he who is naïve and lacking in any critical faculties. You know David refers to him as *born-again Jason, the born-again therapist.* He reckons he had a conversion experience when he met Alexander McDonald on that surf beach. He thinks Alexander McDonald is like a cult leader and Jason has fallen under his spell!'

'David's right, Fran. What's that thing you always say? About holding your ideas lightly? That's the very opposite of what Jason's doing and exactly what you would find in a cult! Have you noticed how dismissive he is if you try to question his practice? He is so sure he has seen the light and we have yet to see it for ourselves!'

'Well, you know what I think, Margaret. I think the same about most therapies, not just Zen Psyonics. You know I keep a little list of all the latest entrants to the market. Practically every letter of the alphabet is covered! Most of the western world has been duped into this cult of therapy. There's a whole load of gurus out there, vying for your custom, selling their apparently exclusive, distinctive wares. And yet when you look at them all, they're all just variations on the same theme. What makes one therapy better than another? Marketing, probably! And there's a whole load of tax payers' money being spent on this nonsense!'

'Aw but Fran, you know it's not all a waste of money. I wouldn't be doing this job if I thought it was, and neither would you.'

'Maybe so, but it's getting more and more like we're required to be agents of social control, especially with these groups, basically promoting conformity and *modifying* people into something society thinks they should be, rather than actually helping people. It makes me wonder how much longer we'll be allowed to work with our patients in the ways that we think will be most helpful. We're only able to carry on doing what we do by keeping under the radar and calling it something apparently legitimate, like cognitive behavioural therapy.'

'Anyway, Fran, I hate to cut this short but I've got to go. I've got a patient in two minutes. Don't let the buggers get you down, my treasure!'

Frances put her lunch box and flask away and opened up her laptop. There already, at the top of her inbox, was an email from Jason letting her know that she was to be the lead facilitator for Life Skills Group Two, and asking for her to clear a space in her diary in order to get the group under way as soon as possible. She raised her eyebrows, to no-one other than herself, wondering how the situation had moved so quickly from the discussion about the patient consultation, to her actually being named as a lead facilitator, despite her numerous and vocal protests. Not only was the consultation not an actual consultation, but now it seemed that disagreement of any form was entirely meaningless. It was as if she hadn't even been present during any of the meetings where this had repeatedly been discussed and she had repeatedly voiced her objections. Is this how it was now, then? That challenges to any activities that had already been decided on, were simply batted away like negative automatic thoughts? Those pesky NATs were to be paid no attention whatsoever and new paths would be furrowed, just like those new neural pathways forged by diligent patients of CBT, trampling on any troublesome ruminations that dared get in the way. Let nothing impede the path to progress! These groups were the promise of a swift and effective cure for every single one of the burgeoning list of modern mental health problems racking up in the latest diagnostic and statistical manual!

Frances closed her eyes and took another long slow breath in, saying to herself, *I am rooted*. She slowly breathed out, saying, *I am strong*, and was just reaching the end of her breath out when Jason's voice shattered the peace.

Attentional Regulation Therapy

Attentional Regulation Therapy (ART) was developed in the late 1990s, as an approach to treat anxiety, and subsequently expanded as a general treatment approach. It is backed by scientific evidence from a wide range of studies. It targets the common experience in psychiatric disorders where thinking becomes difficult to control and attention is biased in ways that lead to increased and prolonged emotional distress. ART recognises how thinking patterns have become fixed, leading to potential behavioural solutions becoming part of the problem.

Through therapy it is necessary to remove fixed cognitive patterns by developing new ways of directing attention towards cognitions and by modifying the beliefs that give rise to the unhelpful cognitive patterns, thereby allowing space for new, regulated and adaptive cognitions which lead to more productive behaviours.

ART has been developed into specific ways of understanding and treating disorders such as generalised anxiety disorder, post-traumatic stress, obsessive-compulsive disorder, social anxiety, depression and health-anxiety.

2

It was a seven out of ten kind of day, Jason thought to himself as he filed out of the team room along with the others. He felt buoyed by the authority Hayley was giving him to get the Life Skills groups off the ground. Admittedly, it felt a little strange, and almost *lesser*, to have this conferred by someone who was young enough to be his daughter. But at this point, he was happy to take all the seniority on offer as it was *his* time now to really play his part in transforming mental health services, even if it was only locally. What would it take to lift that seven to an eight, he asked himself? Undoubtedly, if he could only bring Frances Fisher on board, where others had failed for years, *that* would really be something to celebrate.

He found a free desk at the end of the office near the team managers' workstations and set about composing an email to all those staff he and Hayley had identified for running the groups. He decided he would take a counter-intuitive kind of tactic, going along with Frances' sense that the groups were a done deal, instead of reassuring her that everything was still up for discussion. That way, he would not be demeaning her further by performing some sort of dance of negotiation only to arrive finally at the same position, the *only* position, which was that the groups were going to happen. He would spare her the humiliation and instead give her the opportunity to be an equal partner in this transformation. He would appeal to her years of experience and wisdom, though he really did struggle to understand what her beef so often was. She was getting paid more than him and on paper was way more qualified (for goodness sake, she was a *doctor of psychology!*) and yet it seemed she couldn't grasp many of the fundamental concepts of Zen Psyonics and certainly wasn't using them in her practice, as far as he could tell. He wasn't sure if she actually had fundamental gaps in her knowledge or if it was more a case of wilful ignorance. She just didn't want to understand. Actually not unlike his daughter, Layne, who, at nine years old, could be quite stubborn when she didn't want to know something.

Down the other end of the main office concourse, Jason could see Frances and Margaret huddled closely together, no doubt picking apart the bones of the team meeting. He could tell that Margaret wouldn't be staying for long as her bags were fully packed down by the sides of her chair and sure enough, she was now getting up to go, squeezing Frances' shoulder. Jason would give Frances a moment so that she would see the email and be primed for him.

As he approached, he observed Frances to be in some sort of meditative state. Maybe she hadn't looked at the email after all. Her eyes were closed and she seemed oblivious to the general office hustle. He didn't want to interrupt her if she really was taking some time out for a Five Minute Breathing Space. Gosh, maybe some of his staff training had actually gone in and she wasn't so averse to it after all. But perhaps now would therefore be a good time for dialogue, especially if she was calmer for the breathing. Plus, there was an empty chair which Margaret had just vacated, ready and waiting for him.

'Sorry to interrupt you, Frances', Jason said boldly. 'Have you got a minute?'

Frances slowly opened her eyes and looked mildly annoyed, understandably, Jason thought, if maybe she had been settling in for the *Ten* Minute Breathing Space.

'You're here to schmooze me about the groups, I expect, Jason.'

He found her directness quite disconcerting. It wasn't that he was uncomfortable with people being direct. In fact he generally liked to take that approach himself, particularly with patients, as he felt it was important to have clarity and not dance around the edges of things, which could create too much room for confusion and misunderstanding. No, it was more that Frances's directness had an authoritative quality to it, as if she was positioning herself as senior to him. Which she was of course, in both age and pay grade. But she wasn't senior to him in her knowledge and expertise in Zen Psyonics. In fact, she had very much chosen to have as little to do with Zen Psyonics as possible. He struggled to understand just what in fact her problem was with it. Whenever they had discussed it, whether in team meetings or just between the two of them, she would usually trot out the same line about the evidence base, dismissing everything in the clinical guidelines and writing off not just Zen Psyonics but pretty much all other psychological interventions, sometimes coming out with what seemed grossly exaggerated figures about the numbers of different therapies being practised now. *'You do realise there's over five hundred different psychological therapies now, Jason?'* She would say the number very slowly for emphasis. She would also often talk about how you couldn't put people into boxes and sometimes, if she seemed to get really exasperated, she would just close the conversation down by repeatedly saying, 'I think you'll find it's rather more complicated than that, Jason.'

'I wouldn't know how to schmooze you, Frances', Jason smiled, doing his best to look sincere and friendly. 'I know you're not a fan of Zen Psyonics or the groups. But like I said in the meeting, regardless of our differences, we'd really value your expertise and wisdom and hope you'll be an equal partner in getting these up and running. I'm sure you'll be able to find a way of delivering them that fits with your own practise and means you can preserve your integrity.' He hoped that the mention of integrity would resonate with her, as this was often a kind of bottom-line for her, where she could occasionally find flexibility and bow to other people's agendas as long as it didn't challenge her integrity.

'Ha!' Frances threw her hands up at the same time as rolling her eyes and shaking her head. 'Honestly, Jason! If you had any idea! Obviously I will find a way to contort myself into some sort of strange robot therapist who can deliver Zen Psyonics without completely losing my integrity but I must say, I'm going to feel like a prostitute for those two hours every week and I fear this is a very slippery slope. I can see those two hours becoming four hours, becoming eight hours, becoming sixteen hours and soon I'll no longer be recognisable! Are you sure you can't get someone in IT to work up something using AI to deliver the groups? It would probably be much better than me. There would be way more fidelity to the model. Much cheaper too! Free in fact, after the initial outlay.'

'Maybe one day this *will* all be delivered by AI and I guess to some extent that's already very much with us, in terms of all the apps and digital interventions being used now. But I think there'll always be a place for the likes of me and you, for those people you often remind us about, who don't fit into boxes and need adaptations to what we're offering. Those little tweaks that are needed in the group situations too. Those are the things I'm thinking of when I talk about your skills and expertise.'

'Do me a favour, Jason and please stop the sales pitch. I've already said I'm going to do it. But you'll have to allow me to do it my way. You can think of it as me making the necessary adaptations, if that makes you feel better. But I won't be using those handbooks which were proudly unveiled a few months ago. They contain factual inaccuracies and it's against my code of conduct to knowingly give false information to patients.'

'*One* factual inaccuracy, as far as you've pointed out. And I'm not sure I even agree with you on that, assuming you're talking about the personality disorder brain thing.'

'That *thing*, as you know very well, was the bold claim that *people with personality disorders have a more active amygdala and smaller frontal lobes.* That is patent nonsense and problematic on so many levels. I've no idea how many other wild statements there might be in those handbooks, but it's not for me to mark somebody else's homework. Besides, all that should have been done before the money was spent getting them all printed. We could have given that money to people instead of making them attend the group. That probably would have made them feel a lot better!'

Jason could feel himself getting impatient. He sometimes thought Frances was arguing just for the sake of it, simply because she enjoyed an argument, or perhaps because she was angry about something else and it was safer to displace it onto this, which she cared less about. Frankly, most of the time, it just felt like she was nit-picking. People coming to the group probably wouldn't even notice that statement about personality disorders. And in any case, there were peer-reviewed neuropsychological studies cited in the Zen Psyonics manual which proved, or at least came close to proving, that people with personality disorders did indeed have smaller frontal lobes.

'I appreciate that you haven't yet read it, and perhaps you never will read the Zen Psyonics manual, Frances, but with all your knowledge of clinical guidelines you must be aware of the growing number of studies demonstrating exactly the evidence for smaller frontal lobes in personality disorders. It's no longer really a matter for debate.'

'That's a very simplistic take on a very complex situation, Jason. Would you like to borrow my book *Seduced by Neuroscience*? It's all about how the public and non-experts are duped by neuroscience. Even irrelevant neuroscience information fools people! I mean, you're not on your own at all in being seduced by neuroporn. I guess that's the whole point of porn. But you must surely be aware that porn is all it is. It's no more than a reductionist approach that sees brain activity as the truth about what goes on inside the skull, when really it's simply a reconstruction of readings of changes in the electro-magnetic field in different parts of the brain.' Frances wasn't finished yet. 'It's generally accepted that science as a whole is unable to explain all aspects of human life, just as brain-scans are unable to explain the workings of the mind. You need to consult the great artists and writers for that. They have far more to say about the human condition than any neuroscientist!'

'I'll pass on the book, thanks', Jason responded, tersely. 'I guess we can expect this debate to run and run. But in the meantime, thank you for agreeing to lead one of the groups. I'll send another email out later with all the paperwork and instructions. I've got to dash now.' He turned and walked slowly back along the concourse, pondering how although it hadn't been the most successful bit of negotiation, he was still inclined to award himself an eight out of ten, because he had, after all, got Frances on board. She had clearly said she was going to be involved in running the groups. So he could count it as a result, of sorts.

Balint Spitz Reprogramming

Established in 1978 by Zoli Balint and Beata Spitz, Balint Spitz Reprogramming (BSR) stands as the most advanced therapeutic system for emotional re-education and restructuring. BSR facilitates the healing of past emotional deficits through distinctive processes known as 'Scaffolding' and 'Microlocating™,' aiding clients in recognizing emotional gaps and constructing new realities. These symbolic realities serve as a fulfilment of fundamental developmental needs such as home, care, shelter and boundaries. The incorporation of 'Gaps and Traps,' a recent innovation in BSR theory and technique, equips therapists with a highly effective and streamlined approach to diminish opposition and relational overload. Many elements of BSR theories and techniques exhibit close parallels to recent neuroscience findings related to mirror neurons, compassion, morality and theory of mind.

3

When Frances first qualified as a psychologist, there had been plenty of time for further learning on the job. Nine years of training (if you counted the three year bachelor degree, three years as an assistant psychologist and the three year doctorate) provided a basic grounding in working psychologically with a variety of people experiencing a range of problems. But it was only *that*, a basic grounding, which, whilst useful in enabling students to understand and critically appraise psychological theories and research, only took practitioners so far. This meant opportunities for further learning were very welcome, not least because they offered occasions to build relationships and connections with colleagues, to get to know each other and forge alliances.

There was a particularly rich tradition of continuing professional development in the department where Frances got her first qualified job. She hadn't actually ever left her first employer, but the director who employed her had long since retired and the organisation itself had been subject to a series of mergers, making it unrecognisable from the form it was when she arrived. Back in those days, the department regularly organised conferences with nationally, and sometimes internationally, renowned speakers. The director was editor of the profession's in-house journal and ran a weekly writing-for-publication group. Staff were encouraged to innovate and try out different ways of working, running groups for GPs, developing books on prescription schemes, hosting film clubs and walking groups and writing groups. It was a hive of creativity and it seemed like there was something for everyone. Frances was convinced that if it were possible to compare data on patient outcomes from those times, thirty or so years ago, with patient outcomes now, when the world had gone mad for branded therapies, the outcomes (and cost) would compare very favourably, if not considerably better. This wasn't just a hunch. It was from her direct experience of trawling through referrals, seeing the patterns of people repeatedly being offered this therapy, or that therapy, according to the so-called evidence base, only to return sooner or later (often within the space of year) because the therapy hadn't worked or even made the person worse, or the benefits had not been maintained, or in some cases, the therapy had been so good, the person wanted more. In those cases, Frances would always try to raise the issue with the referrer, asking how much more they thought would be enough. Or did they think perhaps the person needed to be permanently having therapy? In which case, was it really effective? It was also very apparent to Frances that often the people who struggled the most with trying to make changes in their lives were those who had the least access to resources. All sorts of therapies might be helpful to people who had the wherewithal to do something about their situation, but many of the people she saw had been dealt a shoddy hand of cards which meant they were playing a game of catch up right from when they took their first breath in the world, and perhaps even before that.

It was particularly irritating to Frances that Zen Psyonics seemed to have been heralded by the mainstream psychological community as one of the most effective new therapies to treat the large and growing numbers of people being referred to secondary mental health services. David was quite right to see the whole movement in terms of a cult, where any critical analysis of either theory or method seemed to be sadly lacking. Once a year, though, Frances got to teach a current crop of psychology trainees on the local doctorate course and remind them about what they had learned as undergraduates, as well as ask them a few questions that didn't seem to get asked much elsewhere in clinical training these days.

'Would anyone like to have a go at recounting the history behind one of the psychological therapies you've been taught on the course so far?' Frances invited the group of twenty varying degrees of keen faces. At this point in their training, most had become entirely comfortable with silence which sometimes meant nobody volunteered for anything as they were all just happy sitting and waiting. Frances didn't mind. She was happy to have exclusive use of the soap box if nobody else wanted it. 'It's good discipline, I think, to go back to the source of a theory or practice, to get properly acquainted with its genesis. Sometimes it can be illuminating to go even further back and look into the history of how the latest new thing has emerged, and the key players. It's a big ask for something like psychodynamic psychotherapy, I know, but easier to give a potted history of one of the newer therapies, of which there are many to choose from. Neurolocation Reprocessing and Release, anyone? No? Bilateral Stimulation Therapy? Zen Psyonics?'

A few hands were raised at the mention of Zen Psyonics.

'I'm suspecting many of you've probably come across Zen Psyonics in your assistant posts prior to training? It's perhaps more interesting than some of the other new wave cognitive behaviour therapies, at the same time as, in my opinion, being more of the same.' Frances chose one of the three male trainees. 'Steve, what can you tell us about it?'

'It was developed by Alexander McDonald, who had started off using surf therapy for people with addictions.'

'Yes, Alexander McDonald apparently discovered that his passion for surfing was something he could get paid for. What do you know about Alexander McDonald's professional background?'

'Didn't he start out in addiction services as a support worker and he took the opportunity when it arose to train in Cognitive Behavioural Therapy? Then he felt the CBT was a little limited, for a variety of reasons, so he started experimenting by adding short surfing sessions into his practice with particular clients. He explains on his website that the surfing offered a far more holistic approach to human wellbeing and addressed the need to integrate mind and body, something which he felt was lacking in CBT.'

'Yes, indeed, that's the story on his website. So how did he get from that to Zen Psyonics?'

'Well he decided to make the move away from the public sector and began to build up a private practice, branching out with small-scale surf retreats, where they did group therapy interspersed with surf sessions. I think he was in Portugal somewhere. I think his clients were quite wealthy people with drug and alcohol problems. The sort that might rock up at private rehab clinics. I can see why they might have chosen these surf retreats over rehab clinics, if money's no object. Surfing kind of sounds more fun than rehab! Maybe they worked out they could get their hits from surfing instead of drugs.'

Emma, the woman sitting next to Steve joined in. 'But his website does also say about how his retreats involved a lot of psychoeducation and his clients got a better understanding about why they felt the way they did and how to move forward in their lives. His programme and interventions were always grounded in evidence-based therapy and built on the latest neuroscience and bio-feedback techniques.'

'Yes his website makes those claims,' interrupted Frances, 'but claims about evidence are what we're here to look at in more detail today. There's a lot of people making a lot of claims and as psychologists we have the ability to separate fact from fiction, but in our busy lives we don't always get the opportunity. So, Steve, carry on. How did he get from surf therapy to Zen Psyonics?'

'Well I think basically he realised that surf therapy was a rather niche market and that by honing the CBT part of his work, the surf sessions became more of an optional extra but not necessary for the full therapeutic gains. He showed how you could get all that from other physical activities and mind-body practices, which meant you didn't need to be living by the sea to do the therapy.'

'Yes, which would be a serious constraint on the growth of his business otherwise,' Frances remarked pointedly. 'It's quite a good example of how the therapy was possibly shaped at least as much by marketability as it was by evidence base. So by the time he launched it officially, a typical ninety minute Zen Psyonics session involved a careful blending of four elements:

meditational practice, communications exercises, physical activity, and selected thought restructuring exercises drawn from cognitive therapy. With surf sessions no longer a requirement of his treatment, and with a fully articulated, distinct therapy, Alexander McDonald was now able to tap into a much bigger market. Does anyone have any reflections or opinions about this?'

Emma spoke again. 'I think it's just an accurate reflection of the world we live in now. We all need to make a living and everything has a price. Why not get the best price for your product rather than down selling yourself?'

Frances was saddened, but not the least surprised at the Emma's neoliberal take on the story. This was one of the reasons she continued to do her teaching at the university, so that she at least got to put forward an alternative view. Whether anyone actually heard it or not was a different matter.

'Well, yes that *is* very much the way of the world now. But my answer to your question, which I think was probably rhetorical, but I'm going to answer it anyway, is that it's a moral and ethical issue, and a question of integrity. I know from many years of studying psychology that Zen Psyonics is simply another variation on a theme, a mongrel offering it could be said, hardly distinguishable from any of the other hundreds of therapies flooding the market. I don't have much of a problem with any of the elements of Zen Psyonics in particular, apart from the generally overstated claims about the transformative effects of meditation, or exercise, or communication training, or cognitive restructuring. It's the *lie* that bothers me. The promise that *this* will transform your life. That and the ridiculous amount of money being made on the back of it. Who is Alexander McDonald, or anyone else, to *sell* surfing to people, anyway? The audacity that someone, *anyone* seemingly, can package together a set of age-old practices for managing life's problems and sell them back to an insatiable audience, under the guise of the latest science, punctuated with a trademark which means it's now owned by the inventor who has just stolen it!'

'Okay, well you can have that view about the market, if

you want,' Emma was clearly going to take her on, 'but are you suggesting that we all just ignore the evidence and we all just go away and have endless rambling conversations with patients, and forget about any proven psychological techniques and strategies?'

'Well firstly, they aren't necessarily endless rambling conversations. They're conversations about what is going wrong in the world and people's lives, which have led them to feel and behave the way they do. And as far as the evidence is concerned, I'm quite comfortable that evidence-based practice makes sense in *physical* healthcare,' Frances responded. 'There need to be robust ways of making decisions about effective treatment, as well as considering cost implications, particularly since healthcare budgets have been eroded by successive governments, and anything profitable's been outsourced to private companies. But evidence-based practice in the realm of mental health and psychological wellbeing is a much more nebulous affair. Need I remind you? We've all been undergraduates in psychology, which itself was founded upon attempts to measure and predict human experience and we have indeed learned much about cognition, perception, memory, the brain and behaviour. I hope you're all as fascinated by this as I am! And yet, despite this vast and growing knowledge about the nature of being human, it's often no more conclusive than a physicist's eternal search to explain things like why we travel forwards in time or what came before the big bang, questions great and small that even the finest minds have not been able to explain. Perhaps amazing discoveries will eventually be made, as has been the case throughout human history. But I imagine that, at least in my lifetime and for some way beyond, many aspects of human life are going to remain a mystery and something probably better articulated by those with a talent for expressing the ineffable.'

'Ineffable?' Emma asked.

'Something which can't be described in words, or yet by science, I would add.' Frances at least admired Emma's confidence. 'But you're also right of course. The clinical reality is that whilst healthcare may not have started out in this way, it's now very much an industry and operates the same as any other, with the basic aim being about selling products and services to make a profit. The thing is, if you're buying a product like a coffee maker, it will either make coffee or it won't and if it doesn't work, you get your money back. If you're buying a service, like a mechanic to fix your car, you won't pay him until he fixes it. With CBT on the other hand, its fifty percent success rate is not actually that good. And apart from not getting our money back, what about the question of *why* it isn't that effective? Because the forces of the world outside are so much more powerful than CBT! You're all probably familiar with stories about how this has gone wrong where pharmaceuticals are concerned. Critical psychiatrists have been exposing dodgy practices for years, so it's common knowledge, at least in our line of work, that drug research has been selectively published to make antidepressants appear more effective than they actually are. Hopefully you're already aware that pharmaceutical companies covered up research about Selective Serotonin Reuptake Inhibitors leading to suicide in a small but significant number of cases. But the psychological therapy industry has largely escaped similar criticism, almost as if the act of talking couldn't possibly be powerful in the way that psychiatric drugs are. That says something in itself, doesn't it, about the power of language? *Sticks and stones will break your bones, but names with never hurt you.* Some agree with that, others don't. I take a *both-and* position myself. Words are not real, but they have real effects. Words can be very important and also not so important. They're the tools of our trade. But it's the actual, material conditions of people's lives that underpin all this. Solid foundations and resources create the conditions for human beings to flourish. That's not to ignore profoundly powerful examples of human creativity arising out of the depths of despair and adversity, but ultimately, to ensure that human beings are able to live relatively healthy and comfortable lives, a certain level of access to resources is needed.'

'So wait,' Emma came in when it seemed Frances had finished her point, 'you're saying the evidence base for psychological therapies is dodgy, then? Even though there are countless eminent professors out there proving various therapies work?'

It sometimes astounded Frances that other highly intelligent, highly educated colleagues failed to grasp the basic flaws in the research into psychological therapies. 'Remember your psychology degree, Emma? Any undergraduate student of psychology should understand the basic premises of the scientific method. We'll all hopefully have learned those by conducting several psychological experiments early in our degrees. So we all should be knowledgeable, if not adept, at selecting participants, isolating independent variables, selecting measures and so on. We would therefore know that when it comes to looking at psychological therapies, the field is replete with problems. Can anyone point out some of those problems, based on the research paper sent to you prior to today's session?'

There were a few murmurs. 'Who were the participants in that study?' Frances asked directly. Some of the trainees looked bemused, as if they didn't know why Frances was even asking the question, but eventually someone called out, 'people with depression and anxiety.'

'Thank you. People with depression and anxiety. So in case you're not already aware, it's not uncommon for information to be rather vague, even in research trials, about what participants are suffering from. There are some instances where participants cover a great range between mild to moderate depression and anxiety and crippling depression and chronic anxiety *in just one study*! So that's our first problem. And then what about diagnosis itself? The clinical guidelines openly acknowledge how even the seemingly uncontentious condition called depression constitutes a very broad category, which means it's got limited validity as a basis for effective treatment plans.'

'But this is the whole point of peer review,' Emma came back in. She seemed to like a good argument as much as Frances did. 'There may be some problems with methodology, but the peer review process can give us the confidence that the findings are largely good enough.'

'Okay, so you're happy with the selection of participants, as people with anxiety and depression, and you're happy with the robustness of the diagnoses of anxiety and depression. What about the independent variable then?' Most faces in the room looked blank. 'The independent variable being the thing that's manipulated in an experiment, in this case the type of treatment being investigated, for those who might have been struggling to remember from undergraduate days.'

'Yes, I can see where you're going with this,' Steve said. 'How do we know the treatment is the same for each patient? In fact, surely we'd have to say that the treatment is never going to be the same for each patient, even if we're following a manual, because there's always going to be little exchanges and non-verbals and different environments and the rest of it which are confounding factors, so it's never going to be a very tightly controlled setting. Unless we start using robots, maybe!'

'Exactly. So we can pretend that there are distinct, highly defined illnesses called depression and anxiety and whatever else. And we can pretend that participants in research trials are people all diagnosed with illnesses using the same screening tool by the same expert psychiatrist. And we can have something like CBT as the independent variable. But what sort of CBT? It's practised in so many different ways now, with so many varieties. We know ourselves, working in mental health services, that the clinical guidelines recommend CBT for both depression and anxiety. But the guidelines are clear that there are significant limitations to the current evidence base, that they include very limited data on long-term outcomes for most, if not all, interventions. And they're clear that these limitations are due to the problems associated with the randomised control trial methodology in psychological research. So yes, these are peer reviewed studies. But at what point do we say, the methodology is shoddy and it's not good enough?'

When Frances tried to raise these objections at work, she was used to people rolling their eyes and closing the discussion down with an offhand comment about the research not being a precise science, insisting that it was indeed *good enough*, adding, *and in any case, we have a service to run.* But these were trainees. Could they afford to be more critical and bring new energy and challenges back into services? Or was it inevitable that they would just get sucked into the machine, along with most others? To Frances's delight, not all of them were there yet. Steve, for one.

'It's interesting that you said about being comfortable with evidence-based practice in physical healthcare, Frances,' Steve said. 'I was reading just the other day about this guy, a biologist, who quit his job to pursue his hobby of finding flaws in scientific papers. And he uncovered all this stuff about cancer research, where findings couldn't be replicated and positive outcomes were far smaller than originally claimed. And this was in a number of prestigious cancer research institutions. When people are donating all those billions of pounds and dollars and euros to cancer research, I bet they think the scientists doing the research have very high standards and they're very careful. But apparently not! So if it's like that in cancer research, imagine the mess in psychological therapy research!'

It was moments like these, where someone, and what's more, someone young and energetic, appeared to be as bothered as she was, which gave Frances some hope that all was not lost.

Behavioural Analytic Therapy

Behavioural Analytic Therapy (BAT) is unique in its focus on the genuine relationship that forms during therapy as a mechanism for modifying troublesome behaviours. Using the therapeutic alliance as a catalyst for change enables BAT to be used as a standalone treatment or complement other therapeutic approaches.

Four functional rules guide the treatment protocol and central to this are the in-session occurrences of the clients' problems referred to as Clinical Target Behaviours. CTBs are divided into those which are manifestations of existing troublesome behaviours and those which are improvements or behavioural progress. At the beginning of the therapeutic process, clients are prompted to articulate their treatment objectives. This involves exploring their aspirations and profound desires—defining their ideal selves and identifying what they are driven to achieve throughout their lives. Through this dialogue, behavioural targets are jointly established: understanding which entrenched problematic behaviours contribute to their current challenges and discerning new, adaptive behaviours that will propel them towards the envisioned life and desired self.

4

The conditions were almost perfect. The water was probably around seventeen degrees and there was a slight offshore wind. The sea was smooth as glass, carved with perfect, generously-spaced barrels, and despite this joyful day there were only a handful of locals out there sharing the glory. Alexander McDonald was sitting astride his board and caught a waft of weed over from his left where Regan, probably one of the best surfers around, was chilling in the line-up. Alexander paddled closer to Jamie, a journalist from *The Outdoor Cure* magazine, who had come to interview Alexander about his work. Seeing as Jamie was also a surfer, Alexander had suggested they go and ride some waves together, to give the article some authenticity.

'You can probably smell that too, yeah?' Alexander said quietly to Jamie. 'Don't know about you but I don't smoke myself. I prefer the pure experience. And from the people I know, it's the clean living surfers who are always the mellowest, in and out of the water.'

'Yeah,' said Jamie. 'I was wondering about the whole dope-smoking vibe in surfing and how that played out when you first started introducing surfing to people with addictions. I wondered whether it might just encourage people to take up a weed habit on top of everything else.'

'Well it was a condition of the retreats that people didn't use any substances stronger than tea or coffee. And most people hadn't ever tried surfing before so it was a new experience, and generally very powerful. Clients really quickly recognised how there was no need for weed, or any other drug, when the surfing itself prompted the body's own chemicals, releasing endorphins and providing a natural high as well as decreasing stress. I mean, I don't have to tell you, right? You're a surfer. I'm sure you get this.'

'Absolutely,' agreed Jamie. 'I'm sure it was so much more

convincing, them actually feeling it for themselves, than just being told about it. And on that note, look at this set coming in.'

Today, like the weather, the break was working nicely. Jamie had already taken to it and aside from him being a slight distraction, Alexander felt in harmony with the ocean, his board simply an extension of his body. He could see the next wave barrelling towards him and locked his eyes onto it, beginning to position himself. As the wave approached, he started paddling with a smooth and powerful rhythm. His arms sliced through the water like a machine, propelling him forward with precision and grace. At just the right moment, he sprang to his feet, in a dance-like movement. He felt weightless, suspended on a liquid wall of energy. He was fixed on the unfolding path ahead, calculating every subtle shift in the wave's shape, carving graceful turns and generating a spray of water as he banked off the wave's face. The ride seemed to last forever, but eventually, as the wave lost its energy, Alexander guided his board back towards the white water and completed a stylish dismount. He paddled back out towards Jamie with a satisfied grin, ready to catch another wave. After *three more good ones* which as usual turned out to be more like five or six, they retired to the Coffee Shack just above the beach to continue their conversation.

'So yeah, after making sure the clients had all thoroughly immersed themselves in the joy of surfing, I'd give them a bit of background,' Alexander explained. 'I used to like teaching clients about the mammalian dive reflex and how it's triggered by being in the ocean.'

'Remind me about that,' Jamie asked.

'It's about how cold water immersion causes the heart rate to drop by up to fifty per cent, and how it reduces blood flow away from the extremities and reduces blood pressure. Clients were often amazed to hear me explain how the mammalian dive reflex completely changes your physiology and reduces stress hormones. It's an involuntary response, so it's de-stressing you whether you like it or not!'

'So tell me a bit more about how the business developed, how you combined the surfing with psychological therapy.'

'Well I've always liked the idea that surfers get that profound sense of having *found their true north*. That thing about discovering their authentic self, the combination of purpose and belief, putting their values at the head of their journey. I think there was something about the clients being on this journey at the same time as me being on my own. When it first started taking off, I felt fairly sure I'd found my unique path in life, and was answering a calling to transform the lives of hundreds of people through life-changing surf therapy programmes. It was really gratifying when I started winning awards and endorsements from the big players in both mental health *and* surfing industries.'

'I know that these days people are more likely to know you as founder and clinical director of Zen Psyonics and The Green Room but back then we knew you as the surf therapist. How did surfing take you to Zen Psyonics? And does surfing still have a place in The Green Room?'

The green room was that mythical place, inside the barrel of a wave, the ultimate Zen surfing experience. But it was also a place Alexander had created, where people could transform their trauma and unlock the secret to healing through his unique combination of surfing, group therapy, psycho-education, mindfulness, and bonding in a small, intimate group. His programmes were suitable for everyone, but especially those recovering from addiction, dealing with PTSD, or struggling with issues from childhood. He had helped so many people turn their traumas into opportunities for growth and positive change.

'I hadn't expected The Green Room to be quite so successful but in the space of just five years I was employing seventeen staff, a mixture of yoga teachers, surf instructors and counsellors. But as the business grew though, I found myself getting really busy, with not enough time for surfing, which made me feel a bit out of balance. At the same time, I was really pleased to be getting all the recognition for my business. I was being contacted by people from all over the world, asking for my expert opinion or to present at events. The money they were offering was off the scale compared to when I was support worker in drug and alcohol services! But interestingly, the bulk of interest in my work was about the therapeutic practices outside of surfing. I think people were drawn to my work from seeing it in magazines and newspapers, with it having that unique surfing element, but mostly people wanted to skill themselves up with the additional practices, as the majority of them weren't likely to incorporate surfing into their practice. It takes years to carve the waves like we do, right? The surfing was just a bit impractical and didn't lend itself well to therapists practising in landlocked areas, or none-surfers, or people who were doing therapy mostly online, which is probably becoming the norm these days.'

'So it was the market then, mainly, that caused the shift from surf therapy to Zen Psyonics?'

Alexander didn't know Jamie. There was a connection between them, simply because of their shared love of surfing, but he wasn't sure what to make of him. Jamie had been enthusiastic and polite in securing the interview with him, explaining that *The Outdoor Cure* magazine was doing a special issue on water-based therapeutic activities, so Alexander felt it was a genuine request to learn more about his work. But mention of the market made him feel slightly uncomfortable, as if Jamie was suggesting that making money was more important to Alexander than healing people. Over time, Alexander had honed his brand, so that surfing was more of an underpinning philosophy, which continued to mark him apart from the many other psychological therapies in the increasingly crowded market. He was aware how important it was to both keep hold of surfing as the foundation for his brand, at the same time as letting it go, in order to maximise his share of the market. He had a mixed reception from within the surf community, where some of his friends were proud of what he had achieved, but others felt he had sold out and was turning his back on the whole vibe of surfing. He was annoyed about this but told himself that this was the nature of life. In fact, he saw himself as *surfing the therapy industry*, in a similar way to how he would approach the shape-shifting nature of a beach break, knowing that it is precisely the forces of nature bigger than ourselves which demand us to adapt and move with the flow. Like many surfers, he could find some beach breaks incredibly frustrating. Being in a constant state of flux, one of his favourite secret spots could have world-class surf-producing sand bars one day and be absolute mush the next. So he liked to adopt an attitude with his evolving and fluctuating business interests; accepting that sand moves (and fashions and fortunes change), observing patterns before paddling out (scanning the competition horizon for the latest big hitter therapies), and keeping in mind that waves move quickly (as does the market).

Alexander decided he may as well say to Jamie what he truly believed. 'I don't think one outweighs the other. Both the market, and the evolution of the therapy to heal people, are important. And I think it's just a mirror of the reality of today's society. We're all striving to support ourselves, and every commodity holds a value. So, why settle for less when you can maximize the worth of your product or service?'

Jamie seemed satisfied that he had got enough for his piece in the magazine and promised to send Alexander a copy for approval before publication, then they said their goodbyes.

Around an hour later, Alexander was settled on his kneeling chair, coffee brewing on the sideboard, checking through his inbox. Buddha, his little brown dog, was scrabbling about in his basket under the desk, trying to rearrange the covers which had been recently laundered and therefore, annoyingly for Buddha, had all their comforting aromas removed.

'I know, Bud', Alexander made sympathetic noises. 'It sucks when someone messes with your place. It'll come right again. You'll get those smells back!'

Buddha whined in response and made a move to settle on Alexander's lap, which was no longer possible with the kneeling chair.

'Aw Bud, it's all change, isn't it? I'm sorry, man. You'll adapt. We can cuddle on the sofa later. How about you settle back down there whilst I try to sort through my own stuff up here? You're not the only one who's being messed with!'

Alexander was scrolling through the latest email from Ed Burrell, his lawyer, who he had recently instructed to represent him in surely the most annoying and unwarranted legal case ever in the therapy business, against him, Alexander McDonald. It was being brought by someone who had stolen and been using, no, bastardising, the practice of Zen Psyonics. Clemmie Service (and what sort of a nonsense name was that anyway?) had had the audacity to bring a defamation case against Alexander, claiming that he had injured his reputation by slandering him on *Couch and Client*. Alexander had been a regular visitor to the therapists' social media forum for so many years he felt himself to be a founding father. He had initially grown his business via the forum and he had many admiring followers. He had made some genuine points about Clemmie Service, which he knew to be true from insider information from other therapists and clients even. Under the guise of Zen Psyonics, the conditions of Clemmie's clients worsened and he exploited this to sell them more therapy. There was even a story going round that one of Clemmie's clients had killed themselves, though people were careful to avoid conjecture on a social networking site, even if it was a closed group. At no point did Alexander name Clemmie. So he felt he had no case whatsoever to answer. But not only was Clemmie suing Alexander for defamation, but also for engaging in deceptive trade practices. The very same thing that Clemmie was actually guilty of himself!

Alexander was so outraged simply going through the material again that Buddha must have picked up on the rise in adrenalin in his master's body and started whining and fussing again.

'It's okay, Bud, don't you worry. We're going to sort this mess. We're going to nail this fucker.'

Alexander and Ed had discussed how their most sensible option at this stage was to make a counterclaim. Clemmie Service was engaging in deception by operating a therapy business claiming to offer the trademarked therapy, Zen Psyonics, but in fact not adhering to Zen Psyonics standards or those established by the corporate entity of The Green Room. Further to that, he had engaged in intellectual property theft. Ed's latest email was asking Alexander to furnish him with the details of Clemmie's practices in order to build up evidence for the case against him.

Alexander was rather irritated by the amount of time he reckoned it was going to take him to trawl through the internet for the dirt on Clemmie Service. He made a mental note to check with Ed that part of the claim would include recompense for the amount of work he was having to put into the case. The most obvious place to start was Clemmie's website. The homepage opened with a large head and shoulders of Clemmie looking vaguely smug. His name was below in bold letters, followed by a string of credentials which were not dissimilar to Alexander's own, apart from Clemmie having achieved higher academic status with his masters degree. It went on to describe him as *a Zen Psyonics therapist, author, trainer, supervisor and consultant who understands the challenges and opportunities of implementing Zen Psyonics in real-world settings. He has been an invited speaker for large national conferences and private events of all sizes and has trained numerous professionals in the UK and beyond. He has provided specialised Zen Psyonics training and consultation to mental health services, addiction services, hospital settings and forensic settings.* Further down the page there was a video of Clemmie introducing his business, *CentreFlow*, which was tagged with the header, *CentreFlow – who we are and how we are different.*

Part of Alexander wanted to relax into the task and have a good old look at how Clemmie was presenting himself to the world, as he knew he would find plenty of gold for Ed Burrell. But he had a whole load of other pressing needs to attend to, as well as having two colleagues booked in for supervision today. So he decided to go through his file on Clemmie Service, where he had already saved various documents from *Couch and Client*. It was some of his followers on the forum who had initially alerted him to Clemmie's practice, concerned as they were that Clemmie was confusing the families of suicidal children and other individuals into thinking that his treatment was the same as Alexander's own time-tested and proven therapy. One of them had even covertly recorded an online supervision session with Clemmie where it was very clear that he was being rather slap-happy about the delivery of Zen Psyonics, to the extent that the person being supervised felt he wasn't delivering Zen Psyonics at all. More than that, she was concerned that his practice was actually dangerous as he was not giving his clients the proper tools and resources to manage their severe emotional dysregulation. She could see it all ending very badly indeed.

The video was one of the most compelling aspects of the evidence Alexander planned to send to Ed. There were all sorts of other bits of evidence though, which taken together led him to conclude that as Clemmie clearly wasn't practising Zen Psyonics, he had no right to be using the trademarks of Zen Psyonics. This was plenty. He clicked reply to Ed's email and attached the best documents from his folder and pressed send. Then he poured himself another coffee, picked up little Buddha and took him to the sofa for a cuddle.

Behavioural Reprocessing and Reconditioning

Over the past 15 years, Behavioural Reprocessing and Reconditioning (BRR) has evolved into an innovative and highly effective therapy, grounded in the latest neuroscientific research. Drawing on empirical studies and brain imaging insights, BRR aligns with the actual functioning of the brain, freeing us from outdated models that have dominated psychotherapy.

BRR primarily focuses on the unconscious creation of states of mind and being. Habits are formed in state creation, and individuals can become trapped in habitual states like sadness, rage and anxiety. BRR allows an exploration of the mental, emotional and physical resources associated with each state, examining their interplay. Each state unconsciously pursues a specific purpose, forming neurocircuits that intertwine thoughts, feelings and physiology. These circuits become automatic and strengthened through repetition, leaving the individual feeling powerless and confused. BRR sheds light on the unconscious intentions behind these states by bringing them into conscious awareness, enabling behaviour to be swiftly reconditioned.

BRR isn't reliant on sophisticated methods or techniques; instead, it is grounded in the liberating truth. BRR is characterised by its speed, simplicity and permanence. Sessions do not dwell on the past, avoiding the need to repeatedly revisit painful events. It is virtually content-free and, therefore, not a protracted process. Remarkable progress is achieved in just six sessions, as evidenced by the testimonials of satisfied clients.

5

Paula knew she should have taken her phone. As she came down the hill and rounded the corner, past the pub, the sunset over the river took her breath away. What had started as an orange glow in the west as she set out for her walk, had now become an even more beautiful pinky-red. It had been so hot that the clouds were gathering for thunder, but that seemed just a threat and the clouds themselves added to the light show, floating in various shades of purple. Below the bridge, the pink light was reflected in the river which was particularly pretty, being so low it was exposing the rocks, making patterns of shimmering water as it flowed down towards the weir. This would have been the point where she took a photo of her walk, had she brought her phone. In its absence, she stood there for a while on the bridge, taking in the scene. Above her, the whoosh of a chain of swifts took her attention and she watched them make their way south, maybe to Spain, maybe to Africa. It reminded her of the evening sky and the birds leaving in the Sandy Denny song, Who Knows Where the Time Goes. She hummed the song to herself, and felt something, not being sure whether it was sad or resigned, or something else. She wondered whether the lyrics actually meant the opposite of what they were saying about counting the time. It felt like it to Paula. I might not still be here when the birds have gone, she thought, and I *do* count the time. *All* the time these days.

Paula had had a particularly difficult day. Most days were difficult at the moment. But today she had to do a sixty-mile round trip to the hospital for a meeting with the oncologist, to review her treatment. She had been expecting it to just be a brief conversation about side effects and next steps but the topic of vaccination came up. Covid was on the increase again and a new strain had been detected and seemed to be spreading rapidly in the south east. The oncologist asked if she would like to be vaccinated by one of the nurses there and then, which had taken Paula by surprise.

'Oh,' she said, flustered, 'I'm not sure I want the latest vaccination. I've begun to question it a bit.' She felt sheepish saying that. 'I had all the other doses. I'm not an anti-vaxxer,' she added hurriedly. It's just part of me wonders, you know, whether it might be causing harm that we don't know about yet.'

'It's really very safe', said the doctor. 'And certainly a lot safer than not having it, as obviously you'd be aware of your vulnerability with weakened immunity.'

'Yes, I know. It's a dilemma really. But another thing is I think I'd probably rather die quickly of Covid than slowly of cancer.'

The oncologist looked shocked. Gerry stepped in at this point.

'Paula has actually been feeling very depressed and anxious, and quite suicidal at times. I guess it's normal in the circumstances, but she's been finding everything really difficult to deal with.'

The oncologist nodded at Gerry and turned back to Paula. 'I know your GP offered to prescribe you some anti-depressants a few months back when you were anxious about the treatment not starting soon enough. Do you think it might be helpful to start on those now, if you're feeling like this?'

'No. I really don't want to put any more toxic chemicals into my body. It already feels too much with the chemotherapy. And anyway, I've got cancer. Like Gerry said, it's hardly surprising I feel depressed and anxious.'

The oncologist paused as she continued to look at Paula, almost waiting for her to say something else, though nothing was forthcoming. Paula hated these appointments and the intrusion into her soul was worse, if anything, than the physical examinations and exposures.

'I don't really feel comfortable leaving you like this', the oncologist eventually said. 'If you don't want medication, would you be okay with me referring you to mental health services? You're probably aware we have a limited counselling service in cancer care but it's more for people who are struggling with... who have got...'

'...a terminal diagnosis', Paula filled in for her. 'It's okay. I wouldn't really want to waste people's time. I don't really think mental health services could do anything for me. It's not as if they can cure cancer, is it?'

'But they can help with how you're coping with the cancer, with dealing with the thoughts and feelings about it', the doctor urged.

'How do they do that?' Paula asked, though she wasn't particularly interested in the answer.

'Well it's not my area at all, but I do know that many patients I see talk about how helpful it is to be able to talk things through with someone trained to deal with the effects of what you're going through.'

Gerry stepped in again at this point, looking at Paula rather than the oncologist. 'You don't really think it's your thing, do you?' he said, as a way of showing solidarity with Paula and to endorse the message that Paula would be declining this offer.

'No, it's not really my thing, but you know, maybe I could just go along out of interest, to see what they do, see what they say. It's probably not the best attitude to have, starting out thinking it's not going to be helpful, but I guess I've always been a bit curious about what they actually *do*, what it would be like to be on the receiving end of something like that. I'd probably feel a bit like a mystery shopper, but anyway, it might at least make people *here* feel better,' Paula looked back at the oncologist, 'to know that at least it's been offered and I've been assessed, or whatever they do.'

The oncologist smiled. 'Ok, I'll make that referral. You should hear from them within the next few days when they'll do a telephone triage and discuss next steps. You might be surprised. I think you're a similar age to me. You might remember those adverts. It's good to talk!'

Paula smiled back. 'I guess it depends on who you're talking to. And why. And what about. But anyway, like I said, I'll try to keep an open mind!'

'Gosh, I wasn't expecting that, Paula', Gerry exclaimed as soon as they got outside of the oncology centre.

'No. I thought you might fall off your chair!' Paula laughed.

'Well it's good to see you smiling, at least!' Gerry said, reaching for her hand as they walked towards the car park.

'I mean, I do still think it's a bit ridiculous and with the state health services are in, they could do with prioritising money on getting people faster cancer treatment, and then maybe less people would need the counselling! But anyway,' she trailed off.

'I so wish you weren't going through this. It's so horrible and scary. It's so unfair. I wish I could be more helpful.'

'Well maybe you could've not said about me feeling suicidal. I doubt it's that unusual for people in this situation to feel like that. It's not as if I'm going to do anything about it. It's just how I feel. I don't think I'm quite like the typical person turning up at a mental health service. Also, it's kind of private. But look, it's okay. I know it's just that you care and you're concerned.'

They got in the car and Paula immediately pulled her wig off and scratched her bald head. 'Thank fuck for that. I hate that thing!'

It was ten days later when Paula found herself sitting in front of her computer screen looking at a woman in her late fifties, early sixties possibly, but certainly not the bright, young corporate thing she had somehow imagined. She wasn't sure what to think about the fact that this was a video call, rather than the telephone triage the oncologist had mentioned. Had the referral led them to think she was more of a risk and therefore needed to be actually *seen*? Needed to be viewed for signs beyond language that she was someone to worry about? This woman, who introduced herself as Frances, was wearing a black t-shirt underneath a burgundy collared shirt. No jewellery, no make-up, as far as Paula could tell from the video quality which wasn't bad. She had a fairly short hairstyle, a kind of grown-out short cut, of a rather lovely grey colour. She didn't have the appearance of someone who went for six-weekly appointments at the hairdresser. Her voice was slightly gravelly, probably signalling her age. She was smiling, but not too much. Not overdoing it. The whole effect was quite comforting to Paula, but they hadn't even started yet, so she reminded herself to be on guard.

Frances explained what Paula could expect from their conversation today, that they could discuss the referral, and Paula's expectations about the appointment, what her difficulties were at the moment and what sort of support, if any, might be helpful. It all seemed fairly low key to Paula, thankfully.

'So Paula, can you tell me a bit about your understanding of the referral? Whose idea it was, what you think about it, that sort of thing?'

This was interesting. Paula had been expecting whoever she met to get straight into asking how she was feeling, not what she thought about the referral. But maybe this was what they did, as part of the warm-up, before they went into the heavy stuff.

'It was the oncologist in my recent review who suggested it. She was concerned as my husband mentioned that I'm finding the whole cancer thing difficult. He used the word suicide and I guess that's one of their red flags.'

'And you've come to the appointment, albeit virtually, so would I be right in assuming you thought it was a good idea, that there might be something we can help you with?'

Paula was a bit disarmed. They seemed to be talking *around* the appointment, not about her actual situation and feelings. She wasn't sure whether this was a good thing or a bad thing but she thought it might be difficult to maintain her mystery shopper position. She had planned to just give some minimal details, agree that she had been feeling very low, yes, a bit suicidal, but who wouldn't, and see what came back.

She hesitated. 'Well yes, I guess I must have thought it was a good idea, seeing as I'm here, though I'm not sure what you offer, so I'm not sure what you might be able to help with.'

'The reason I ask, is that we get all sorts of referrals that are often somebody else's idea and not necessarily the person's who has been referred. But I'll take your point that you've attended the appointment as kind of being in agreement, or at least open to finding out. So, would it be helpful to talk about how the breast cancer has affected you?'

What on earth am I doing here? Paula asked herself. No, it wouldn't be helpful to talk about the breast cancer. It wouldn't be helpful to talk about anything with you or anybody else. For some reason, I thought it might be interesting to meet with you but I was clearly out of my mind. I think we should just end this appointment right now! Could this Frances woman actually read her mind and hear everything she had just thought privately to herself? Speak! Paula urged herself. But before she could, Frances continued.

'Or maybe you'd like me to ask you some questions? Sometimes people prefer that.'

There was something about this older woman on the screen in front of her that Paula couldn't quite articulate. It wasn't just that she wasn't what Paula had been expecting. It was also that she wasn't lots of things that Paula sometimes found difficult about other women. Despite the fact that Frances's job meant she was in the business of probing very private areas of people's lives, Paula didn't feel intruded upon. She didn't feel like this woman was trying to get something from her. She didn't feel like she was trying to use power over her. She felt that this woman had the ability to look after her, though at the same time that her care would not be forced upon her or suffocating. How on earth could she feel all of this from what had so far been barely more than three minutes on a video call? The urge to be completely honest and just tell Frances everything about how she was feeling was incredibly strong. She wished she could just wait and think, instead of feeling compelled to jump in and at least say something, anything, which she was then likely to regret.

'I'm not really sure what to say,' Paula managed eventually. 'I'm not really sure I'm in the right place here and I don't want to waste your time. You're probably right. It wasn't my idea and I probably don't agree with it.' *I just thought I'd be a mystery shopper for a bit to take my mind of this horrendous thing that's happening in my life.* Paula was so close to saying that. She had never before quite realised how biting your tongue might actually be a necessary strategy.

'Do you think you'd be here if it weren't for the fact that you're currently going through treatment for breast cancer?' Frances asked gently.

'Absolutely not', Paula said without hesitation.

'So maybe that's one thing that makes it seem you're in the wrong place. A sense there's nothing wrong with you, were it not for the cancer, and so why on earth would you need referring to mental health services?'

It was impossible to be the mystery shopper. If she was playing that role, in order to get her foot through the door instead of being signposted elsewhere, Paula knew that with the state of health services these days she would need to be really emphasising the suicidal thinking, the endless pondering about different ways to die, preferable things to die of and how she could see no alternatives. But it was impossible to disagree with what Frances had just said because it was almost precisely what she herself had said to the oncologist.

'Yes. That's pretty much what I said to the oncologist. I've got cancer, not a mental health problem.'

'And they can't offer you any counselling in cancer care services because they only have a limited service. Though it sounds like maybe you wouldn't have taken that up anyway? Which leads me right back to wondering why you have attended the appointment. What do other people think? Have you told anyone about this appointment today?'

'Well my husband knows because he was there at the appointment. He's definitely in the camp of thinking it's a good idea, because he's worried about me. He's the one that sees me weeping and wailing all over the place and struggles to know what to do with me.' So, the filing cabinet was now well and truly open and Paula was flinging out the contents. 'I haven't told anyone else. I thought I'd see what happened first.'

'Who would you be likely to tell? Do you have parents still alive?'

'My mum's in her 80s, still in fairly good health. I haven't told her. She can be a bit much sometimes. She likes to know lots of details and it can feel quite intrusive. Plus, she's not a massive fan of *therapy*. She thinks people should talk to *each other* and support each other. And also that God will look after us all, or at least, that everything is God's will.'

'Any siblings?'

'I've got a sister and two brothers. I guess some people might say we're a fairly happy family. But I've been trying to avoid that *Team Paula* kind of situation, where everyone's cheering you on and telling you how amazing you are and how you're going to be fine because so and so did this and that and they're still alive today! Like they've got a bloody crystal ball. I find it so thoughtless and it totally invalidates and minimises everything I'm going through. Well, I don't mean that to sound horrible. I know that some people really appreciate that kind of thing. But not me. And unfortunately it's the kind of thing my family tend to do, getting manically invested in a situation where it becomes the main topic of conversation, so...' Paula trailed off, but not because she thought she had revealed too much. She had indeed revealed far more than she intended but she was beginning to not care. Frances was kind of low key, the opposite of Paula's family. There was plenty of space and time to breathe. She seemed curious, but not overbearing.

'As if the cancer isn't enough itself, there's the whole circus around it and how you deal with all of that. I wish I could say something helpful.' Frances paused. 'I'm not sure how familiar you are with mental health services but your referral was sent through to secondary care, which is usually because someone thought there might be more risks involved, or that the situation is more complex than can be dealt with in primary care. What you and I need to establish today is whether you think it would be helpful to have a chance to talk through what's going on in more detail and find ways of trying to alleviate what you're going through. The problem is, if you did want to do that, you wouldn't be able to do that here in secondary care, because we have very long waiting lists and have started to only offer groups as a first step. There are counsellors and therapists in primary care but they might not accept a referral as they might think you're too risky or complex, hence why you've come through to me anyway.'

Paula's heart sank a little. She had been beginning to open up to the idea that it might genuinely be helpful to talk more with this Frances. It certainly wasn't making her feel any worse. It wasn't clear exactly what was on offer now.

'So are you saying that I wouldn't be able to get counselling in primary care but I might be able to join a group in this service?'

'Well, sort of. The problem with that though is the groups aren't really for people like yourself, dealing with cancer. They're more for people with long-term problems managing life, for want of a better way of putting it. People who struggle with managing their emotions, for all sorts of reasons, and the consequences of that. I'm not getting the sense that's something you've struggled with, though I might be wrong. I haven't even asked!'

'I guess I don't really fit into that. Though I can say I've been a complete wreck these last few months after getting this diagnosis and my husband would definitely say I'm not doing a great job of managing my emotions. Do you think there might be something in the groups that could help me with that?' Back to being the mystery shopper then, Paula thought.

'The groups run over twenty weeks and cover four different modules. Meditation, communication, physical activity and thought restructuring. Not all the elements are helpful to everyone but maybe everyone can find something helpful in some of it. That's the hope. It's not everybody's cup of tea. I don't want you to feel pressurised and it's perfectly understandable if you think it's maybe not for you.'

Paula was finding the conversation a little strange. It reminded her of occasions when Gerry had tried to persuade Paula to do something or go somewhere and then *de-selling* it after he himself had changed his mind, by which point Paula really wanted to do it herself. Gerry had learned about de-selling when he used to work in sales. He explained to Paula how salespeople are traditionally entrusted with the job of communicating a product's values and benefits to the customers, whereas de-selling is the process of communicating the opposite, letting the customer know why they should not buy your product. And this is the way they earn customer trust. Was this what Frances was doing?

'I kind of get the feeling you're trying to persuade me not to sign up. Is that just me or...?'

'Oh, I'm sorry. No, I'm not trying to do anything. It's more that I got the sense you might prefer just the opportunity to talk, rather than the structure of a group, but unfortunately I can't offer you that', Frances said rather apologetically.

'Okay. Well I'm happy to give it a try. Does that mean I won't see you again?'

'It depends. We have individual meetings prior to the group starting, then a review half way through and then again at the end. You also get assigned to one of us as a point of contact in case of a crisis. So it's possible you could get assigned to me but I really can't say. I'm sorry, that's not very helpful.'

Frances shared a few more bits of practical information then they agreed to end the appointment. Frances suddenly disappeared from the screen and Paula was left, momentarily wondering what had just happened.

Bilateral Stimulation Therapy

Bilateral Stimulation Therapy (BST) is a ground-breaking and world leading approach to resolving trauma, using bilateral stimulation as the key ingredient. The therapy comprises six phases, with bilateral stimulation employed during a specific segment of each session. Once the clinician identifies the targeted trauma memory, the client is instructed to hold various aspects of that memory or thought while tracking a visual, auditory or tactile stimulus. This process triggers internal associations, allowing clients to process the memory and associated distressing emotions. In successful BST, the emotional significance of painful events undergoes a transformation. For example, a person surviving a road traffic accident may shift from experiencing terror and helplessness to adopting a resilient belief such as, "I survived it, and I am strong."

Unlike traditional talk therapy, where insights often stem from clinician interpretation, BST relies on the client's accelerated intellectual and emotional processes. Consequently, clients emerge from BST feeling empowered by experiences that once caused debilitation. Their wounds not only heal but undergo a profound transformation. As a natural outcome of the BST process, clients' thoughts, feelings and behaviours become robust indicators of emotional health and resolution. Remarkably, this transformation occurs without the need for detailed verbal communication or homework assignments commonly found in other therapeutic approaches.

6

Around eighteen months ago, when the team took the first cohort of patients for the Zen Psyonics pilot group, there were just over two hundred people on the waiting list for psychological therapy. With the equivalent of only two full-time psychologists for the whole service, and around a thousand people on the books at any one time, there was only one direction that number was going to go, which was up, and swiftly. Since Jason had trained up some of the nurses and support staff to help him run the groups, he was now about to discharge people in the sixth cohort. Those two hundred people waiting to be seen had all been contacted, with the offer of starting work sooner, if they opted to join a Zen Psyonics group. Most had chosen to stay on the original waiting list, but around twenty of them were now on the group list, along with all the new referrals. Originally, it had been agreed that groups would have a maximum of twelve participants, but as they were now running them online and physical space was therefore no longer an issue, the team agreed to increase the maximum to twenty, which was similar to what mental health services were doing elsewhere.

The list that Jason now had in front of him were new referrals for group work; the people who had been referred since the team had made the decision to close to referrals for individual work. Jason wanted to check through them, to see that these were appropriate, before sending them their pre-group appointments. The majority were standard personality disorder type referrals, even if they didn't have this formally recorded as a diagnosis in their notes. Their histories typically involved a background of trauma, often childhood sexual abuse and family violence, which had led them to develop pathologically unhelpful ways of coping, like self-harm and risky behaviour. Jason noticed that a couple of the referrals were people who had been to his first and second groups eighteen months ago, and so had been discharged around a year ago. He felt disappointed to see that they had been referred back, but perhaps it should be considered a successful result that they had managed to stay out of mental health services for a year and maybe a top-up would be all that was needed to get them back on track again.

Jason was rather irritated to see that Mandy, a patient he had only recently discharged from the service, had been referred to the group by Dr Williams, one of the psychiatrists, who had been very supportive about the delivery of Zen Psyonics. This was tricky. Jason didn't want to have any conflict with Dr Williams, but it was not the best use of his time trying to engage with people like Mandy, who were clearly not showing any degree of responsibility for themselves or likelihood of engaging with services. He made a mental note to raise it in the next team meeting, and perhaps issue guidance about appropriate referrals. There was another anomalous one which had come through from Frances Fisher, of all people. This was a woman recently diagnosed with breast cancer, with no signs of mental illness, nor any history of it. This person shouldn't even have been assessed by their team. And now that they had, it was another annoying demand that he would have to address. Keen not to waste any more time, Jason copied the twenty names and numbers and emailed them off to admin with a request to book them into pre-group appointment slots with him. When he met with them, he would try to dissuade both those two from the group and encourage them to go elsewhere for support.

The day Jason met Mandy again a couple of weeks later, he had hit nine out of ten on arriving at work, having been greeted by a lovely card from a patient, thanking him for running the group she had just been discharged from and saying how much it had helped her turn her life around. Jason welcomed the feeling of warmth and pride, at the same time as accepting that he should enjoy this moment and not try to hold on to it, for it was simply part of his *river of feelings*. He liked to use that metaphor, which he had learned through his Zen Psyonics practice, being aware of how every drop of water is a different feeling, and each feeling relies on all the others for its existence. *To observe it, we just sit on the bank of the river and identify each feeling as it surfaces, flows by, and disappears.* Of course, this was much more welcome with unpleasant feelings that we might want to chase away. So he was grateful of the practice a couple of hours later, after doing the pre-group appointment with Mandy.

When Jason first started working with Mandy, he felt some connection to her background and was hopeful that through Zen Psyonics he would be able to help her get her life back on track. Both of them had experienced difficult childhoods which made it hard for them to find their path into responsible adulthood. In Mandy's case, she had witnessed years of violence from her father towards her mother. Her mum eventually escaped, leaving Mandy with her father. Although he was never violent to her, there was rarely any affection from him and when Mandy got pregnant at the age of eighteen, following a one-night stand, she was offered a flat through the local housing association and was glad of the opportunity to get away from her father. But despite being in a rather more secure position for the first time in her life, she found it hard being a mother, especially because the few friends she had were going out and having fun, which she was unable to do with a baby to look after and no parents to help her. She devoted herself to looking after her daughter and felt that she had done a good job as a mother in some ways, especially as her daughter went on to university. But she also resented her daughter, feeling she had missed out on forging her own path in life, not having anything much in the way of work experience or qualifications and not having the money to get any. In turn, her daughter resented her and they grew further and further apart. Mandy never had any problem getting boyfriends. She was naturally good looking, but the men she attracted were often only interested in her for looks and her body, not for herself. She fantasized about living off grid and being self-sufficient, but it seemed so far out of her reach, destined to remain only a dream.

Unsurprisingly, given her ongoing situation, Mandy often seemed angry, bitter and hopeless. Jason struggled to get her to accept that she needed to let go of the past if she was ever going to move on. He tried to get her to see that change was possible, sharing some of his own story about his less than ideal childhood and his sense of not having a place in the world. But he soon learned that Mandy was always ready for a fight, always ready to blame her situation on something outside of her, and she just didn't ever seem able to hear what Jason was saying to her.

The pre-group appointment was just more of the same.

'So you're telling me that I should just go to a support group and have a cup of coffee once a week?' Mandy shouted when Jason suggested that she would be better off accessing support that she didn't need to commit to and could just turn up whenever she liked. 'I'm not going to be fobbed off by you!' she continued. 'Has it ever occurred to you that it might not be *me* who is failing to take responsibility for myself but that it's actually *you* who is not very good at your job and have no idea what it's like to have a personality disorder?'

Jason had no chance of persuading Mandy that the group was not for her. He would just have to wait until she failed to attend two sessions consecutively and he would be able to discharge her.

He focused on facing his anger and irritation with care, affection and nonviolence. He was neither drowned, nor terrorised by the feeling, nor rejecting of it. Breathing in, he knew there was an unpleasant feeling in himself. Breathing out, he released his unpleasant feeling into the air. His breathing was light and calm and his mind and body slowly became light, calm and clear as well. He was pleased to be ready for the next pre-group appointment with Paula Vale.

'So the appointment today is for me to tell you about the group and about what you need to do to get the most out of it. This leaflet gives you more information and sets out the aims,' Jason read from the leaflet, 'to teach you skills to improve your ability to regulate your emotions, get along with people, cope in an emotional crisis and decrease the likelihood of emotional crises.' He handed the leaflet to Paula who had been very quiet so far. 'I'm wondering, though, bearing in mind the background to your referral, whether you think this might not be the right group for you?' he asked tentatively.

'Yes, I discussed that in my appointment with Frances Fisher but in the end we both agreed I may as well give it a try.' This woman, Paula, wasn't giving too much away and Jason got the sense that she was quite guarded, which was not unusual.

'Is that something you struggle with, getting along with people?' Jason asked.

'No, not particularly, but it is very difficult for me to manage my emotions at the moment.'

'That's obviously understandable and I'm sorry to hear that you're going through such a difficult time. I guess it's maybe helpful for you to know that most people referred to the group have personality disorders or at least long-standing mental health problems. I'm not sure you fit into that category...'

Jason hoped he would have more chance dissuading Paula than he had with Mandy. But he wondered whether it was actually making Paula *more* keen, if anything, to get into this group and see what they were trying to hold back for only the select few. At any rate, she kept quiet and waited for Jason to continue.

'It's important for you to know that you'd need to attend the group on time and let us know if you can't attend or if you'll be late. You need to be willing to try things out and complete the tasks and practices at home, as well as share your experiences in the group. Are you in a situation where you'll be able to commit to that?'

'It depends what the tasks are but I'm off sick from work at the moment so I can't imagine that would be a problem, as long as it's not too onerous.'

'I understand you're currently going through chemotherapy. Might that make it difficult for you to complete the home practice?'

Jason sensed her digging her heels in further. It seemed that the more he tried to put her off, the more eager she was to voice her commitment. Perhaps she wanted to actually see him in action. Perhaps she had heard good things about Zen Psyonics.

'I think it'll be fine,' she said confidently. 'It astonishes me that there are women with young families going through chemotherapy and still managing to look after their children and do the housework. I imagine this won't be as time demanding or energy consuming as that, unless I'm wrong?'

'Well I guess it depends on what support you have around you, but some people do struggle to commit to the home practice and if you miss two sessions or you don't complete the home practice for two sessions, unfortunately we'd have to discharge you from the group.'

'So what would happen if you were discharged from the group? Would you be offered some other type of therapy?'

'No, that would be you done here, unfortunately. Though of course you could find further support from groups out there in the community. I can give you another leaflet about those if you decide this isn't for you.'

Paula declined. 'So what sorts of things do you do in the group? You haven't really said.'

'Well, it's not a *therapy* group, where people sit around and talk about their histories or the details of their illnesses. It's focused on learning skills to enable you to live more of a fulfilling life. There's a space on the back of the leaflet for you to complete before you attend the first session, so that you can share your ideas with the group about what you want to get out of attending and where you want to get to in your life. We also encourage group members to share specific examples of how they've used the skills we've been focusing on each week, whether they've been successful, what has got in the way, and so on. The skills are for things like managing emotions and communicating more effectively. Running alongside the skills work is mindfulness practice and daily exercise plans which Zen Psyonics has shown are key to leading a fulfilling life.'

'I'm an English teacher. It sounds more like my school's personal and social education curriculum than a therapy group. Though to be fair, you already said it wasn't a therapy group and I haven't always paid much attention to the PSE curriculum, being in the English department. I often think it's a bit wide of the mark though for the children in most need. Communication skills aren't necessarily going to get children very far if the adults around are not in any fit state for constructive dialogue themselves. Maybe it's different for adults with mental health problems though. Sorry, I'm rambling a bit. So what happens if it doesn't work?' Paula asked.

'Oh it *will* work', Jason said emphatically. 'There's a very strong evidence base for Zen Psyonics and we've been getting great results locally, which is why we're expanding our programme. It also means that we're confident about discharging you from our service at the end of the group. But don't panic. That's twenty weeks away and you'll be in a totally different place from where you are now.'

To Jason's annoyance, Paula persisted and seemed to be playing him. 'Do I get my money back if it doesn't work?' she smiled.

Brief Dynamic Healing Therapy

Brief Dynamic Healing Therapy (BDHT) represents an accelerated form of dynamic psychotherapy designed to swiftly alleviate symptoms of emotional distress and enhance mental health. This approach targets the unconscious emotional processes underlying various psychological and somatic challenges, employing powerful interventions in a cost-effective manner.

While BDHT shares historical roots with classical psychoanalysis, it diverges significantly. BDHT therapists are not neutral; instead, they actively advocate for change and health. Rather than relying on interpretations, therapists highlight the importance of experiencing core emotions, utilizing non-interpretative interventions to address anxiety and defences. This approach strengthens emotional processing, leading to freedom from distressing symptoms and maladaptive behavioural patterns concerning oneself and others.

A substantial body of published research supports the efficacy of BDHT in treating a range of emotional issues, including depression, anxiety, psychosomatic illnesses and personality disorders. Notably, these benefits not only endure in the long term but may even increase after the termination of therapy.

7

'Jason! Good to see you!' Alexander smiled warmly at the screen. 'It's been a long time! How you doing?'

'Yeah, good thanks, Alexander. I'm just snatching this hour from the family before it's time to do the bedtime routine. Sharlotte's doing the homework shift. How about you? How's life leading the Zen Psyonics charge?' Jason heard his youngest, Kelly, shouting at his mother about homework. He briefly muted his connection, not wanting to bother Alexander, aware that his guru was not a family man himself and could get irritated with young children. He was also careful to address Alexander by his full name, knowing how he hated it being shortened to Alex. Alexander had once said something about the abbreviation cheapening him and who on earth ever referred to *Alex* the Great?

'Life is busy! You know, I thought streamlining ZP by clearing the surf element would free up more time for me, but woooo!' he made a whooping sound, 'we're busier than ever! You know, I could retire right now but I want to take care of my baby until she comes of age and can take care of herself! No seriously, I'm in the process of negotiating my participation in a third wave CBT conference in Colorado next spring. They are mad about ZP over there. Shame it's not California but that will come later, hopefully. I *really* want to go back to Malibu! Still, I'm going home to my folks up in Farwater at the end of the month so I've got that to look forward to. Anyway, enough about me. This is *your* time. What can I do for you?'

'Well, you know we've been rolling out the ZP groups for the last eighteen months and we've been getting pretty good results.' Jason made a point of calling it ZeePee, using the American pronunciation like Alexander, even though for some reason it made him feel a little silly. 'You've seen our results anyway. I've still got an assistant inputting them onto the ZP database and I'm really pleased they compare so favourably with your own.

You must have taught me well!' Jason wouldn't normally be so deferential to someone, but he knew he was lucky to be in this position, having a video consultation with Alexander, the founder and creator of Zen Psyonics. It was admittedly a meeting at his own expense, but Jason considered the one hundred and fifty pounds (*mates rates*, Alexander had said) a price worth paying, because apart from anything else there was much kudos attached to being able to say he *knew* Alexander McDonald and had been involved at the *beginning*, when ZP was being developed, before The Green Room even existed.

'Nice work, Jason! But you're not here just to shoot the breeze with me, are you?'

'Well it's nice to celebrate the successes, of course. But you're probably aware the public health service is quite a different beast to the world of private practice. And we do sometimes encounter problems that you might not experience in The Green Room. So,' Jason paused. He felt a little uncomfortable, embarrassed even, at broaching what he was about to say next. 'The thing is, I've had a couple of referrals recently which I don't think are appropriate and I want to discuss them with you, to work out whether you would be doing anything differently to what I'm doing.'

'Fire away!'

'Okay. The first is someone I only discharged from our service a couple of months ago, due to repeated DNAs, but unfortunately she was referred back by one of our psychiatrists, who, I have to say, has been a big supporter of the ZP groups. So it's great that I've got the backing of a key, senior colleague. But it's not so great when they send inappropriate referrals. Basically this woman, Mandy, had already been sent a pre-group appointment, as we've got quite a slick system now and our admin send the letters out and book them in as soon as they go on the list. Of course, Mandy actually attended this appointment. She always complies with the system just enough to keep herself in it, but then she doesn't engage. I've been round this circle with her twice already. So she was on the attack right from the off and when I suggested she would be better off accessing groups in the community, which didn't require reliable attendance, she started accusing me of fobbing her off and even suggested that the problem was that I'm not very good at my job! In the end, I just went along with her signing up, knowing that I'll be discharging her soon enough when she fails to attend. But it feels very unsatisfactory, so I was wondering what *you* would have done?'

'Mmmm...it's a tricky one,' Alexander shut his eyes briefly and sank deeper into the sofa, slowly stroking his dog who had settled onto his lap. 'You're correct, of course. It's not the sort of problem we typically encounter in The Green Room because with us people are spending their own money to attend and therefore they value the product more and want to get their money's worth.'

'What about in years gone by, before The Green Room was born, when you were developing ZP and working in drugs and alcohol? Didn't you get people who were ambivalent then?'

'Sure. That's where the surfing was helpful to hook people in. The starting point was something people wanted to engage with and once they were in, it was easier to introduce the other practices. But you're a bit land-locked where you are and even if you were down here on the coast, that psychiatrist would probably raise her eyebrows if you started incorporating surfing into the groups!'

'Mandy wouldn't be interested anyway. She seems to lean more towards an alternative lifestyle but I can't see that including something like surfing. She's more the type to enjoy watching the surfers whilst she's smoking a spliff on the beach! She's just one of those permanently chaotic people, lurching from one crisis to the next. I once did a home visit and her house was a tip. I don't think she ever bothers to get out of bed until the afternoon and she's one of those people who seems to collect animals, making out she's rescuing them, but really she just has no insight into the fact that she's bored because she has nothing to do all day, because she doesn't work and has an aversion to it. At the end of the day, we can only treat people who want to be treated, who are properly committed to their recovery. Six months of intensive support should be enough for anyone and if they don't get anywhere with that, they're basically not suitable for mental health services.'

'I completely agree, Jason. People need to be ready and if they're not they need to go away and come back when they are. It's frustrating that you have to waste time on these people, not to mention scarce public health service resources. I think all those campaigns to de-stigmatise mental illness has led to basically healthy people excusing themselves from the responsibilities of life by saying they've got mental health problems. I remember working with people like your Mandy. I could always tell, working in drugs and alcohol, the moment I met someone, whether they were going to take on board the programme or not and I quickly dropped the ones who weren't. But I guess in your situation, you don't have much choice if your service is the last port of call. I might not have done anything much different. You can factor in that she's not going to stay the course and maybe have one extra person in the cohort because of that. I'd exclude her from the stats too as she's an outlier and shouldn't be in the group anyway.'

'Oh well, it's reassuring that you wouldn't necessarily have done anything different', Jason concluded, feeling a little deflated. He had half expected Alexander to talk about time wasters, but he thought there might have been some more about the specifics of who was suitable for ZP. He had hoped that Alexander might furnish him with some advice that he could take back to the team to bolster the case for them not accepting referrals of people who were not prepared to engage with the programme, but the general category of non-committed time-wasters was not really the clinical or technical language he was looking for. 'How about the next one? This is actually a cancer patient. You remember that colleague I've talked about, the psychologist? Nearing retirement? Burnt out and not wanting a bar of ZP?'

'Remind me.'

From what Jason could see on his screen, it looked like Alexander now had his feet up on his coffee table and Jason felt he could detect a slight boredom in his demeanour.

'Frances, the psychologist who always seems annoyed with everything and is always banging on about the evidence base yet doesn't seem to know much about diagnosis or neuropsychology or trauma or the newest recommended therapies.' Jason paused, then added, 'and she gets paid a lot more than me and is on the collective leadership team, just by virtue of being a psychologist. Remember her?'

'Ah, Frances, of course! So what's she got to do with this other referral?'

'That's the thing. Frances has repeatedly voiced her objection to ZP, especially to the groups, and now that she has to join the team facilitating the groups she has said it will be like being a prostitute and that I would be better off getting AI to run the groups! And after all that, she referred a woman with *cancer* to the group programme! For fuck's sake!' Were it not such a sensitive issue, it occurred to Jason that this would be a perfect example to share for the emotional regulation module, where participants are asked to generate uncomfortable feelings by imagining a particular situation. Jason knew that were he to have a blood test right now, it would register an increase in cortisol, simply having talked about Frances Fisher.

'Do you think she referred her deliberately, to be awkward, or to prove some other point?' Alexander seemed to be getting interested now.

'Honestly, at one point I started thinking Frances had actually recruited this woman, deliberately as a disrupter but that's obviously far-fetched as the woman could have just as easily ended up in a group with Frances. Anyway, I did ask Frances and she said there was no other option for the woman, now that we're no longer offering individual work and the group is default for all referrals where psychological therapy is indicated. She also made the argument that the woman was struggling to manage emotions and so she might get something from the emotional regulation module. I tried to point out that the group was intended for people with personality disorder but I've had way too many arguments with Frances about diagnosis and it was just a repeat of everything she's already said about that particular topic. Honestly. The amount of time I've wasted with that woman!'

'I'd just take the referral and enjoy! She will probably be a good patient and do her homework and won't give you any trouble and generate some nice scores for your group stats, so it's a win-win really!'

Jason had been so wrapped up in his irritation with Frances that he hadn't seen this now obvious point that Alexander was making. He nodded sagely and could feel his vagus nerve being activated, triggering the relaxation response, calming his heart rate and breathing, restoring balance to his nervous system. He enjoyed a deep, slow breath in and on releasing it, sighed, 'yes, of course. I hadn't even seen it like that. So, what about the other modules? Should I be thinking about adaptations for a cancer patient?'

They spent the rest of his allotted time talking through various tweaks and pondering the possibility that this challenge was a new opportunity. ZP might grow a new branch into cancer care and Jason could be instrumental in this venture.

The following Monday, Jason had the opportunity to raise the issue of group referrals in the team meeting. He had been looking forward to it, since meeting with Alexander. He was still curious about why Frances had referred Paula to the group and privately thought it wasn't for the benefit of the patient, but rather to make yet another point about the fallacy of group work and indeed Zen Psyonics itself. Jason knew that Frances probably wouldn't be ready for him to actually voice his agreement with her and he felt it was important not to take her by surprise, as she was likely to get defensive. He therefore decided to *warm the context* (one of Frances's own tricks) and catch her before the meeting actually began. He hung around in the office just before the hour and sure enough, prompt as usual, Frances was making her way down the concourse to the group room.

'Frances!' he stood up and beamed at her as she was passing his desk. 'You're probably going to be surprised to hear me say this, but on reflection, after our discussion the other week about the groups and that cancer patient, I had a bit of a discussion with

Alexander McDonald in supervision, and he actually agreed with you, that she is likely to benefit from the group and the fact she doesn't have a personality disorder is not really an issue.'

'Ahhhh,' Frances responded slowly, knowingly, 'the great man himself, Alexander McDonald. So he doesn't mind a bit of mission creep?'

'Mission creep?' Jason didn't know what she meant and he realised he should have sought her out sooner for this conversation.

'I'll explain later,' Frances whispered as they entered the group room and seated herself next to Margaret, leaving Jason to take the only spare chair tucked in the corner at the back.

Hayley was soon in full swing, zipping through the referrals and allocating new patients to staff who, as usual, had barely any space to take on more work. Usually at least once in these meetings, she was likely to say something along the lines of, *if nobody volunteers I'm just going to have to allocate them, and this will be based on my knowledge of your caseloads*. Some of the nurses did volunteer and clearly felt the need to be as helpful as possible to Hayley, even though it was likely to be at some detriment to themselves. There was a scheduled discussion about patients who had been admitted to the wards and a few who had recently been discharged. Then Hayley moved on to *any other business*, and as it was already nearly two o'clock, she was clearly keen to wrap things up.

'Yes, Hayley. I wanted to flag up referrals to the Zen Psyonics groups. Obviously this is now our default for people referred to the service and in need of psychological therapy. But I do want us to avoid taking inappropriate referrals for the groups, because if we do, we're likely to just get clogged up with people who don't need to be here and leave less space for the hundreds of people waiting who do need therapy.'

'What sort of inappropriate referrals, Jason?' Hayley was twizzling her long brown hair with her perfectly manicured fingers and looked rather disinterested, if not impatient.

'Well, I've already discussed one with Frances, and we did agree that this person may benefit from the group, but she's actually a woman who's undergoing treatment for breast cancer, with no history of mental health problems. How on earth these referrals get through to secondary care, I don't know.'

'It was the risk of suicide', Frances answered, 'and the fact that she doesn't fit the criteria for counselling in cancer care.'

'So she got dumped in secondary care, like all the others who don't fit anywhere else,' Hayley concluded. 'I've got a meeting with service managers next week. I'll raise it with them. In the meantime, she could be referred to self-help groups. There's plenty out there for cancer.'

'She was already in our system and she fits our criteria in terms of risk so I think we have to offer her a service and the only one on offer, since our team decision, is the Zen Psyonics group', Frances responded, somewhat triumphantly, Jason thought.

Hayley looked annoyed. 'Well we'll have to make an exception this time, but I'll make sure these sorts of referrals don't get through in future.' She went on hurriedly. 'I'm just aware of the time and this room is booked. We'll have to put this on the agenda for discussion at the next meeting, sorry Jason.' Hayley stood up, an emphatic gesture to show the meeting was now closed. 'Thanks everyone. Have a great week!' she said in a sweet voice and was gone.

Jason felt deflated. He decided he would Google *mission creep* when he got back to his desk.

Cognitive Construct Therapy

Cognitive Construct Therapy (CCT) involves developing the capacity to pay attention to mental states within ourselves and others as we seek to comprehend our actions and the actions of others based on intentional mental states. Identifying cognitive constructs enables us to grasp the workings of our own minds and the minds of others, understanding how this influences emotions, thoughts and actions. This comprehension of both our own perspectives and those of others contributes to more effective interactions and social relationships.

In certain mental health conditions, such as personality disorders, individuals may experience limitations in their ability to identify cognitive constructs. This impairment can lead to misconceptions about emotions, thoughts and actions, resulting in breakdowns in interactions and relationships. It is crucial for individuals to develop the capacity to identify cognitive constructs to enhance mental health and social functioning.

This evidence-based treatment has proven highly effective in addressing Borderline Personality Disorder (BPD), gaining recognition nationally and internationally. While initially designed for BPD, CCT is now utilised for various disorders. Training programmes are available for CCT across the range of personality disorders, and with families, groups, adolescents and more.

8

Frances and David were tucking into a delicious supper of slow-cooked beans and butternut squash. With David retired, it was very rare that she didn't arrive home to yet another amazing dish.

'I'm not going to spoil this fantastic food by telling you about the born-again therapist's latest move!' Frances declared resolutely. 'I swear I must be the best fed wife in the country! What's the catch?'

David raised his eyebrows and smiled. 'No catch, my dear. You're not at work now. I'm not trying to schmooze you!'

'Well you'd probably do a much better job than Jason if you were. Maybe he should just bring me food like this and I'd be won over. I doubt he's much of a cook though. He spends too much time meditating and cosying up to his heroes.' Frances fell silent and savoured the food. David had cooked a large dish, enough for another meal, though they were both tempted to carry on until it was finished.

'I'm going to move this away from us', he said, putting it on the stove, 'and you can tell me about your day.'

Frances sighed. 'There's really not that much to tell, other than Jason has decided that me referring that cancer patient was not such a bad idea after all. But I smell a rat. He said he'd been talking to that hustler, Alexander McDonald, who he is completely in awe of. And that he agreed with me after all that this person would benefit from the group. Which isn't quite the main point I made. I said that she had no other option than the group now that we're no longer taking individual referrals. He only hears what he wants to hear. He still seems to be trying to get me on side, for some reason. I have no idea why. But anyway, I'm actually more bothered about what sort of experience this poor woman will have in the group. She's going to be in Jason's group which I think makes it even worse. If she'd been in a group with me, I would at least have been able to adapt it and try and make something useful out of it for her. And I would have been able to use the individual meetings to try and give her some time for talking about things she might have found helpful. As it is, I can just imagine Jason repeatedly reminding her of the proven benefits of Zen Psyonics. Oh well, it will all come out in the wash, although that will probably be some years down the line and in the meantime it will be hundreds of patients who lose out.'

'What about what's happening elsewhere in the country? Didn't you say they've adopted this ZP in lots of other places? Aren't there results coming out from there which suggest it's not all it's cracked up to be?'

'Not really. The problem is, services tend to get on these tracks and keep going. And whilst some of them might collect pre- and post- group measures, they don't seem to get published anywhere externally or publicly, and even if they did, they'd be replete with problems. They wouldn't include the people who were not admitted to the group in the first place, because they were either too ill or not ill enough. And they wouldn't necessarily include the people who dropped out. And they wouldn't include the stats on how many of those same people get referred back to mental health services not so long after they've been discharged. And even any positive stats don't necessarily mean that it's the group programme itself that makes a difference. There's so much included in the programmes that the measures can't possibly capture what are the so-called *effective* aspects of the *treatment*.' Frances paused for breath. 'Am I boring you, David? You've heard all this before, surely. I'm definitely boring myself!'

'Frances, you never bore me. Even after thirty-five long years! You frustrate me sometimes and you can be hard to argue with sometimes, but that's the beauty of you. That's what I love about you. You never bore me! Do I bore you? What do you love about me?'

Frances looked directly into his wonderful brown eyes. 'I can safely say you never bore me either. And that you frustrate me sometimes and can be hard to argue with! And I love your wonderful cooking. I am very much enjoying your retirement! And looking forward to when I can spend more time arguing and being frustrated by you!'

'Nil desperandum,' David said to his wife the next morning as she was leaving for the gym before work. 'In other words, don't let the buggers get you down!' He said this to her most mornings and she found it strangely comforting, even though she did, often, find that the buggers got her down. But it appealed to the rebel in her and she needed that more than ever this morning as she was going to be starting her first Zen Psyonics group that day. She was mainly not looking forward to it, such as it was an assault on her professional practice, but there was a part of her that was determined to give her group the best she possibly could in the circumstances. Hopefully her gym session would be the necessary kick start to her day.

The local Freedom Leisure centre was busy as usual just after opening its doors. The demographic of the early morning brigade was generally the full age range of working people, getting their exercise in before the start of a busy day, alongside retired folk who liked to rise early. Frances was pleased to see a free stationary bike where she could begin her five minute warm-up with a light cardiovascular effort to get the blood flowing to her muscles and loosen up her stiff joints. There was a young man, thirties maybe, clearly pushing himself on the bike next to her and whilst part of Frances wished she was young again and could put in an effort like that, she was content to do her own routine which generally left her feeling energised and ready to face the next eight hours of work. Before moving onto the strength training section of her workout, she did her little stretching routine, which she had followed religiously since signing up with Freedom Leisure over ten years ago now. Then she made a beeline for the leg press machine which had just become vacant and found herself next to John, the secretary of the local Labour party, on the leg curl machine.

'John!' she greeted him. 'I haven't seen you for ages. I heard you had an accident. How are you?'

'Recovering slowly, Frances. Feeling better for getting back to the gym. I was going mad lying around at home!'

'Oh tell me about it! I thought I'd end up sectioned when I broke my leg all those years ago. What would we do without our daily dose, eh?'

'Indeed, although the convalescing did give me time to catch up with some of the constituency business. I honestly thought I'd have more time in retirement but I seem to get ever busier!'

'David's the same, John. I keep wondering whether I'm misguided in looking forward to joining him in retirement. It doesn't sound like you lot get much rest!'

'No rest for the wicked, is there? We must have been very wicked in our past lives!'

'How's the campaign beginning to shape up, anyway? Not long to go now. A year will fly by, I imagine.'

'That's going slowly too. Lots of internal wrangling, the left fighting with the centre, as usual. And how about yourself and the health service, these days? Are you still hanging on by the skin of your teeth?'

'Something like that, John. That's why I'm here in the gym. I need to get the endorphins going just to get me through the door these days. So I better crack on and stop nattering with you, otherwise I'm going to underperform today!'

'I can't imagine you ever underperforming, Frances! I'm sure you do a great job even when you're below par. I hear good things about you, you know!'

'I wish my colleagues could hear you say that, John. Sadly I don't think they share your view, but anyway. You know me. I see it as my duty to keep that little subversive space open for the people I see, so that we don't all get sucked into the big, black neoliberal hole!'

'Keep the faith, comrade,' John winked at her as Frances moved on to the bench press.

'Always, John!'

Frances hadn't done enough cardio yet for any endorphins to

kick in but she was already feeling good, simply having had a little chat with John. That was the thing about this gym habit. So often there was the added bonus of bumping into a friend or neighbour and sharing a bit of love or strengthening solidarity. She wouldn't be without it. She did a twenty minute hard blast on the rowing machine, working at threshold, her maximum heart rate. When she climbed off she felt renewed and strong and powerful. She chanced skipping the cool down and went straight for a cold shower, hoping she would still feel the glow when she arrived at the office.

'Hello,' Frances said as cheerfully as possible to the people arriving on the screen. She felt conflicted about hosting the group virtually now that Covid was no longer really a factor for consideration, and knowing that some people would have much preferred to meet in real life. At the same time, others welcomed not only the convenience of attending sessions by video call, but also found it less anxiety provoking. It was horses for courses and just not possible to please everyone in a group.

'I can see that we've got twelve people here already and we're expecting twenty today so we're just going to hang on and wait for the rest to arrive. Please feel free to take the time to look through the handbook we sent you, whilst you're waiting.'

Even after years of running groups and melding strangers together, Frances still felt slightly uncomfortable at the beginning, with the sense of the unpredictable, not knowing whether the group would gel, not knowing their own personal motivations for attending, what they were hoping to get from it. But she knew most would quickly be revealed, even if it was only that some people didn't want to reveal much.

Jess, the support worker who was co-facilitating the group with Frances, sent her a private message to say that admin had been in touch. Two people had said they were unable to attend today and one person had changed their mind and decided they didn't want to attend the group after all. Three more people had arrived so they were just waiting on the final two. It was already five past ten and they had a lot to get through. Frances knew, through experience, that the final two might simply not turn up and not have any further contact with the service, so she signalled to Jess that they would get started.

'Thank you for coming everyone and good to see that you got onto the call okay. I'm Frances, one of the psychologists in the team and I'm co-facilitating this group with Jess, one of our support workers. You've all had your pre-group meeting with a member of the team and been sent the information about the group and the handbooks, so you'll be aware of the ground rules of the group. Please say if there's anything you're not sure about. You'll also know that we start off with the mindfulness module. So today is just going to be a gentle introduction to that, with a few exercises, some sharing of our experiences and then we'll talk through the home practice. But before we get into that, please can we just go round and say something brief about what you're hoping to get from attending the group?'

Frances allowed space for people to think and knew it was likely there would be some people keen to share their hopes and others not wanting to speak at all until they had sized up the social situation, or perhaps would not ever get to the point of feeling comfortable enough to share anything for the duration. That was fine. It normally relaxed into a space that everybody could get something out of.

A youngish man called Kevin put his virtual hand up.

'Well I'm not sure what I'm hoping to get from this group. I had been wanting to see someone for individual work but I was told that the waiting list for that was around two years so I would have to come to the group if I wanted to get seen sooner.'

A couple of women and another young man nodded and said that they had been told similar.

'I'm sorry about that,' Frances acknowledged. 'It is a very long time to wait to see someone, which can be incredibly difficult if you're feeling really distressed. I really hope that we can make this worth your while and that you and everyone else will get something out of it. There's such a lot of material to get through.

It won't all be everyone's cup of tea, but that's okay. If some of the elements don't work for you, hopefully there will be other elements that do. It's also worth saying that although it can be really daunting to attend a group, when you're dealing with what might feel such private difficulties, actually the other people in the group are often the thing that people end up valuing most, knowing that you're not alone and that there are other people out there who have some idea about what you might be going through. I don't want anyone to feel under any pressure though. So let's just go gently with each other.'

Karrie, a woman who looked close in age to Frances, unmuted herself and spoke with confidence.

'Actually, I've been really desperate to attend this group. I've got a personality disorder and this is the recommended treatment for me. They've been doing Zen Psyonics groups in other places in the country for quite a while now and it seems like they've taken ages to catch up here. So, bring it on!' Karrie said with gusto.

Frances inwardly flinched, though smiled warmly at Karrie. 'Well it's good to see you, Karrie, and I hope it lives up to your expectations.'

With no other contributions forthcoming, Frances gave a little spiel about mindfulness and then invited Jess to read from the script. She knew that even though mindfulness was such a simple and straightforward practice, it was not unusual for people to find it quite challenging and she wouldn't be surprised if the person challenged the most was Karrie, the keenest. Time would tell, Frances mused, and despite her coming from the polar opposite position of not wanting to *bring it on*, she was determined to make whatever this was, worth everyone's while.

Cognitive Framework Therapy

Every individual shares an innate yearning for connection, understanding, and personal growth. When our efforts are hindered by factors like deprivation and trauma, our longings can intensify. Fundamental to our well-being is the inherent need for growth, healing and the realization of our best selves.

Cognitive Framework Therapy (CFT) encompasses the full spectrum of neuropsychology in its approach. Neuroscience reveals our inherent capacity for growth and healing. Positive, responsive and secure relationships trigger the release of chemicals and hormones that enhance emotional regulation, stress management and neural firing. The brain's ability to change, combined with the transformative influence of a secure therapeutic relationship, holds the promise of fulfilment.

Many clients may have previously engaged in various therapies, feeling frustrated by limited progress. Cognitive Framework Therapy proves particularly effective in addressing chronic mental illnesses and preventing relapse among substance abusers. It offers a pathway to change for those who feel trapped in self-destructive patterns, where problematic behaviours seem deeply ingrained in their identity.

People with mental illness have cognitive frameworks which lead to low self-esteem, relationship problems, emotional dysregulation and poor life choices. Through a series of assessments, clients in CFT learn to identify the most impactful cognitive frameworks and initiate lasting changes. Therapists provide validating relationships, fostering a healing and transformative process.

9

A young, lithe woman was making great headway up the road past the Gwel An Mor campsite and Alexander was determined to catch her before she reached the crest of the hill at the crossroads. He hadn't seen her around before and presumed she was a tourist, probably substituting her surf session for a run, seeing as the sea was pan flat and the sunshine of the previous day had given way to drizzle, damp and monotone. It was definitely not his preferred way to start the day and it annoyed him that he was not gaining quickly enough on her, as he was usually able to execute the victory once he had locked on to his target, especially if it was a woman. He put in a massive effort and reached her about thirty yards from the junction. He made a point of controlling his breathing so that she wouldn't hear how out of breath he had made himself.

'Hi,' he greeted with forced nonchalance as he passed her.

'Oh, racing are we?' she glanced over at him and then suddenly engaged her turbo and sprinted past him to the turn and was gone.

Probably some GB athlete, or something, he consoled himself and trotted slowly on home. He was at least prepared for Ed when they connected on screens half an hour later.

'So, we're here to examine the evidence, Ed, something crucial to both our professions!'

'Indeed, Alexander. So, let's recap on where we're up to, shall we, and then I'll set out further sources we might need.'

Alexander was psyched up, probably more so having been overtaken by that woman, so maybe she had done him a favour after all, even though it hurt his pride. There was no way Clemmie Service was going to get him like that.

'I'm just going to share my screen,' Ed continued. 'Here are the facts, as I understand them so far. You, Alexander McDonald, created a new treatment for people with drug and alcohol issues, back in 2011 and coined the term, Zen Psyonics. You have devoted your life over the last ten years to the development of ZP treatment and training of therapists in ZP treatment. So far, so correct?'

Alexander nodded.

'You earned your Masters in Cognitive Behavioural Therapy from the Anglo-Euro College of Psychotherapy in 2010. You have been the director of Zen Psyonics since 2011, where you lead research and further development of ZP treatment. You also founded The Green Room, which trains practitioners in ZP treatment, in 2011. As clinical director you train and certify practitioners and programmes in ZP treatment. You have published, produced and presented dozens of academic papers, manuals, video and audio programmes, journal articles, lectures and workshops on ZP treatment. You are well known and widely recognised throughout the community of psychotherapists as the creator and foremost expert in ZP treatment and you have received multiple awards for your ground-breaking work in treating people with substance abuse problems. You own the trademarks, Zen Psyonics and ZP. You filed a trademark application for ZP based on your use of the term with educational services, research and healthcare.'

'That's a fair summary, Ed,' Alexander felt his mastery restored and that woman dismissed as an irrelevant interlude in his morning practice.

'So, now we get into more detail about your ownership of the Zen Psyonics and ZP trademarks. The further facts are that the practitioners who receive your education and training, participate in development and research and seek certification in ZP, immediately recognise Zen Psyonics and ZP as originating from and relating to you, Alexander McDonald. What's more, within the field of psychological therapies, you and ZP are famous due specifically to the widespread recognition of your work and ground-breaking treatment. As far as the defendant, Clemmie Service is concerned, he has used your name and the goodwill associated with ZP and Zen Psyonics trademarks to promote his professional profile and business interests.' Ed paused for breath and scrolled down the screen he was sharing. 'Stop me if any of this needs correcting. I'll tell you what, I'll let you read through it yourself. Tell me when you're done.'

Alexander scanned through the text Ed had prepared. *Defendant Service has never studied with, taken a course taught by, trained with, or been certified by Alexander McDonald in his ZP treatment. Despite this fact, Defendant Service holds himself out as a self-anointed authority on ZP treatment. He has written at least six papers since 2018 on ZP treatment. He offers consultation and training on ZP treatment through Clemmie Service & Associates, CentreFlow and other business interests. He regularly presents at conferences focusing on ZP treatment, which he markets and promotes throughout the country and further afield. Defendant Service formed CentreFlow in 2018 to offer a certificate programme for practitioners in ZP treatment. Since 2018 he has promoted and offered certificates under the logo shown below (the 'infringing logo') and the acronym ZPCF to practitioners throughout the UK.*

Alexander needed to make a point. 'On the matter of the infringing logo, it was brought to my attention recently that Clemmie has started using his own logo which is remarkably like mine. Can you let me screen share and I'll show you?'

Alexander pulled up Clemmie's website and zoomed in on the logo. Alexander's own ZP logo was a circle, denoting the world, struck through by a horizontal curved line representing a wave, with the logo itself being close to the eighth letter of the Greek alphabet, *theta*, which in ancient times was considered the symbol of death. In ZP it was symbolic of the death of the old life and old, drug using, ways.

'See how Clemmie's logo is also a circle with a line through, albeit a vertical one and that line apparently represents a tree, for whatever reason. Either way, it looks like a modified version of mine. So are we also going for him using that *modified* logo, bearing in mind your explanation last time that anyone who uses an important component of your logo may be legally pursued for infringement?'

75

'It's covered,' Ed reassured, taking back control of the screen and sharing the next part.

In 2018, knowing of Alexander McDonald's creation of ZP treatment, his publications, presentations and trainings, and his ongoing use of ZP and Zen Psyonics, Defendant Service filed trademark applications through his CentreFlow organisation claiming the exclusive right to use ZPCF (Serial No. 76/230438) and the Infringing Logo (Serial No. 76/030814) for certification services related to ZP treatment. In preparing and submitting the trademark applications for the ZPCF mark and the Infringing Logo, Defendant Service, through counsel, declared, under penalty of perjury, inter alia, that no other person had a right to use either mark or a confusingly similar mark.

Ed appeared back on the screen. 'Now the interesting thing is the evidence you gave me last time, that Clemmie consistently uses your name in his training and his ZPCF certification requires candidates to have read *your* ZP manual. I actually found some additional stuff after we last met and have this journal article where Clemmie states that *Alexander McDonald's work is the genesis of my work and without him I would only be me*! He sounds like one of your surfing bros, Alexander! Could almost be a bromance! Though I guess it's maybe unrequited love! Anyway, I've included all the other pieces where Service promotes himself as a ZP expert, he uses your name in close proximity to his own photo and uses your name on his brochures, which you had no knowledge of and certainly didn't authorise. So our finishing point is this.' Ed highlighted the text on his screen.

Practitioners seeking education, training or certification in ZP treatment are likely to encounter Defendant Service's professional practice and his businesses offering, promoting and marketing their services under the ZPCF mark, the infringing logo, the ZP mark, the Zen Psyonics mark and the founder of ZP, Alexander McDonald's name. These circumstances are likely to result in confusion. The use of these marks, symbols and Alexander McDonald's name are likely to result in the mistaken belief that Alexander McDonald is affiliated, connected, or associated with Defendant Service and his businesses, or that Alexander McDonald otherwise sponsors or approves of his services.

'Right. So what next?' Alexander was keen to get this legal case dealt with as quickly as possible but never having pursued anything like this before he felt he had no option other than to go at Ed's pace. He wasn't massively interested in wading through all the information, the processes and the legal niceties. That was Ed's job. That was what Alexander was paying him handsomely for, or at least would be, assuming they won the case. But Ed seemed keen to take a fair amount of time explaining things to him and it was difficult to do anything other than listen.

'So then we set out our cause, or causes, of action. This is the legal claim that gives us the right to seek a remedy. So in your case, our first cause of action is the trademark infringement, for which you should be entitled to damages which will be determined at trial. The second cause of action is the false endorsement, where Clemmie has continued to use your name in association with his services which are in direct competition with yours. I will word it to the effect of capitalising on your fame and success in the field of psychotherapy as well as misleading the public. And again, if we win, you will be entitled to damages decided by the court. The third cause of action is violation of the Trade Descriptions Act, which most laypeople are aware aims to safeguard consumers against misleading claims about products and services. To do otherwise is an offence. So there you have it. I will get my assistant to check for any errors and have her send them through to you. I'll need a signed copy in order to proceed.'

At last, Alexander exhaled quietly, feeling the relief of finally moving on to the next stage. He was curious about the damages element though. Whilst his main aim was to relieve his indignation that Clemmie Service brought the defamation case against him, and to send a signal to Clemmie not to mess with him, he did hope that he might come off profitably from the action.

'Can I just check, Ed, about the damages? How does that work? What exactly are we asking for?'

'Absolutely. Always an important question. Basically we're going for damages resulting from the trademark infringement, for any profits, gains or unjust enrichment due to the infringing activities and for legal costs in bringing the action. I can't say what sort of amount this would be. It depends on how the trial goes and on the evidence from Clemmie's accounting which can often be rather messy. And of course, he would be prohibited from using ZP, Zen Psyonics or any other confusingly similar trademarks in future.'

Not even any ball park figures then, Alexander conceded. 'Obviously I'm aware that this is probably not your typical intellectual property case, Ed, but do you think we've got a pretty solid case?'

'It's as solid as it can be. You're right in that it does stray somewhat into trade descriptions territory, which might make it a little more complicated than a standard *stolen goods* case. But we will hopefully at least see off the defamation case this way. And return to you what's rightfully yours.'

He couldn't quite put his finger on it, but something didn't feel quite right today. Alexander wasn't sure whether it was the unfortunate start to his day, having his arse handed to him on a plate by that woman running up the hill, or the general malaise of the weather which meant he had gone without a decent surf for over a week now. Or was it this business with Clemmie Service? It was almost fine when he was meeting with Ed, because it was a straightforward situation of Ed drawing up the case on his behalf. But he was uneasy about what colleagues and friends might make of the fact that he was taking someone to court for stealing what was, essentially, his *brand*. It was unsettling to be in the position of having to fight his corner and he resented it especially when it was *years of his own hard work* that had transformed so many lives and pulled people out from the gutter.

He had many loyal followers, including those who had been helping him gather evidence for his legal case. He also had absolute certainty that Zen Psyonics was the most successful market-leading therapy of the last ten years in treating people with substance use problems and latterly personality disorders.

ZP was perfect for these two patient groups, as they had similar problems, particularly around emotion regulation and impulse control. Alexander was very clear that it was the unique, four-pronged module approach of Zen Psyonics, with its meditation, communication, physical activity and thought-restructuring, that ensured its success. Other new wave cognitive behavioural therapies were lesser, for not taking the sort of holistic approach that ZP advocated, and in particular not addressing the psyche at the level of the *body*. The more woo-woo body psychotherapies, on the other hand, did not give sufficient attention to meaning and cognitive restructuring. Zen Psyonics packaged it all together beautifully.

But, very occasionally, Alexander would be challenged, usually at some conference he had been invited to speak at, where a truculent member of the audience, maybe a direct competitor, had clearly come prepared to rip him apart. One time, there was an older, rather shabbily dressed man, who appeared to have come to the wrong conference. At least, he had spent the whole of the morning taking to the floor when it was time for questions. He said he was a psychologist himself, but he certainly didn't seem to be much of a fan of CBT. He had an annoying manner of being almost deferential at the same time as making an attack. Alexander, like the other presenters, batted his comments away, but some of the man's words had gnawed at him ever since. The man had begun by acknowledging the competitive nature of the psychotherapy market place and went on to question whether Zen Psyonics was in fact a distinct therapy or just more of the same. Alexander had responded by returning to a few of his slides, highlighting once again what made Zen Psyonics distinct from other products on the market. The man was clearly not finished and came back with his almost apologetic voice, asking: 'Would you be in favour of the psychotherapy industry in the UK being more tightly regulated, and to move responsibility for its interests out of the Department of Health and into the Department of Trade and Industry?' Alexander had said that he wasn't sure what the man was getting at and the Department of Trade and Industry wasn't really his field. He had signalled to move on but the man kept a firm hold of his microphone. 'PsySuNUK, the psychiatric survivor network, have advocated that the pharmaceutical industry should be regulated by the Department of Trade and Industry. Do you think the same should apply to the psychotherapy industry?' Alexander had decided it was time to shut this nonsense down and so declared that the topic needed to be saved for another time and signalled to one of the assistants to retrieve the microphone.

As if that wasn't enough though, the man was relentless and had made a beeline for him at the lunch break.

'I thought your talk was very interesting, Mr. McDonald. I find it difficult to tease out the differences between the different therapies, with there being so many on the market now. It makes it quite a challenge for us practitioners. And it does genuinely make me wonder about industry regulation. I think PsySuNUK have got an important point.'

Alexander had wondered whether the guy was actually playing Columbo and if in fact he was a fully paid up PsySuNUK service user.

'The thing is,' the Columbo man had continued, 'for all their apparent novelty, it seems to me that third-wave CBT approaches all share the same magical belief that we can overcome deeply entrenched personal problems, caused by a toxic and punishing world, through *insight*. And in fact, the development of psychotherapies has reflected the efforts of practitioners to market their skills, rather than it being a result of scientific advancement. I'd go as far to say that the third-wave therapies have a deliberate mysteriousness about them, when in reality there's nothing mysterious about the world being a cruel and damaging place, though various people would be happy for us all to believe our problems are entirely within ourselves.' The man had paused and looked innocently at Alexander. 'Do you think there might be some truth in that?'

Alexander had surmised that this strange, bumbling-not-bumbling man had no interest whatsoever in his own opinion and wanted to get away from him as quickly as possible. He had no intention of engaging with him any further, so pulling his phone out of his pocket he had pretended to take an urgent call and headed off towards the toilets as quickly as he possibly could, with *the efforts of practitioners to market their skills* ringing in his ears.

Cognitive Restructuring Energy Alignment Method

Cognitive Restructuring Energy Alignment Method (CREAM) is a well-established, highly effective and non-invasive brief therapy method developed and honed over the past 35 years. CREAM involves self-tapping acupressure while recalling a traumatic event. This process induces the relaxation response, allowing individuals to confront and think about their problems. The positive changes are typically rapid and often enduring.

For therapists or health practitioners, delving into Cognitive Restructuring Energy Alignment Method can be particularly advantageous. In therapeutic settings, clients are encouraged to identify problematic thoughts or memories for healing. Clients then observe a reduction in the intensity of these disturbances as they tap on specific areas of the face and hands in a prescribed sequence. Even sceptics often report a decrease in the intensity of unwanted feelings, and clients typically find it challenging to revert to their original state of upset. Self-treatment between appointments is recommended for addressing addictive urges and physical pain.

Cognitive Restructuring Energy Alignment Method has been embraced by numerous professionals worldwide, including psychotherapists, medical doctors, nurses and others in caring professions, as a complementary alternative technique to aid those in need. There is growing evidence from research conducted around the world to support the effectiveness of Cognitive Restructuring Energy Alignment Method as a psychological intervention.

10

We have four pebbles and the first pebble represents a flower. Begin by picking up the first pebble representing a flower. Put the flower on the palm of your left hand. Breathing in, I see myself as a flower. Breathing out, I feel fresh. Flower, fresh. Take time to breathe in, flower, and out, fresh. We human beings are a kind of flower. We can be very beautiful, very fresh, as a human being. Every one of us has our flowerness, that makes us beautiful, that makes us fresh, that makes us pleasant, that makes us loveable. If you have freshness and beauty, you can offer your freshness and beauty to the world, like a flower. Practise with this pebble, breathing in I see myself as a flower, breathing out, I feel fresh. Three times, and you restore your freshness. Then take the first pebble and put it down on your right.

Now take the second pebble. The second pebble represents a mountain. Put the mountain on your left hand. Breathing in, I see myself as a mountain. You are seated in a very stable position. You are quite stable, solid. Even if someone comes and provokes you, you stay solid. You are not carried away by your anger, your fear. Solidity is very important. Solidity makes it possible for us to be happy. Someone who is unstable, someone who is not solid, cannot be a really happy person. That is why solidity is very important. When you are solid, people can rely on you. Breathing in, I see myself as a mountain. There is a mountain in me. Breathing out, I feel solid. Practise this three times. And then put the pebble down on your right.

Now pick up the third pebble. The third pebble represents still water. When the surface of a lake is very still it reflects mountains and clouds and trees. When you are calm, when you are still, you see things as they are. You don't distort things. You can see things as they truly are. You are not a victim of wrong perceptions. Wrong perceptions bring about fear, anger and despair. But wrong perceptions are there because you are not calm. If you are calm, your perception is perfect. Therefore we want to cultivate stillness and calm, because we know stillness and calm is the foundation of happiness too. Breathing in, I see myself as still water.

Breathing out, I reflect things as they are.
The last pebble represents space, freedom. Without freedom, happiness is not complete. When you arrange flowers, you know that each flower needs space around it to radiate its beauty. A human being is like that too. We need some space inside and some space around to be truly happy. And if you don't have enough space for yourself, how can you offer space to others? Therefore it's very crucial that we know how to cultivate more space for us, because space is one of the basic conditions for happiness. Breathing in, I see myself as space. Breathing out, I feel free.

Jason struck the bell cleanly with the wooden wand and as the initial strike faded, the bell continued to produce a soft and rhythmic tone, slowly diminishing in volume. He hoped that it was carrying its warm resonance and wrapping the group in its gentle vibrations.

'Allow the bell to invite you to pause and be fully present in the moment, drawing your focus away from distractions and worries. Allow yourself to be in the here and now, free from the constraints of past and future concerns.' Jason looked at the screen of faces, some with eyes closed, looking quite serene, others fully alert, staring right at him. 'And when you're ready, return to the group.'

Jason felt all the better for the mindfulness exercise, as he often did. It was such a great way to start the group and even though he was aware that many people, particularly in a group like this, struggled with being in the present moment, it was a good starting place for him at least, to talk through difficulties with the practice.

'Anyone want to share with us how they found that pebble meditation?' he asked, hoping for a few positive responses.

'I found it really difficult,' Mandy piped up.

Jason had been hoping someone would get in before Mandy. He'd experienced this a few times in groups, where one person's negativity seemed to infect the rest of the group and it could ruin not just the session but the whole course. This was another reason why he had not wanted Mandy to take part in the group programme.

Jess, who was co-facilitating the group with Jason, got in before him.

'Thanks Mandy. Do you want to say more about that?'

'Well it was pretty much from start to finish, really. I don't feel like a flower or a mountain or still water and I'm not sure I agree with all that about these things being necessary for happiness. I thought the whole point about this mindfulness was that we're not trying to make ourselves happy but we're trying to be okay with whatever's happening at the time. It just doesn't make sense and I found myself getting irritated with it and then it was even harder to imagine myself as a mountain or whatever!'

'I agree, it can be confusing and really difficult to practice,' Jess acknowledged. 'That's why we try out a variety of different exercises so that hopefully everyone will find something that suits them. I quite liked this one today, but remember I really didn't like the raisin one last time?'

'It's also important to remember,' Jason joined in, 'that we need to practise these exercises regularly, because the mind is like a muscle that needs exercise. The same way we do certain exercises to strengthen our body's muscles, with mindfulness we train the brain's muscle, which is attention. So even though you might struggle with particular exercises, it should get easier with regular practice.'

'I'm with Mandy,' Owen, one of the keener group members said. He was an older, flamboyantly dressed man, and over these first three weeks had been a dream group member. He was punctual, did his homework and had plenty to contribute during sessions, as well as showing an interest in the other members. So it was disappointing for Jason to hear him siding with Mandy. 'I've been practising mindfulness for many years now so I would hope that my brain's muscle was disciplined and obedient by now. But I don't feel like a flower or a mountain or still water either. I'm more of a wobbly jelly most of the time!' he laughed and generated lots of smiles from the faces on the screen. 'I guess you might say, Jason, that I need to be mindful of being a wobbly jelly and smile at it! But that's difficult when you're telling me to be a mountain!' he laughed again and was clearly carrying the audience with him.

'I agree with Mandy too, but for a different reason.' This was from Paula, the group member that shouldn't even be here, Jason reminded himself. 'I found I was able to be a flower and a mountain and still water, or maybe not *be* them, but bring them to mind, so I was quite absorbed in that. But it was that repeated reference to happiness. I'm not here looking for happiness. And anyway, isn't it said that pursuing happiness can make you unhappy?' Jason didn't have time to respond before Paula went on. 'I'm here because I'm finding it hard to *survive*. If I could find a way to survive what I'm going through, that would be a result, but talk of happiness just seems trite and irrelevant. Obviously I'm in a bit of a different position to others, with me being in the group because of breast cancer, but I could imagine that many of us here are trying to find ways to survive, and probably some of you have been trying to do that for a very long time. It must be really tiring.'

'Actually, I think that's a really good point, Paula, and I think that's what I'm looking for in a way,' Mandy responded, clearly connecting with what Paula had said. 'It's reminded me, has anyone seen that reality TV show, *Team of One*? It's about people being dropped in the wilderness on their own, with only a few things to help them, like a fire striker and a gill net. And they've got to build their own shelters and hunt for food and all that. But I've actually been finding it really helpful, tapping into their experience, because one of the things lots of them seem to find most difficult is not the practical skills to keep them alive but the fact that they are *on their own*. And that's one of the things I've found so difficult over the years, that so much of the time, I feel so *alone*. I felt alone when I was growing up and my mum left me with my dad because he was so violent. And I felt alone when I had my daughter because I was a single parent and didn't really have anyone to help out. So yeah, I'm in my own *team of one!*' Mandy tailed off.

'Yes I've been enjoying it, Mandy', Owen said. 'I *totally* agree with you. I feel incredibly *alone* at times. I guess that's one of the reasons I'm pleased to be here in this group. Even if the content is crap, the company is great!'

'That sounds really interesting, Mandy,' Paula sounded buoyed in a way she hadn't done in the group up to this point. 'I've seen it advertised but thought it was probably just another one of those reality TV shows and I'm not a massive fan of them. I also thought the name, the idea of *Team of One*, was a bit off-putting. So many things these days seem to be about self-reliance and individual resilience and independence. But I don't think that's healthy. I sometimes think the worst place anyone can be in, is alone. I'm more into *inter*dependence and community. Anyway, I'm rambling a bit now. I'll check it out, if you're both recommending it.'

'Yes, definitely do!' Mandy seemed pleased to have made a connection. 'Notice where they start to crack. It's usually because they can't cope on their own but if they were in a group, if they were all looking after each other and being looked after, they'd probably keep going!'

The calming effects of the mindfulness exercise on Jason were beginning to wear off. These three group members were monopolising the space and had gone way off at a tangent. Jason needed to bring them back to task.

'This is one of the great things about being in a group,' he found himself saying. 'The learning from each other, the comfort of others and the power of the group. There are so many added benefits from our Zen Psyonics groups, simply from being with other people. And it seems like the three of you have just demonstrated that, sharing your experiences.' Jason could hear Frances's voice in the background, needling him. *The benefits come from being with other people. It doesn't matter what they do together.* 'But I need to emphasise the *added* there. None of us would survive in the wilderness if we didn't first have those skills, regardless of whether we are on our own or with other people. And here in this group, we also need to work on our life skills, so maybe this is a good point to move on to our next exercise.' Nicely brought back to task, Jason congratulated himself.

As he was cycling home later that day, Jason pondered the group session. It was definitely a different dynamic to all the hundreds of sessions he had delivered to individuals. It was much easier to keep things tight whilst doing Zen Psyonics with one person. There was an obvious positioning where he was the teacher and they were the student. But with twenty people in the, albeit virtual, room (though the current group had reduced from seventeen to fourteen by this third session), and two facilitators, it was more of a challenge to keep control because powerful characters could coalesce and the central purpose, for participants to learn new skills to enable them to deal with challenges in their lives, could easily be derailed.

It had taken a while for Jason to become comfortable with this very structured approach. Growing up, his parents had been very busy with work. His father had been a primary school head teacher and his mother a professor of education. But despite their very educated and middle class existence, it seemed that his parents were more bothered about their careers than their children, and they didn't put a lot of time into nurturing Jason and his brother, Scott, who were largely left to their own devices. Unlike Jason, Scott seemed to just *get* life, in a way that didn't make sense to Jason. Scott excelled at school and there was never any doubt that he would achieve his ambition of becoming a doctor. Jason, on the other hand, went through school rather aimless and having little direction from the adults around him. He struggled in the classroom and was often in trouble. Whilst both his teachers and his parents often told him he had the ability to do really well, he became less and less interested in anything at school and scraped an E grade in A level History before he was finally released into the world. He went off travelling, with no plan, taking each day as it came and finding work here and there, in order to continue his journey. Eventually he found his true calling (or what he thought was his true calling at the time) when he came upon Alexander McDonald, delivering *surf therapy* in what was once a fishing town on the Portuguese coast. The small community of surfers was the first place he felt he belonged somewhere.

He loved the laid-back vibe of the town and the way people just weren't really bothered about mainstream things like careers and property and marriage. He spent a month with Alexander as an assistant. The pay was only just enough to cover the rent for his room and food but this mattered little to him as he was learning such a lot and was energised in a way he had never experienced before.

It was also through this work that Jason found that structure wasn't necessarily a boring thing, getting in the way of him having fun, but it was actually helpful and allowed him to get more out of life. Alexander had encouraged him to join the teaching sessions he ran as part of the surf therapy package, suggesting that it would be helpful to Jason in assisting the surf activity if he had an understanding of the problem backgrounds of his paying clients. In fact, Jason found that he could identify quite closely with some of the stories he heard from these people. It occurred to him that his approach to life so far, of having no plan and not investing in anything in particular, was a way of protecting himself from the pain of not being cared for. In one particular session, an introduction to trauma, he was quite alarmed to find himself almost in tears as a long-buried memory surfaced. It was fairly insignificant as these things go, but that made it all the more surprising to find himself having such a strong reaction. He later confided in Alexander.

'I had the most weird experience back there in the session today, when you were asking them to connect with a time when they had felt ashamed. For some reason it brought back this memory of when I was little, at primary school. I must have been around eight at the time. We were on a school trip and when the time came for lunch all the other kids got their lunch boxes out and apart from the fact that some of them had very fancy actual boxes, with superheroes and cartoon characters on them, they all seemed to have a proper picnic with nice drinks and pies and cakes and chocolate bars and crisps and basically all the things kids love in their lunch boxes. And I got my own out and it was literally, the same as every day, four small sandwiches on white bread with a bit of cheese inside, in a plastic tub which had been saved from ice-cream or something. *And that was it!* And the thing was, as if that wasn't bad enough, a few of the teachers noticed and they felt sorry for me and started trying to find extra things they could give me to make my lunch nicer. *And it was that!* Not only feeling that my parents didn't give a shit about me, but *that shame* of being the kid whose parents didn't give a shit about him.' Jason found himself welling up again as he recounted his tale and felt embarrassed. He shook his head vigorously to shake away the feeling and let out a growl. 'So I guess it was then, really, that I just stopped allowing myself to be bothered about being the same as everyone else, trying to achieve like everyone else, because if I didn't care about anything, I couldn't be ashamed about anything.'

'It's powerful stuff, man,' Alexander said. 'Sounds like that was some profound learning for you today. Instead of blaming the world or your parents for not being where you want to be in life, you can see that it's down to you and the way that you think about yourself that's the problem. And now that you've recognised the link between that event and how it shaped your thinking, you can begin to challenge that. And once you start challenging that you can begin to grow.'

On returning to England, Jason managed to find his way into adventure therapy with troubled kids, as a support worker, which meant he could enjoy activities like surfing, skating and climbing whilst he was actually working. He kept in touch with Alexander who became a kind of mentor to him and was instrumental in Jason getting work in a drug and alcohol service and training in ZP. Life had unexpectedly began to make sense to him after all, and although his parents still didn't show the same interest in him or seem to have the same pride in him as they did for his brother Scott, despite the fact that he was now on a well-defined career path, his relationship with them improved because he at least felt better about himself. ZP had absolutely delivered on its promise of post-traumatic growth. Jason felt wiser and stronger, knowing that he had been able to use adversity to transform himself into a better person.

Dhyana Focused Rational Therapy

Dhyana Focused Rational Therapy integrates cognitive behavioural therapy (CBT) techniques with dhyana meditation practices. Its roots can be traced to traditional Indian religious and philosophical traditions.

In Western scientific and medical communities, there is growing interest in mindfulness meditation practices, leading to the development of innovative mental health approaches. One such method is DFRT, particularly effective in addressing negative thought processes like false beliefs and rumination.

DFRT incorporates elements of psycho-education; teaching participants about depression and the role of cognition in it. CBT is then blended with dhyana practice, encouraging people to become aware of incoming thoughts and feelings, accepting them without attaching or reacting. The goal is to help individuals disengage from self-criticism, rumination and dysregulated emotions triggered by negative thinking patterns. Robust evidence from neuropsychological research shows that DFRT strengthens functional and structural connections between the amygdala and middle frontal gyrus, and this increase in communication correlates with improvements in clinical symptoms.

11

So far it seemed, Mandy was right. Paula was well into watching the second series of *Team of One* on TV catch-up. There were some amazing and fascinating people and it was a surprise to see that those who started out with great credentials for the task of surviving alone in the wilderness, were some of the first to go. Many had significant experience of living on the land, often using ancient skills lost to most people leading modern lives. But even with all these skills, it was easy to come to an unanticipated, abrupt end.

In the first series, there was a man who seemed supremely confident and intent on harvesting a big game animal to sustain him long enough to win the competition. Such was his hubris that he was making fun of other contestants, calling them wood nymphs and tree huggers. Then on day four, as he was describing how great it was going to be when he got to tuck into his first moose stake, he tripped and injured his knee. Following much groaning and tears he was swiftly stretchered off the island. Paula felt a little guilty, like she suspected other viewers might have done, feeling some satisfaction at this man's hasty downfall. At the same time, she thought the episode was a great mirror of life in general. You can have all the skills and all the resources in the world, and they will help you in greater or lesser ways, but simple bad luck can ruin all of that. Of course, she was aware that she was inclined to make that particular interpretation at this point in her life because of her own, essentially, *bad luck* in getting this dreadful breast cancer. She did pretty much all the things that everyone was constantly reminded to do, by health experts, the media, celebrities, politicians, in the quest of keeping healthy. She had a varied diet with plenty of fruit and vegetables, didn't smoke, drank occasionally, walked an hour every day, more on weekends, swam three times a week and went to bed early. She had no family history of breast cancer. And yet here she was.

It was noticeable, again probably due to Paula's own permanent body consciousness with the awful side effects of the chemotherapy, that another strong factor for success or failure on *Team of One* was the degree to which the contestants found their *bodies* were able to cope, or not. A fair few people seemed to be doing okay, albeit having lost a significant amount of their body weight, sometimes around the thirty percent mark, but their bodies felt *wrong* and the fear of doing any permanent damage was too much for them to continue. Paula really identified with that. The chemotherapy felt wrong. She felt she was doing her body more harm than good. It seemed like one of the most alien experiences she had ever encountered. *To deliberately do something damaging to your body* to undo some other unknowable and unquantifiable damage.

But where Paula thought Mandy was so right, was in her assessment of the social factor, how being *alone* was the thing that finished off some of the strongest contestants. Again, in the first series, there was a thirty-year old man who surely seemed like he was going to go the whole way to victory. He was skilled, creative, adaptable, humorous and for the first month or so, apparently at ease with his own company. In one of the earlier episodes he had filmed himself doing some sort of war dance around his campfire and exclaiming how much he loved the place. But then, around thirty days in, he slowly started to fall apart. He got frustrated when things went wrong. He started talking more to the camera about how he was missing his family and his girlfriend. And he could be seen wandering around ranting, asking himself, *what is wrong with me*? He was clearly experiencing something that he wasn't able to articulate, even though to the viewer it was more obvious what the problem was. He had plenty of food, an impressive and sturdy shelter, an abundance of fire material, close proximity to water and basically all the essential elements for his survival. Except other people. He asked to leave on day thirty-five, in a tearful call to the programme team, saying over and over, *I don't know what's wrong with me. I'm just missing my family and my girlfriend.* It was as if he thought that wasn't enough reason, that survival is just a material thing and other people an irrelevance. He certainly wasn't on his own in this respect. Three other contestants in that series also threw the towel in, saying they missed their family or partner or they had only just realised they should be with their mother instead of on their own in the wilderness. *In order to survive, they needed to be with people.*

Paula could have quite happily carried on watching the entire series of *Team of One* but she decided to ration herself and use it as a reward for getting other things done. There were plenty of those others things, including housework and shopping and cooking, and now, since joining the Zen Psyonics course, homework. Gerry kept telling her she didn't need to do any housework or anything else, that he would do everything so she could rest if she needed to. But she preferred to get things done so that Gerry could spend time with her at weekends and when he was back from work, instead of doing jobs. Plus, she hated to be seen as a sickly cancer patient and it was one small way she could resist this awful identity, for as long as she possibly could. She was also making sure she took her daily walk which now more than ever she saw as essential medicine.

Paula considered herself very lucky to live in such a beautiful part of the country. She could walk from her house in any direction and very quickly be out on footpaths through fields and hills, along streams and rivers. Even her original thirty-minute romp up and down the common overlooking her house always offered some new delight or different perspective. Before the cancer diagnosis, her walks had generally been about getting some exercise and fresh air and setting her mind straight before what was usually a challenging day at school. She would rise just before six o'clock, which meant that in winter the sun was only just appearing as she got home. She loved that magical time though, with the changing of the light and the stillness gradually being broken with bird song and small sounds of activity as people and animals began to wake up and go about their days. Since the cancer diagnosis, and for the time being no longer facing challenging days at school, Paula tended to walk around lunchtime, often going further afield into the forest above the common. She was amazed how many new paths she had found, never having gone that way in the twenty years she and Gerry had lived in this town. She had taken to choosing a tree each day to *commune* with. That arrogant guy on *Team of One* would have put her in the tree-hugger category as she liked to fully embrace the tree, stretching both arms around its girth, with her cheek on its trunk, and stand there like that for a good couple of minutes, fully taking in the strength of the tree. She sometimes liked to think she could feel the tree's heartbeat, by which she visualised the osmosis of water from the ground through the roots and between cells, and the photosynthesis of sunlight through the leaves, the exchange basically, between inside and outside, between the tree and the elements, taking in, and giving out, like breathing. She would look intently into the patterns of the bark, and feel a deep connection to the age of it. And before loosening her embrace she would always tilt her head back and stare at the branches above, the canopy and the patterns of light between the fluttering leaves. It was both magical and very real. And it was comforting, the sense that grand old tree, for she always chose a grand old one, had been here long before her and would continue to be here long after she was gone.

Not quite so nourishing was her Zen Psyonics homework, the task to which she was now attending. She had a worksheet to complete, giving daily examples of times she had practised the skill of being fully aware of the present moment whilst engaged in particular activities. She had to write down body sensations, emotions and thoughts whilst engaged in the identified activity and then write something about her experience after using the skill. It felt very tedious. She had seen similar worksheets some of her pupils had worked on for mindfulness classes at school. She had even sometimes helped if a child had struggled to write about what they had observed. But she felt uninvested in this herself. It seemed rather pointless. Was this to help her distract herself when she was troubled by terrible thoughts about cancer, or horrible pain from all the drugs? Because if so, it was nowhere near powerful enough. Was she maybe not doing it properly and did she need to choose something more attention-grabbing, or would that defeat the purpose, that the skill was to pay more attention to the mundane? She wondered about using her tree-communing as an example but thought it was probably the wrong kind of thing and in any case, it wasn't a skill she needed to learn, focusing on her awareness of being with the tree, as it just came completely naturally.

It was Friday now and the group was on Tuesday. She had half-heartedly completed the row of observations after the group on Tuesday, using the washing-up as an example. The homework had then completely slipped her mind over the next couple of days as she was happily distracted by spending time with Gerry who had some time off work. So she needed to invent a couple of things for Wednesday and Thursday as well as decide on today's activity, then she would be back on track, wherever that was likely to lead. She filled in the boxes to record the activities, deciding on *making coffee* for Wednesday's task and *sweeping the floor* for Thursday. Today could be *peeling potatoes*. She completed for Saturday, Sunday and Monday as well, deciding it was easier to get the thing done now, so allocated *picking raspberries* to Saturday, making jam on Sunday and *cleaning the bathroom* to Monday.

There was a whole stream of thoughts she could have written all across the page about how she was finding the experience of completing the worksheet. She thought this was not dissimilar to those children at school who would sit there staring at the page or out of the window, or muck about with the child next to them, anything other than the task in hand, and then get called up and told they have a bad attitude and asked whether they care about their future. It wasn't at all new to Paula. It made sense to her that children often struggled with what their schools required them to do and couldn't see the point that adults seemed to see. She had often felt like this herself as a child at school and it wasn't much of a surprise to find herself back in this position. She reminded herself that it didn't really matter, that there didn't need to be any point particularly, other than she was attending the Zen Psyonics group out of interest, to see what actually happened there, to see what this therapy was all about, not to actually *cure* herself, because of course she had cancer, not a mental illness. She did feel a little disingenuous though, a little guilty. She decided she would make up for it by being a decent member of the group and being as supportive as possible to the others attending.

Tuesday came round quickly. Paula was ready to report back on her homework and waited as Jason went round, asking each group member in turn. It seemed that the others had settled on similar tasks to Paula, to practise the skill of awareness, though Paula wondered whether some of them seemed to be hastily noting down comments made by other people, as a way of disguising their blank sheets, which weren't so easy to check online. That was another strategy familiar to Paula after online teaching during Covid. Mandy didn't follow suit though, when it came to her turn.

'Obviously you know Jason I've done this before with you and you might remember I found it difficult last time and this time was no different.'

'Okay, well let's just go through it together and see where we get to. Can you share your examples with the group please, Mandy?'

'Well that's the thing. I actually don't have any. My sheet is blank,' Mandy declared, with comfortable honesty. 'I dug out the same worksheet from last time to see if that would help. Do you want me to share that?'

'That's great that you checked back to see your work from last time, but what we need today is to hear how you got on with the skills practice during this last week,' Jason remained gentle in his firmness.

'Yes I know but that's the problem really. I couldn't get past feeling like it was a bit pointless and wasn't going to work for me. I'm still not that sure what the purpose is. I mean, if it's to distract me from what's going on in my head most of the time, or from the massive row I've just had with my best friend, which completely derailed me this week, it's not really powerful enough. I wasn't sure whether I should have been choosing something different, like something I wouldn't normally do which might be more likely to distract me, but I remember you saying that just routine activities are the best. And then I just got fed up thinking about it. I did wonder about using that as an example, being aware of my thoughts and feelings whilst filling in the worksheet, but I had got too annoyed by then.' Mandy paused. 'Sorry. I know it's an important part of being in the group and it's one of the rules to do the homework. I've just had a really difficult week this week and wasn't in the right frame of mind.'

'Thank you, Mandy,' said Jason. 'We appreciate your honesty. But I do want to remind you and everyone else that two weeks' homework not completed is treated the same as two missed sessions, which would mean you would have to leave the group and be discharged from the service. Is there anything we can do to help you make sure you don't miss any more?'

'Switch off all the other things which are stressing me out?' Mandy half-joked.

Paula decided to speak up, even though she hadn't been invited. 'I haven't shared my homework yet but can I just say, what Mandy described was similar to my own experience. It felt a bit pointless to me too and I found myself thinking of my pupils at school, the ones that don't do their homework, who are often told they have a problem with their attitude. I don't mean to say there isn't a point to it and I don't mean to criticise *you*, Jason, as I know you're just teaching the course and it's not as if you invented it. But I just wonder whether it's maybe more helpful for people who aren't at the strong end of distress, people who aren't up against so many other powerful factors.'

Even through the medium of the computer screen, Paula thought she could detect Jason bristling. It was probably little micro-movements of his face that were impossible to detect in this impoverished communication environment but she was fairly sure it was there. Or perhaps, Paula thought, he might be thinking Mandy and I are connecting too closely and he's worried

99

we'll become a disruptive force.

'It's a fair point, Paula,' Jason said eventually, 'that obviously this stuff is going to be easier without other challenges going on in your lives, but I can say very confidently, both from my own experience of running these groups, with people like yourselves, with significant mental illness, and from the evidence base from populations similar to yourselves, that Zen Psyonics *works*. And if anything, it's probably even *more* effective with people with more severe difficulties because they have got the most to gain. I've worked very closely with the founder, Alexander McDonald, who developed it specifically to help people with drug and alcohol problems, people who had been written off by other services because their difficulties were so apparently entrenched. So I don't think it's helpful to go down the road of *this can't possibly work for me because my difficulties are too severe*. In fact, you will learn when we get to the cognitive restructuring module that allowing thoughts like that is a form of therapy-interfering behaviour, a kind of excuse that people can give to themselves to let them off the hook, to avoid doing the difficult work. So I think it's important for all of us to commit firmly to all of the homework, and notice that if you have a thought like *this is pointless,* you need to bat that away, knowing it's a therapy-interfering thought.'

After the energy of his little lecture, Jason seemed to have forgotten all about checking Paula's homework. She decided not to say any more but wasn't entirely convinced. Mandy had also gone quiet. The break was very welcome when it came. The first couple of weeks Paula had turned off her camera and microphone during the break and gone to get a cup of tea and dealt with some emails. This time though, she felt she wanted to be there for Mandy, though she wasn't sure what it would be possible to talk about, given the public nature of the situation. Luckily though, Jason and Jess seemed to have absented themselves and Paula was saved by the lovely Owen, who was keen to follow up on last week's conversation about *Team of One*.

'Well, Mandy,' Owen started, 'I think you need to take a

leaf out of Jose's book, darling,' he said with great conviction. 'Have you seen series two? I'm *so* glad you recommended that programme. It's part of my new evening routine. I'm *loving it*! Jose, though. Apart from the fact that he is so *dreamy*. He talks such a lot of sense. I even wrote down one of the things he said and it's perfect for what you were just talking about, in my humble opinion. Is it okay? Can I just read it to you?' Mandy told him to go for it. 'So Jose was talking about the massive undertaking of the competition and he said *I'm expecting this to be a miserable time. It feels weird to say this but for this experience, I think it's good to be negative. I'm expecting nothing. I'm starting in a very miserable place so that way, if anything good happens, then I'll be thankful.* So as you and Paula were both talking about finding the homework pointless, I thought about Jose saying this and thought you could apply it to the homework or even the whole course if you want. What I mean is, maybe if you stop expecting there to be a point, maybe if you don't expect anything from this and just go along with it, then if anything good happens it will be a bonus!' Owen looked out from the screen with his eyes wide open, smiling and looking as hopeful as he possibly could. And then suddenly his face changed and he frowned and asked, 'Or is that a bad attitude? Is that therapy-interfering behaviour?'

Mandy smirked. 'Owen, can you just run away with me to the Canadian wilderness? I think that would sort out all my problems!'

'Darling, I wouldn't even survive the journey! The closest I'm going to get to the Canadian wilderness is watching it on *Team of One*, from the comfort of my armchair!'

'Just thought I'd ask,' Mandy teased. 'I don't think our cats would be too happy there anyway!'

'I've been loving it too,' Paula joined in. 'I've actually bought a book that Jose wrote about survival, and I agree, Owen, he makes such a lot of sense. He's so humble too! I wouldn't say I agree with everything he says but in general it seems he has taken bits of this and that from everything and just come up with a recipe which works for him. I guess that's what he's urging everyone else to do, to find what works for you.'

'Isn't that what they say about Zen Psyonics though?' Mandy asked. 'That not all the exercises will work for you but everyone should be able to find something in order to learn the skills? But that's confusing, because at the same time they say you've *got* to do this and that, otherwise you'll be thrown off the course.'

'I know,' Paula agreed. 'That's why I said that thing about children at school. I think for some kids, if school doesn't work for them or doesn't fit for them, they can end up thinking there's something wrong with them and that makes the whole thing worse because then they feel really alienated because there's nothing and nobody to validate them. The school sees them as being difficult, there's often similar problems at home and all there is for them is to get with somebody else's programme.'

'Yes it does feel like that Paula, almost like you've just told the story of my life,' Mandy sighed. 'I don't want it to sound like I'm always making excuses but it often feels like I am. I was one of those kids who just didn't get on at school. But a lot of that was because I was so distracted by what was going on at home. My dad was basically a nasty, violent thug who used to regularly beat up my mum, until she escaped but left me with him. But he wasn't violent to me and there's plenty of other people who've grown up with men like that and they're not fucked up like me. Well that's what my friend said to me the other week at any rate and she knows me pretty well, so if your friends say that to you, you'd think they were right, yeah?'

'It does sound like you've had a most horrible week, Mandy,' Owen sympathised.

'Mmm,' Mandy murmured. 'There's so much I could say, about my week and about trying to do that homework, but...' she paused, and added, lowering her voice although anyone present could hear, 'I think we're only allowed to talk about certain things in certain ways. I'm probably breaking the rules just by saying that.'

There was nothing particularly earth-shattering in the second half of the session and Paula noticed that Mandy was quite subdued. She certainly couldn't be faulted for not contributing, as she was always completely attentive and made plenty of comments, as well as responding to other people. But Paula did genuinely wonder how helpful this group was to Mandy - it sounded like it would have been more helpful for her to have the chance to talk through what had happened with her friend and have someone help her make sense of that. But Zen Psyonics was the only thing on offer, which was fine for Paula, as she was fairly certain she didn't really need it, but not so fine at all for someone who was dealing with who knows what, in their life outside. Paula was troubled too about the rules. She kept coming back to her pupils. It was good to have rules. It created safety and security, particularly for those children who maybe didn't have that in their lives outside school. But she also knew that the best teachers, the ones that were really able to draw the child out from their difficult circumstances and enable them to *become themselves*, were the ones that knew the importance of sometimes bending the rules, of crafting the environment in a particular way for a particular child. She remembered the poster on the wall at the entrance to the science block, a quote from a Buddhist monk: *When you sow seeds, if your garden does not grow well, you don't blame the seeds. You try to find out why they are not doing well. They may need fertiliser, or more water, or less sun. You never blame the seeds.* Paula wasn't sure, but it seemed that despite drawing on the teachings of that very same Buddhist monk, Zen Psyonics was probably quite inclined to *blame the seeds.*

Embrace and Adherence Therapy

Enveloped in a cohesive theoretical and philosophical foundation, Embrace and Adherence Therapy (EAT) stands out as a distinctive, empirically supported psychological intervention. It employs techniques of mindfulness for embracing difficulties, alongside adherence to behaviour change strategies, aiming to enhance psychological flexibility. This flexibility involves fully engaging with the present moment as a conscious individual and, depending on situational possibilities, adjusting or persisting in behaviour aligned with chosen values.

Drawing on behavioural analytic theories, EAT sheds light on how cognition ensnares individuals in futile attempts to combat their internal struggles. Through the use of allegories, contradictions and experiential exercises, clients are guided to establish a healthier connection with thoughts, feelings, memories and physical sensations that they may have previously feared and avoided. The therapeutic process equips clients with the skills to re-evaluate and embrace these private experiences, gain clarity regarding personal values and adhere to necessary behavioural changes.

12

'Kevin, I'm not being funny or anything, but I found the homework hard, too, and I think that's exactly what it's supposed to be. This is supposed to be hard work. There's no point in making excuses as if we were still at school. If we want to change ourselves we have to follow this programme. Just like doing our exercises if we were going to physio. The people that don't do the exercises don't get better. We're all lucky to be on this course. This is our opportunity!'

Kevin could barely respond to Karrie as she was hardly pausing for breath, such was her zeal for Zen Psyonics.

'When I'm finding it difficult, I find it helpful to go to that page of quotes at the back of the handbook. There's one in the mindfulness handbook that says *when you fully embrace responsibility for every aspect of your life, you gain the power to transform any part of it*. That's what I think a lot of this is about. We need to *take responsibility!* I checked out where that quote came from and it's from a guy who has survived a terminal illness and he's all about teaching people to wake up to their full potential.'

Kevin looked stunned and eventually managed to get a word in. 'I'm not sure that's quite my thing, Karrie, but great if you've found that helpful.'

Frances didn't want to intervene too soon as she knew through experience that there could be so much wisdom amongst the group members that any of *their* ideas and responses might well be just as helpful, if not more so, than her own contributions. There was also Jess, who was doing a great job of co-facilitating, and she hoped that Jess might have confidence to add something.

'When I first got diagnosed with personality disorder,' Karrie continued, 'I was really relieved because I thought at last there's a reason which explains why I am like I am and it's not my fault. But for a while that meant I made excuses and when things went wrong I would tell people that I couldn't help it because I had a personality disorder. But now I can see that I was blaming it all on everything else and not taking responsibility for it. It's only when you start taking responsibility that you can actually change anything,' Karrie said triumphantly.

'I think it's fine if you're okay with the personality disorder label and I'm happy for you, Karrie. But I don't really agree with that label,' Kevin said quietly. 'I mean, I agree that I've definitely got some of the problems that would get me that diagnosis, like I can be very impulsive and not very good at controlling my emotions, but I don't think that's an illness. And it might be something that's a problem with me, but there are also lots of things wrong with the world, that make me mad, so I think that if we all took it on ourselves as being our fault, we might never do anything about all the stuff going on in the world that needs changing.'

'But we can't change anything about the world if our lives are in chaos and we can barely control ourselves!' Karrie implored.

'This is a really important conversation,' Frances cut in eventually. 'I hate to interrupt because I suspect you both might have much more to say on this, but I do want to hear how others got on with the homework and it might be that some people have a similar view to Karrie, where others might have a similar view to Kevin. I wonder if anyone has an in-between view? Can we work on changing ourselves at the same time as changing the world?'

Karrie and Kevin fell quiet and the rest of the faces on the screen remained silent. Frances decided to stick with the session plan and returned to going through the homework, person by person. She felt frustrated, once again, to be in this situation, delivering this material, knowing that it had been oversold and that even Karrie, the person who was most passionate about it, might come to the end of the course and feel short-changed. What she really didn't want to happen was for the group to get to the end of the course and for Karrie to complain that Frances hadn't delivered it properly, so she felt added pressure to stay fairly close to the material and not be tempted to diverge into areas that might be both more interesting and more potentially helpful.

Frances was also fundamentally uncomfortable that the people in the group were repeatedly being given the message that there was something wrong with them that they needed to change, rather than something wrong with their worlds. She was fine with it being a bit of both, but ultimately was bothered by this increasing focus by successive incompetent governments to turn the attention away from their own corporate failures and instead switch it on to individual citizens, making each and every one of them solely responsible for the course of their lives, regardless of the very different circumstances that people could be born into; happily wholesome and benign through to distressingly toxic and dangerous. She was also infuriated by the way government ministers increasingly made claims about the numbers, the science and the evidence, when they patently had no idea what they were talking about, but clearly it was persuasive to some sections of the electorate. And then these ideas had trickled down over the years, much more successfully than the wealth that many politicians promised would similarly be distributed, so that it had become pretty much a wholesale national narrative, that *we are all individually responsible for our own wellbeing and success in life.*

That same narrative had saturated health services in recent years, in the guise of staff wellbeing schemes. All over the country workers were being encouraged to use apps to manage physical and mental health and to find support from colleagues or social media and to *practice self-care by being kind to yourself.* Staff *guilds* for baking, doodling, gardening. *Pulse checks* on staff wellbeing. Glitzy award ceremonies. *Listening Into Action* events where the listening never led to any action but everyone who attended got a party bag of non-biodegradable plastic crap made in China. All these stupid initiatives, Frances argued, failed to address the absolute basics that were causing staff so many difficulties. She knew from various national forums that it was the same everywhere. Workers were tearing their hair out, unable to find parking spaces when they arrived at work, then not being able to find desks to work at as everything now was about *hot-desking*. Not being able to book rooms to see patients as the building was completely crammed with too many teams, but working from home being either not allowed or if allowed, certainly frowned upon. Then not being able to offer patients what, in their humble but autonomous professional opinion, they needed because that was not what the pathway offered now. It's all seriously fucked up, Frances thought, every single day.

Now that the Zen Psyonics groups had been expanded and were up and running, and apparently unstoppable, the group facilitators were required, in order to demonstrate fidelity to the Zen Psyonics model, to meet fortnightly for *Covision*, where they could discuss any problems delivering the material, issues with group dynamics and individual group members and generally support each other in providing quality interventions. Frances was surprised to hear that Jason himself was experiencing a number of difficulties with one of his own groups, bearing in mind he had talked in that team meeting many weeks back now, about what fantastic results they had been getting and how there had been so many added benefits to doing Zen Psyonics in groups.

'I'd like to discuss my Tuesday group, if that's okay with everyone,' Jason said as soon as they got to the Covision section on client behaviour in the group. 'It's hardly surprising, but I'm foreseeing problems with this group, which I think are largely due to the fact that it includes two inappropriate referrals, the ex-patient of mine and the person referred from cancer services.'

Frances, along with the other facilitators, waited for him to continue.

'As I expected, Mandy, my ex-patient, has been quite difficult, saying she finds the homework pointless and I'm fully expecting her to either not attend a session within the next few weeks, or be a repeat offender for non-completion of homework.'

Frances was waiting for Jason to say something he hadn't already said about this Mandy in other meetings. So far, he was just reiterating what he had already predicted and if Mandy did drop out, or break the rules meaning she would have to leave, that would be his problem solved and Mandy would have proved his point.

'I'm aware I've already made it clear that this was always likely to be a problem but I think it's worth repeating, so that we can all work to ensure we only get suitable referrals for these groups. The annoying thing is, is that Mandy knows what the Zen Psyonics material consists of, she's already been through the programme with me, so she knew before coming to the course what to expect, yet she insists on complaining about what she argued was her right.'

Did Jason want other facilitators to join with him and agree what a difficult position he had been put in? Frances wondered. She applauded the others for refraining from jumping on board and was also curious about why they weren't doing so.

'What is making it especially difficult is that in this particular group we also have Paula, the cancer patient, who now seems to be in cahoots with Mandy and the two of them together have brought along Owen, an older gentleman, for the ride. And Owen is someone I referred to the group myself and I *know* that he has a lot to gain from this group, but I'm concerned that he's going to be derailed by these other two.'

'I think I know what you're getting at, Jason, but I'm not seeing it quite like that,' Jess spoke up, 'yet', she added, almost as a way of exercising caution, in case Jason was offended by her daring to take a different point of view.

'Say more please, Jess,' Jason invited. 'I struggle to see it any other way myself.'

'I actually think it's really nice what's going on between those three. Just to explain to everyone else, they really seem to have connected over that reality TV show, *Team of One*. Not sure if anyone's heard of it?' Jess waited and then continued after seeing a few nods of recognition. 'It was Mandy who brought it up first because they had been talking about how they found the pebble meditation really difficult. They couldn't connect with it. And so Paula, the cancer patient, said how she was finding it hard to survive and then Mandy linked that to the idea of survival and the *Team of One* show and they all started talking about how alone they felt and how important it was to have other people around you, and supporting you, if you're going to be able to survive.' Jess paused.

Frances found herself unexpectedly interested all of a sudden. This was exactly the sort of thing she welcomed in any groups she had run, where the people attending found things between themselves which were often way more powerful than some of the exercises she had planned for them. She almost wondered why Jason wasn't celebrating this because it certainly sounded more enriching than what was happening in her own group at the moment.

'Have you started watching it then, Jess? I've been watching it with my children,' Vicky, one of the nurses responded. 'It's really interesting, from a practical point of view, but especially if you're interested in people and how they tick.'

'This is the problem!' Jason burst out. 'This is a Zen Psyonics group, not a reality TV watching club! This is exactly what happened in the group! The session was derailed by those three going on about that show and now our Covision is being derailed by it too!'

'As you know, Jason, I haven't ever fully read the Zen Psyonics manual so I'm not sure what's in there, but are there any rules about what you're allowed to talk about, other than not talking about self-harm or feeling suicidal? It strikes me that the people in your group are getting those added benefits we've always noticed, learning from each other and finding comfort in each other. You did say that in the team meeting where we discussed groups, didn't you? I didn't just imagine it, did I?' Frances knew she was being provocative but seeing as she was basically in this situation under duress, she couldn't resist.

'Yes, Frances, you know I said that and I stand by it. But there comes a point when we all need to buckle down and get stuck into learning the skills we need to go about our lives more successfully and talking about reality TV shows is not going to help with that and is just going to delay the work. It's a classic avoidance tactic.'

'That's one way of looking at it, Jason, and of course avoidance is a very useful strategy in some situations. Since we're drawing on behavioural psychology, we might also take into account operant conditioning and the idea that people are more likely to do something when they experience positive reinforcement. So, there's an argument that the people in your group might go about the course more successfully, and even be more likely to attend and do their homework, when they're being positively reinforced by other group members. But maybe you prefer the threat of punishment for not doing homework or not attending? Personally I've always been more into rewards. It's just nicer for everyone if we're all getting rewarded.'

'They *will* get positive reinforcement when they do their homework, attend the sessions and complete the course. And their lives will be much better for it.'

'*If* they complete the course. You've already predicted that Mandy is going to drop out or get thrown out, so she's going to be the rat in the maze that sits in the corner or wanders around aimlessly, because there's no tasty morsel at the end of the track. Unless you think it's still worth it for the latent learning she might experience, just by virtue of being there. So why not use this development as a gift? Incorporate it into the session. It doesn't have to take over, but it can supplement instead.'

'There's plenty of supplementary material suggested in the handbooks, Frances, which I hope you're familiar with, even if you haven't read the manual. I'd rather group members referred to *that* material which has been carefully selected by Alexander McDonald, instead of something on TV which doesn't fit with the course aims. And if you don't mind, I feel that we've actually wasted more time discussing this, so I'd appreciate if we could now move on.'

Frances acknowledged Jason's request and fell silent, deciding to let other facilitators join in further discussions. But her mind was whirling away, going off at all sorts of tangents, mostly from some re-awakened behavioural psychology file stored somewhere in her grey matter from her undergraduate days. She felt uncomfortable with the extent of her dislike of Jason, which she thought was mainly because of how he seemed to think of her as some stupid post-menopausal woman who didn't know much about therapy. She wasn't too bothered about that as she had always been comfortably confident about her intellect and her knowledge amassed through years of studying and training and more importantly, *being with people* and learning from them. But it did bother her when it then meant that Jason seemed to position himself as *the* authority, and when it led to decisions being made, by people with only very rudimentary knowledge, which she wholeheartedly disagreed with. She thought a perfect example of this was the fact that a quarter of the course was a module on cognitive restructuring and yet Jason seemed to have little awareness of his own cognitive processes, or at least an inability to apply any of the lessons of cognitive therapy. If she had been really cruel, she could have carried on the Covision discussion and asked Jason whether he himself might have a problem with cognitive flexibility. She might have pointed out that his own executive functioning seemed to some extent devoid of the ability to produce diverse ideas, or to consider alternative responses or to modify behaviours to manage changing circumstances, *like when someone talks about a reality TV show in a Zen Psyonics group*! So would it maybe be an idea for him to practice some of the exercises in the cognitive restructuring manual as it might help him resolve his own tensions around the group?

But Frances didn't like to be cruel. There had been plenty of people referred to her over the years who presented themselves in certain ways or chose certain turns of phrase that caused her gut to knot up, her eyes to roll and her back to bow up, which she hoped she always managed to hide, though wasn't sure. But through wonderful colleagues and excellent supervisors she had worked on this. The words of one cherished supervisor always stayed with her. *What exactly do you think you already know about this person? Have they ever surprised you? Would you like them to surprise you?* With only one or two exceptions she had usually managed to turn it around and find a connection, often doing the best work with people she had found it hard to like at the beginning. And of course she came to genuinely love and care about these people. So she thought she should at least make the effort of finding the same generosity towards Jason, a colleague in the same field as her, and surely someone with the potential for a connection with her. She also reminded herself of the wider picture, the fact that they were in this crazy system together, even though Jason might not recognise it as such, and it exerted its influence on both of them in ways which were toxic and destructive. Resisting that was tiring and difficult, but it was in her bones to do so.

Harmonic Centred Therapy

Harmonic Centred Therapy (HCT) is a thorough, evidence-based approach for treating borderline personality disorder, substance use disorders, eating disorders, depression and anxiety. Whilst sharing similarities with other cognitive-behavioural methods, HCT has three distinct elements, including a focus on achieving harmony between rational and emotional experiences, and incorporating mindfulness and adherence based interventions.

Developed through the integration of science and clinical practice, HCT originated from experiences with multi-symptomatic, suicidal patients, propelling further research and treatment refinement. Driven by a paradoxical philosophy, HCT emphasises the continuous balancing and synthesis of affirmation and adjustment-oriented strategies. Interventions are embedded in the treatment to convey affirmation of the patient and in turn assist the patient in self-affirming practices related to the self, emotions, thoughts, the world and others.

A large and compelling body of peer-reviewed research shows that HCT is an effective and specific treatment for severe and enduring mental illness.

13

It was gone eleven and Alexander was, unusually, sitting on his sofa, stroking Buddha's belly and talking to him about the latest turn of events in this highly irritating legal case he was having to pursue against Clemmie Service. The previous Thursday, in the *Couch and Client* weekly online coffee meeting, it came to his attention that a rather vociferous group of therapists, and basically *friends* of Clemmie Service, had set up a group intent on not only funding and supporting Clemmie's defence, but aiming to challenge any future cases in order *to protect the free use of the terms 'zen psyonics' and the associated acronym 'ZP.'* Alexander went quietly wild on hearing this. Naturally, he had no problems containing himself in the meeting because he was a master of emotional regulation and cognitive restructuring. But he had to go for an extra-long and fast run when the meeting finished, in order to process the information and metabolise the cortisol which was lingering in his veins.

Buddha was enjoying the extra attention and it made Alexander feel slightly better to be so adored. But it wasn't helping the task in hand. He contacted Ed Burrell immediately after the *Couch and Client* meeting finished and explained what was going on.

'Basically,' Alexander started urgently, 'I've just been in one of the weekly therapist meetings I attend and heard that there's this group, *Free ZP*, which has been set up to fund Clemmie Service's legal case. They're arguing that if I win this legal case, the outcome will harm the public in all sorts of ways, including limiting or denying client access to a diversity of ZP services. I looked on their website, and it says *we cannot allow someone to acquire exclusive trademark rights to the generic name of a form of therapy that has been freely used by researchers, writers, therapists and others for nearly a decade.* It's as if ZP just appeared in the world and was nothing to do with me and all my years of hard work honing and refining it. Apparently there's quite a bit of support out there for Service, not to mention money. I guess there's a lot of interested parties not wanting to have to pay for the privilege of doing the therapy I've spent my career developing.'

Ed Burrell seemed fairly relaxed. 'I've got two questions, but the answer to the first question is potentially problematic,' he warned. 'What did the public do before you invented ZP? Presumably they accessed one of the other numerous therapies you've told me are in existence. You're going to need to provide me with some general information on the sorts of therapies that would be suitable for your client groups, in the absence of ZP. Then we can argue the case that the public will not be harmed, as they'll merely access a different therapy. I realise to some extent this potentially devalues ZP in suggesting it's interchangeable with other therapies and it also calls into question the premise of my second question. What is it specifically about ZP which marks it out from all these other therapies? Can you give me some specifics which detail the exclusivity of ZP? Once you've done this, we can then weigh up the conundrum about how we're going to play this.'

They talked through a bit more detail and then ended the call. Fortunately, Alexander had a file of assignments from ZP trainees which he could mine for some quick answers to both questions. But he was unsettled about what Ed had said about devaluing ZP, and even more concerned about trying to develop a compelling case that ZP was indeed very distinct and absolutely different from *all these other therapies*. Also this was another job and drain on his time. He made a mental note to add this to the costs that Ed would claim once the case was settled. He opened his file of assignments and went to the *HCT vs ZP* file, a task he'd set to make sure people understood the superiority of ZP over HCT, his main competitor. He remembered a particularly good paper written by a very impressive trainee, Anya. She was memorable because not only was she a first class honours anthropology graduate and a two-time British surfing champion but she was also incredibly beautiful. Her words were what he wanted now though. He opened a new document and started copying and pasting.

Origin and Background:

Harmonic Centred Therapy was developed by Dr Arthur Burns in the late 1970s, primarily as a treatment for individuals with borderline personality disorder (BPD).

Zen Psyonics was developed by Alexander McDonald in the 2010s, initially as a treatment for individuals with drug and alcohol addiction. (Alexander bristled at the black and white fact that unlike Dr Arthur Burns he did not hold a doctorate, though was hopeful that he might soon be awarded an honorary title for his work in psychological therapies).

Both therapies integrate elements of cognitive-behavioural therapy (CBT) with mindfulness practices to address emotional dysregulation. But where HCT emphasises the concept of harmonics, which involves achieving harmony between rational and emotional experiences, ZP emphasises exercise psychonautics, which involves using exercise to alter states of consciousness, in order to achieve better balance within the emotionally dysregulated individual. Thus ZP works at the level of mind and body, where HCT only addresses the body via mindfulness practice.

Goals and Objectives:

Both HCT and ZP are used to help individuals who struggle with emotional regulation, self-destructive behaviours and interpersonal difficulties. However, where the main goal of HCT is to improve emotional control, reduce self-harm and enhance overall quality of life through a combination of cognitive and mindfulness skills, ZP also aims to facilitate a more spiritual or experiential exploration of consciousness and post-traumatic growth, leading to patients not only managing their lives as successfully as non-clinical populations, but actually surpassing the average non-clinical individual. As such, it has sometimes been referred to as 'therapy plus.'

Techniques and Practices:

Both HCT and ZP incorporate a range of techniques, including mindfulness meditation and emotion regulation strategies. HCT was initially developed as a group programme but is increasingly offered as an individual intervention. Unlike HCT, ZP crucially involves physical activity as a key component of therapeutic change. ZP was originally developed within the context of surf therapy which involved a mixture of individual and group work. The surfing element has now been broadened to include a range of physical activities which have the potential to affect states of consciousness.

Scientific Basis and Acceptance:

HCT has been extensively researched and has a strong empirical basis for its effectiveness in treating various mental health conditions, particularly BPD. It is widely accepted and practiced within the field of psychology and mental health.

Whilst ZP is in an earlier stage of development to HCT, its scientific basis and effectiveness have already been well-documented and supported by peer-reviewed research. ZP has fast become the therapy of choice for people with addiction problems and personality disorders, often preferred over HCT due to the additional and transformative elements of the physical activity interventions.

Alexander went straight to the references, which Anya had helpfully divided into sections, and pasted the whole chunk of peer-reviewed research supporting the physical activity aspect of ZP. This task was digging up his old dilemma of keeping hold of the surfing in the interests of his brand, versus letting it go, in the interests of making ZP more accessible and maximising his share of the market. He knew that had he stuck with ZP's unique surfing element, there would be no argument about its distinctiveness, but equally, it would not have taken over the psychotherapy industry so comprehensively. There was also the added predicament that some of his friends, or perhaps it was more accurate to say former friends, thought he had sold out and was a traitor to the spirit of surfing. This, he felt strongly, was totally unfair. The tenets *Respect the Ocean, Respect the Land and Respect Each Other* were principles he wholeheartedly continued to live by and there was absolutely nothing in his ZP foundation that ran counter to this code. But he knew that those who had taken against him felt that making surfing into a therapy, essentially commodifying it into something to be bought and sold, was contributing to its growing commercialisation. These naysayers were of the opinion that if surfing was therapeutic, then great, but surfing itself was not, and should not, be for sale. As far as Alexander was concerned, that was patently ridiculous as surfing was already a multi-million pound industry and had been for decades, way before he had even been born. He knew that the whole *spirit of surfing* movement was born mainly out of tribal struggles in Australia, which was fine for them, but it didn't really apply to ancient fishing villages in England, and certainly didn't fit with the commercialism that people were much more comfortable with in the USA.

Alexander checked back over his work, Anya's work, and returned to Ed's email. He had obviously been drawn to addressing Ed's second question first, as the issue of what makes ZP exclusive had always been his concern when he was growing his consumer base. He felt fairly confident that the physical activity module was something that marked ZP out, not just from HCT but from any of the other therapies out there in the crowded market. Nobody was really incorporating exercise as a form of psychotherapy. As far as he could see, the only variants which turned more towards the physical were the body psychotherapies and whilst during the process of developing the theoretical rationale for ZP, Alexander had drawn on some of the psychoanalytic theories underpinning things like vegetotherapy, he got a general sense from the industry that psychoanalytic stuff had had its day. It just took too long, and therefore was too expensive, so was never going to be hitting the public health service markets any time soon. He felt that this might go some way to addressing Ed's first question, about what the public would do in the absence of ZP. They would access something that took longer to get similar results, or they would forego the additional transformative elements of the physical activity interventions. They would achieve an acceptable degree of psychological wellbeing but without the *therapy-plus* benefits of enhanced consciousness and post-traumatic growth. In other words, the public would not be *harmed* were they no longer able to access ZP so freely. They would simply not be quite so well off.

Job done, Alexander decided to take a break and went to fetch Buddha's lead.

'Tatters!' he whispered to Buddha who immediately went mad and started running round the house, out of the study into the hall and round the kitchen, then back through the living room to the study and round and round again. Alexander loved how without fail Buddha was always utterly excited at the prospect of a walk. It made Alexander feel both loved and powerful, in a way that no person had ever really made him feel. He quickly slipped on his trainers and they both trotted out of the door and into the lane. In five minutes they were down on the beach and Alexander was enjoying the wind in his hair and he was sure Buddha was smiling too as he let him off the lead. The beach was fairly empty, as was usual for a weekday lunchtime with no real surf to speak of. They bounded across the hard sand near the frill of the foam and then cut over to the boulders between the east and west beaches. Then without warning, Buddha suddenly shot off across the boulders, clearly having seen a large dog he needed to attend to. This was typical of Buddha, who seemed to have no appreciation of his smallness and never hesitated taking on something twice his size, which had sometimes got him into trouble. Alexander started racing across the rocks after him and just as he straddled the last line of boulders before the sand began again, his foot suddenly went deeper than expected and he heard a snap and was over, groaning in agony. He could hear Buddha barking his head off but had no thought for whatever trouble Buddha might be getting into as he looked, and looked away from the bone protruding from his ankle.

Holistic Phenomenological Consolidation

Holistic Phenomenological Consolidation (HPC) is a therapeutic approach which emphasises the significance of the therapist-client relationship in facilitating the integration of mind, body, emotions and spirit into a cohesive whole. Equal and active participation by both client and therapist shapes the assessment as well as determining the nature of therapy and associated goals.

Practitioners of Holistic Phenomenological Consolidation hold the belief in their clients' capacity to take responsibility for their lives and choices, as well as their potential to consolidate and fulfil their talents. The psychotherapist collaborates with the client to actualise these potentials.

Holistic Phenomenological Consolidation therapists consider the impact of the external world on the client and explore the significance of social, cultural and political experiences. This form of psychotherapy is accessible in various settings within the public, private, and voluntary sectors, providing benefits to individuals, couples, children, families, groups and organizations.

14

Since the discussion in Covision about clients derailing sessions, Jason wanted to find out how close to the model other practitioners were staying, or how far they were comfortable straying, and how they made these judgements. So he was taking the opportunity, during a rare gap between his last patient and the group session coming next, to search online for examples to bolster his position. However, he was instead finding himself increasingly alarmed.

One of Jason's favoured therapist networking places was the ZP discussion list on *Apostle*. It was a great resource especially when most things involving training and supervision tended to cost money these days. It was full of rich contributions and was all the better for having members who were master practitioners, including the founder and creator, Alexander McDonald. Jason generally kept an eye on the latest discussions, in case there was anything of interest and he also posted questions on the list, from time to time, when he was struggling with issues that he had been unable to resolve through his usual sources. So far, he hadn't had anything back which had been of much use, but whilst skimming through the history, he noticed something that had bypassed him previously. He wondered how he had missed it but when he opened the topic he could see that admins, the select group of people monitoring the discussions, had *muted* it. This meant that list subscribers didn't get alerted to the topic and therefore might not be aware of it, even if it was still visible on the page. Sometimes admins did this if there was a topic with heavy traffic which could lead to irritating email updates clogging people's inboxes. And Jason could see that there had indeed been heavy traffic. He also worked out that he had overlooked the original post, because it came under the heading *Free ZP*, which he assumed was advertising some free training or something. So he was quite surprised to see that this was actually about a legal case, involving Alexander McDonald himself.

It turned out that *Free ZP*, according to its website, was a not-for-profit organisation, whose mission was *to protect the free use of the terms Zen Psyonics and the associated acronym ZP*. The website went on to explain that the terms were the subject of a legal case brought by Alexander McDonald against someone called Clemmie Service, whose name Jason was vaguely familiar with. It wasn't clear from the website who was behind *FreeZP*, but it was arguing that the outcome of the case could have far reaching consequences on ZP practice and perhaps psychotherapy in general. They were therefore urging people visiting the website to get involved, as the outcome might affect them personally and professionally. They warned that *if Alexander McDonald prevails in the legal case, he can claim that no one can use those terms without his permission, or he can require practitioners and others to pay him licensing fees to use the terms.*

Jason began to feel quite alarmed and thought his worries about staying with or straying from the model were irrelevant compared to this legal case. What about all the health services across the country, rolling out their ZP groups for huge numbers of patients? Indeed, *Free ZP* was at pains to point this out. The website went on to say: *We believe this outcome is likely to harm the public in many ways, including limiting or effectively denying client access to a diversity of ZP services. If you are a ZP practitioner, you may have to get a license from Alexander McDonald to use the term Zen Psyonics and ZP. This will have obvious and serious implications for practitioners in both public health services and private practice. We cannot allow someone to acquire exclusive trademark rights to the generic name of a form of therapy that has been freely used by researchers, writers, therapists and others for nearly a decade.* At the bottom of the page there was a box urging people to help *keep ZP free* by donating whatever they could afford to assist in meeting the costs of the legal defence.

The mention of harm to the public reminded Jason of why he was familiar with the name Clemmie Service. A few months ago now, in one of their increasingly rare supervision sessions,

Alexander had been railing against someone who he felt was tarnishing the reputation of Zen Psyonics, through his highly questionable and dangerous practice. Apparently, a popular mental health survivors and supporters group had posted an article on its website about abusive therapists. There had been an example of a ZP therapist who had questioned his client's experience of childhood family violence, saying that her emotions were so out of control she was inclined to exaggerate certain things that had happened to her and even to fabricate some events. Tragically that young woman killed herself soon afterwards. In the comments below the article, someone named the therapist as Clemmie Service. The comment was removed fairly swiftly by moderators, but not before various onlookers had spotted it.

Jason desperately wanted to take a moment, or probably more like an hour, to gather himself, notice his thoughts and feelings, identify what was going on in his body and generally calm his clamorous mind. He needed a quiet place to do this but there were no clinical rooms free and it was not possible to book them unless you had an appointment with a patient. The weather was terrible, so bad that he had driven to work instead of cycling. The toilets were not an option as there were only three male cubicles to accommodate the fifty or so male members of staff. It would be noticed if someone was in there for longer than about five minutes and there were bound to be concerned knocks on the door. Besides, a toilet was not the place to find his balance. But nor was the main office, which was particularly busy today. He decided that despite the weather, and despite the fact that he only had half an hour before his ZP group, outside was probably his best option. So he logged off his laptop and took it along with the rest of his things to his pigeon hole and headed out the back door, hoping the trees lining the footpath along the river would keep the worst of the rain off him.

Why am I so unsettled by this news? Jason asked himself as he slopped along the muddy footpath, dodging the puddles, already fairly drenched just in the five minutes it had taken to get from the health centre to the river. He couldn't even begin to imagine why on earth Alexander had initiated this legal case to basically stop anyone from practising ZP without his endorsement and his share of the profit from that. From the first time he met Alexander, he had been so energised by the man's drive to help people, to get them on the right track where they could start building their lives and give them a sense of purpose and meaning they had never experienced before. Jason included himself in the masses of people who had profoundly benefitted from their time with Alexander. He had been forever grateful and credited Alexander for getting him to the place he was now, happily married with two children and a successful career. So how did this unexpected move fit with everything that had gone before? How did it fit with the surfing vibe on which ZP was founded? Jason remembered a conversation with Alexander one weekend in Portugal where the surf was so awesome and the waves so busy that there was some rather nasty jostling going on out back. Alexander was scathing of those fighting for position. *Nobody owns the ocean. It's there for everyone to enjoy*, he had said to Jason. And Jason assumed that Alexander applied the same value to Zen Psyonics because he wanted as many people as possible to benefit from it.

Jason was also bothered about all the ZP groups being run across public mental health services across the country, as well as their recent expansion locally. If Alexander won his case, what would they all do? He thought about the possibility of carrying on delivering the groups in the same way, and was glad they had in fact called them *Life Skills* groups rather than ZP groups. This had been because they weren't strictly following the ZP schedules to the letter as there were various changes they had had to make in order for it to be feasible within their local service. So, for example, *pure* ZP should be delivered by two qualified therapists who were also trained in ZP, whereas in their groups, Jason was the only person trained in ZP and the co-facilitators in all the groups were support workers, not qualified therapists. They also squeezed the content into twenty weeks instead of twenty four.

Jason had always been uncomfortable about this, just as he was about straying from the model generally, which was how he found himself back on *Apostle* less than an hour ago. But perhaps all of this could work to their advantage if this legal case was going to pull the rug from under their feet. They could just carry on doing what they were doing, and call it something else, though they would have a sizeable job updating their handbooks and removing all references to ZP.

Jason realised though that there was another deeper issue bothering him which he was only just beginning to articulate. *What would Frances say?* He could already imagine the broadside from her once she got wind of the legal case. He could hear her saying things like *typical*, and *what did you expect in this cut-throat industry?* And *should I get my No Free Lunch t-shirt out again?* (She had worn that to a team event which had been funded by one of the drug companies and after having no success in getting the funding overturned, she decided to make her feelings known visibly by wearing the t-shirt and standing up to speak in front of the drug rep). She was also likely to make the point about how such action wasn't very fitting of someone from a surfing community. And on top of that, she would now be able to use this as a compelling reason for diverging from the strictures of pure ZP, in other words, going her own merry way, as she had always wanted. Apart from anything else, he hated the idea that she might say this proved her right. And as if all that wasn't bad enough, he really didn't like the idea of Frances getting wind of the fact that someone undergoing ZP therapy had killed themselves.

It was only fifteen minutes before the group was due to start and Jason was still a mile away from the health centre so he broke into a slow run in order to get back in time to get into the room, set up his laptop, log on and compose himself before people arrived. The path was very slippery and each step spattered new globs of mud onto his trousers. Fortunately, apart from his colleagues when he had to walk through the main office, with it being a virtual group, no-one would see the state he was in. He was almost amazed to notice that he felt better for the walk, even in his drenched and mud-spattered state, though he reminded himself that this was precisely the benefits of exercise in action, and decided it was an example he could actually share with the group when they came to the exercise module. He also reassured himself that he was at least, hopefully, early to the party, as nobody he knew at work had mentioned anything about the legal case and he was pretty sure it wasn't widely known outside of the ZP list on *Apostle* which was a pretty select group. So he wouldn't have to suffer the wrath of Frances Fisher just yet, if ever. He resolved to contact Alexander within the next few days and find out what exactly was going on.

Someone was in the room Jason had booked. He usually checked half an hour or so before the group was due to start, because it was common for rooms to be double-booked and sessions to be delayed whilst the affected clinician went around the building trying to find an alternative. This was just what Jason didn't need right now. He couldn't join Jess as she was working from home today, which was reluctantly supported by managers as it eased the pressure on rooms. That wouldn't have been a great solution anyway because he needed his own screen rather than a shared one. Sharing would make co-facilitating difficult, if not impossible. He was sweaty and dirty and couldn't think. He remembered the resource room which had no window but did have a desk and a power point and if no other roomless clinician was in there he could just take it and put up a do not disturb sign. He rushed down the corridor and tried the door. It was locked. He felt the rage and frustration bubbling around his vocal chords and let out a growl which surprised a patient making their way towards the exit. He went in the opposite direction towards the reception, where there was nobody on the desk, so he let himself in using his key fob and searched frantically for the resource room key which, thank God, was where it should have been.

By the time Jason had got back to the resource room and set up his workspace and laptop, which today of all days seemed to take longer than usual booting up, it was nearly ten minutes past the hour. He was late to the group. He was late and angry. Angry about what was happening in ZP world, angry about having had to go out in the rain to find some space and looking a state as a result, angry about somebody else being in the room that *he* had booked, angry that there had been nobody on reception, angry about being late for the group and *angry about being angry*. Jason made a point of never being late for work things. Punctuality was so important because lateness could be interpreted in so many different ways, particularly by patients. He also had little respect for colleagues who were late to meetings and appointments because it wasn't professional, just as his wet, dirty trousers were not professional either. But being late for the group was a massive no-no. The rules on attendance and punctuality were clear for patients, who were required to inform the group leader in advance if they were going to be late or absent. Showing up fifteen minutes late was counted as an absence. Here was Jason, the group leader, nearly ten minutes late, having informed nobody.

He arrived in the virtual room to a screen of faces, about half of which had their eyes closed. Jess was reading through a mindfulness script and clearly had the situation under control. Jason typed her a quick private message to say sincere apologies and thank you, and dropped himself into the mindfulness practice, hoping it would restore his balance and allow him to redeem himself over the rest of the session. After the exercise finished and Jess invited people to *return to the room* Jason thanked her again and explained to the group that he was late as there had been a room booking clash, through no fault of his own. He went on to introduce the theme of the session and the cognitive restructuring exercises they would be doing. As he was talking, another face appeared on the screen. He hadn't noticed up to this point but now realised that he wasn't the only person who had been late. Mandy arrived at seventeen minutes past the hour. She was flustered and very apologetic. Jason knew that she knew this was her second breach of the rules and it meant she would be asked to leave the group. He would need to contact her afterwards.

Innate Needs Fulfilment Approach

Among the pioneers in integrating neuroscientific discoveries into therapeutic practice, Innate Needs Fulfilment Approach (INFA) to psychotherapy and counselling, is a brief and outcome-focused method designed to expedite individuals' improvement and progress in their lives. At its core, this approach hinges on the premise that when a person's fundamental emotional needs are adequately fulfilled, and their inherent mental resources are correctly utilised, they will achieve emotional and mental well-being. Undesirable mental states, such as anxiety, anger, depression, addiction and psychosis, arise when emotional needs are not adequately met, met in unhealthy ways, or when innate resources are damaged or unintentionally misused. These states often involve the misuse of imagination to conjure worst-case scenarios. What sets INFA apart is its focus on identifying what may be missing or misused in clients' lives, aiming to help them discover ways to better fulfil their needs.

INFA therapists also assist clients in recognizing and overcoming barriers that may hinder them from meeting their needs, such as unresolved trauma. To achieve this, and address any presenting issues, INFA therapists draw from a range of established therapeutic methods, including CBT, psychodynamic therapy and hypnotherapy. They also incorporate the latest neuroscientific findings and insights derived from the Innate Needs Fulfilment Approach, enhancing our understanding of human nature and the requirements for maintaining emotional well-being.

15

'Cognitive restructuring involves using techniques to monitor and challenge unhelpful or negative thought patterns and replace them with more productive and accurate thought patterns,' Jess, the support worker, was explaining to the group, in the absence of Jason. Paula thought she seemed relaxed and confident and probably able to conduct the whole session herself if Jason didn't turn up. She didn't even seem phased by the fact that Jason was not there and nobody knew where he was. She said she had seen him in a meeting earlier that day and that he had probably just got waylaid by something or other and would be with them soon.

Having explained that they would be doing some cognitive restructuring exercises in the session, Jess went on to introduce the mindfulness exercise and everyone settled into it. Paula though was aware and slightly distracted by the fact that Mandy was not there. She knew that Mandy was having all sorts of difficulties at home, with a boyfriend who was treating her badly and an adult daughter who seemed to have lost patience with her. Apart from being somewhat concerned about her, Paula also wanted Mandy to be there in the group, for more selfish reasons. She found her refreshingly honest and often quite entertaining, and she had also given Paula the gift of *Team of One*, which she would never have checked out, were it not for Mandy's recommendation. It had become Paula's treat, which she rewarded herself with most days, rationing herself to one episode at a time, so that she could enjoy the benefits for longer. Even Gerry was enjoying it. And apart from appreciating the company and solidarity of Mandy and Owen, Paula felt she was actually getting more out of *Team of One* than the ZP group exercises.

Paula opened her eyes when Jess signalled to return to the room and she noticed that Jason had arrived. He swiftly took up the mantle from Jess, repeating the introduction to cognitive restructuring. As he was talking, Mandy appeared on the screen, apologising for her lateness, which Jason gave only a cursory acknowledgement. Paula herself was relieved to see Mandy and hoped to catch up with her in the break.

The skill they needed to learn today was the three Gs technique, *Grasp it, Grill it, Ground it.* Jason was explaining how the way we think, feel and behave are all linked and continuously affecting one another and that sometimes we develop patterns of thoughts and behaviours that are unhelpful. He said that this could get us stuck in a vicious circle but that we could influence the process and improve our mental health by doing so. The first thing we needed to do was to *grasp it*, which meant recognising and grasping hold of the fact that we were thinking in an unhelpful way.

'Can anyone give examples of having experienced any of the following?' Jason asked the group. 'Have you noticed always expecting the worst outcome from any situation? Or how about ignoring the good sides of a situation and only focusing on the bad? Do you find that you see things as either only good or only bad, with nothing in between, known as black and white thinking?'

The screen was quiet and nobody seemed ready with an example.

Jason explained a bit further. 'Learning to tune into our thoughts like this might feel difficult at first, but even just being aware of the types of unhelpful thoughts that exist should help you start to recognise when you're engaging in unhelpful thinking yourself. Can you think of anybody you know who seems to always expect the worst in a situation, or seems to be in the habit of black and white thinking?'

'I think I've got an example, Jason,' Owen eventually volunteered. 'I've actually been quite aware for many years about my own tendency for black and white thinking and focusing on the bad. I've done oodles of CBT so learned this about myself a long time ago. I was going to share some examples and then I started thinking, *here I go, hogging the space again.* And there you have another example! Me seeing myself as bad for hogging the space, instead of thinking of myself as a good group member for joining in. But then there's another example that follows on from that, because then I start thinking, surely I should have been able to change all this by now, the amount of CBT I've done over the years. But I'm not sure that's a very good example as I think it's *true*, whether it's helpful or unhelpful. Do you see what I mean, Jason? But am I just *overthinking* this? Am I not doing it right? Oh dear! There I go again, you see! I mean, I can laugh about it now, but it's not so funny when I'm on my own at home and in the middle of it.' Owen finished and looked out from the screen expectantly, as if a good student, waiting for the teacher to give the answers.

Jason smiled back. 'They're all good examples, Owen, and it's clear that you've got this part down, *grasping* the unhelpful thoughts. It's maybe the next bit where you're coming unstuck. Once you've grasped an unhelpful thought, the next stage is to *grill* it. This means taking a step back and closely examining the situation, giving it a good *grilling*. So if we go with your first example, *here I go, hogging the space again*, rather than immediately accepting this thought and feeling even worse, take a moment to grill it. Try asking yourself, what is the evidence for you hogging the space? Is it only ever you who volunteers information? If you do speak up more than others, are there other explanations for why this happens, or alternative ways of looking at the situation? What would you say to a friend if they were thinking this way?'

'I actually used this example of hogging the space in my individual CBT a few years ago so I could give you a whole lot of answers to those questions, Jason, but the problem is, even if I can *think* of a different way of seeing the situation and even if I can come up with a more positive thought, like I'm doing everyone a favour because nobody else wants to talk, I don't actually *feel* any different. I still *feel* exactly the same, like I'm hogging the space! Maybe I'm just beyond help! Oh there I go again! I'm sorry, I'm not very helpful, am I? I think I sound like Eeyore!'

Paula found herself beaming back out at Owen because he

was expressing something which sounded very close to how she had been feeling herself and she was struggling to think how *grasp it, grill it, ground it* was going to be a technique of any use to her. She was well aware that she was experiencing cancer in her own particular way, which didn't really fit with so many of the stories leaping out at her from the radio and television and social media. She started to wonder whether there was something wrong with her when the surgeon who performed her lumpectomy declared that outcomes were better for patients who approached their cancer treatment with a positive attitude. This struck her as bizarre. In her own profession of teaching, this would be like telling a child with an average IQ that they would be able to get nine A-star grades in their GCSEs if they adopted the right positive attitude. So when Jason had asked, *have you noticed always expecting the worst outcome from any situation? Or how about ignoring the good sides of a situation and only focusing on the bad?* she had thought, yes I *have* noticed expecting the worst outcome, and I'm not sure if there *are* any good sides to this cancer. I already know that the type of cancer I have is the most aggressive, the most likely to spread and the most likely to come back. And you can bung a whole load of positive stories and statistics at me which are contrary to the *unhelpful* thoughts I'm having, but that's not going to make a blind bit of difference to how I'm *feeling*. Because I'll only believe it when I see it. And I may not live long enough for that.

It turned out Mandy was also reassured by Owen's tangled examples.

'Owen, you *are* helpful,' Mandy approved. 'Hearing you say all that makes me feel like I'm not going mad. I keep trying to tell myself it's not me, that when someone's horrible to me it's something to do with their own stuff, but I can't get away from the feeling that it *is* me, because otherwise why would so many people be like that with me? And why would it keep happening? And by the way, I like Eeyore because he's out there with all the shit that's going wrong and doesn't pretend everything's fine when it's not!'

'Instead of going down a Winnie-the-Pooh track,' Jason cut in, rather abruptly Paula thought, 'I'd like to stick to task and hear if anyone has ideas about what Owen could do differently, or their own examples of grasping their unhelpful thoughts?'

'Yes,' Mandy leapt back in. 'When Owen had the thought *surely I should have been able to change all this by now, the amount of CBT I've done over the years*, I actually wrote that down because I had a different response to that. Owen's unhelpful thought was that *he* was at fault, whereas maybe a more helpful thought might have been that CBT's no good or his therapist was no good.'

This seemed to be turning into a kind of cognitive therapy ping-pong match, Paula thought to herself, and if she was the referee, Mandy would have been awarded the point for that last hit.

'That's certainly an alternative thought, Mandy, but perhaps more of an example of black and white thinking, where something is all good or all bad. Could we maybe have a fresh example from someone?' Jason seemed intent on shutting Mandy down, Paula thought, and yet she herself wanted to hear more from her.

'Mandy, I don't want to put you on the spot, but have *you* got a fresh example? Paula asked.'

'Thanks for asking, Paula. I've got lots, but I think like Owen, I'm going to struggle when it comes to *grill it* and *ground it*. But anyway. One of my examples is that I found out a few weeks ago, and I hope people don't find this too shocking, that my daughter and my boyfriend have been sleeping together. She's now staying at her friend's house and he's staying at his own place and hasn't been round since I found out. He's not replying to my texts but my daughter has just been round screaming at me, which is why I was late to the group. I had everything ready, everything prepared. I'd done the homework and everything. But Sophie decided to come back here to get some of her stuff. I had no idea she was coming. It was just before the group started. She actually threw my laptop across the room and the screen detached from it. She said I was a mental waste of space and was never going to be normal. I told her to get out and then tried to log on with my old tablet but it took me ages to find the links and passwords to get into the session. So amongst my unhelpful thoughts are that I have lost my daughter *and* my boyfriend and neither of them care about me and I am on my own again now. So I guess you could say that I'm ignoring the good sides of a situation and only focusing on the bad, but I'd be interested if anyone could come up with any good sides of this situation, because I certainly can't.'

'Oh gosh, darling, I'm so sorry. That sounds dreadful,' Owen said, full of sympathy. 'It's really hard to think about that in any way other than really bad. I wish I had something helpful to say. It's probably not that convincing with us being on the screen but I do want to at least say that *I* care about you and please remember *we* are here. You are not completely on your own, even though it must feel like that.'

'Mandy, that's awful,' Paula followed on from Owen. 'I don't know where to even begin with that one. I feel like Owen. I just wish I could say or do something to help. You must feel so alone with it all, them being two people who are so important to you. I can imagine it might feel like a repeat of some of the stuff that you've talked about that happened with your mum and dad when you were growing up and left on your own. It just seems so unfair too, knowing how much you've tried to support your daughter and doing it all on your own, only to have her treat you like this. I guess this exercise isn't for these sorts of situations. It's probably for much less serious things because it's not working for me with cancer either - unsurprisingly.' Paula decided to stop at that point as she felt they were in very difficult territory and it was probably more appropriate for Jason or Jess to intervene.

For some reason, Jason seemed distracted or disinterested and Paula wasn't even sure if his computer was working properly because it didn't look like he was hearing the conversation. Jess was still with it though.

'I agree it sounds like you're going through a terribly difficult time, Mandy. And I'm not sure either if this technique would be appropriate for that, or for you, Paula, but there is a related skill in a few weeks' time, the skill of forbearance, where you develop the ability to behave in a calm and sensible way about something that you are understandably very upset or angry about.' Jess paused, as if waiting for Jason to come in, but there was still no response. 'Have I got that right, would you say, Jason?' she asked, respectfully.

Jason at last limped into action. 'Yes Jess, that's right. Forbearance goes along with the skill of *the embrace*. By embracing reality rather than rejecting it, we can break the cycles of suffering, unhappiness, anger and all sorts of other undesirable emotions. But we need to remember that getting through tough times isn't easy.'

'I'm not sure I'm going to be able to keep my shit together for a few more weeks,' Mandy sounded hopeless. 'What about despair? Is despair an emotion? Will forbearance help me with that? I don't think I would be able to embrace it though. I don't think I want to embrace any*thing* or any*one* at the moment. Most of the things I try to embrace seem to end up rejecting me.'

Paula felt quite desperate for Mandy but felt powerless to do anything. She wanted to remind her of how much she appreciated her being in the group and how important Mandy sharing *Team of One* had been to her, however crass that might have sounded. She could hear the hopelessness in Mandy's voice, and the utter loneliness at having been betrayed so profoundly by the very people she might have hoped to rely on. She was astonished by her honesty, that Mandy had shared this most private and devastating of things.

'It must have come as a terrible shock to you, Mandy,' Jason managed eventually to show some sort of compassion. 'If it's okay with you, can I check in with you during the break as I think it might be better for you to discuss this outside of the group?'

'Yes, thanks Jason, I appreciate that,' Mandy said gratefully and Paula herself felt a sigh of relief, feeling that someone would be able to look after Mandy and that she wouldn't be in a place Paula thought might finally crush her, after everything she had survived in her life so far. She wouldn't be in the wilderness on her own. She wouldn't be a *Team of One*. Jason speaking to her during the break meant that she wouldn't be able to catch up with Mandy herself and wouldn't be able to say everything she wanted to her, about how important she felt she was in the group. But Paula thought it was probably better that Jason spoke to her as he would be able to offer extra support from the mental health team, whereas the group members were strongly discouraged from connecting with each other outside of the group, whilst it was ongoing.

So instead of speaking with Mandy, Paula used the break time to look back over her own examples of *Grasp it*, *Grill it*, *Ground it*, in case Jason was going to ask them each individually after the break. No matter how much she looked at it, she found it impossible to arrive at the outcome expected of her, where she had a helpful, rather than an unhelpful, thought about having cancer. She had already had plenty of these arguments, with Gerry mostly, but also with other close friends and even other women with breast cancer. They would go something along the lines of Paula saying, 'I'm going to die a horrible, slow death from cancer,' with the other person saying something like, 'You don't know that' and coming out with a bunch of statistics as to why this was not a one hundred percent certainty, at which point Paula tended to close up and go quiet, knowing that whoever was trying to persuade her had no idea of the utter turmoil she was feeling and it made her feel more alone than ever. Other friends would swiftly change the subject, going into great detail about their own illnesses or challenges, as if to distract her, or suggest they knew how she felt, which again felt like they were completely trivialising and belittling what she was going through. But how on earth did you say that to good friends who you had known for years? She sighed and decided that maybe like Jason had said to Mandy, she needed to be learning the skill of *forbearance* and *the embrace*.

The group slowly began to arrive back on the screen and Jason was ready and waiting this time. But Mandy wasn't there. Paula felt mildly panicked and hoped that Mandy hadn't had a row with Jason during the break. She had been aware of a subtle but noticeable tension between the two of them, right from the start of the group, as if they were both angry at each other, and Paula wouldn't have been surprised if Mandy had simply lost it with Jason, being so close to the end of her tether.

'It looks like we're ready to start back again,' Jason announced.

'Where's Mandy?' Owen sounded a similar concern to Paula.

'I met with Mandy during the break and as she was more than fifteen minutes late today, as well as not having done the homework last time, I've had to ask her to leave the group, as per the rules. But I know that some of you will be concerned for her, bearing in mind her news today, so I want to reassure you that she hasn't just been left and we will be having a discharge planning meeting with her, as we clearly specified to all of you in your pre-group meeting, and we will make sure that she has all the necessary supports in place. If any of you do want to discuss this any further, please can you do that in your half way review, which will be coming up in a few weeks. But for now, I'd like to crack on with today's skill.'

Paula was stunned. She looked at Owen and desperately wanted to speak with him privately but there was no channel for doing this and she couldn't even tell if he was looking back at her. All she could come up with, for the moment, was WHAT? The talk coming out from the laptop was like white noise and she found herself almost in the previous week's exercise, naming her feelings. Outraged. Indignant. Appalled. Speechless. *What?* She asked herself again. How does *that* work? Jason was over ten minutes late to the session himself and he's the group leader! Where is the fairness in that? How come there's one rule for him and another for us? How come what made *him* late was somehow more excusable than what made *her* late? Where's the flexibility of thought in *that* decision? How is *that* not anything other than black and white thinking? Paula seethed and was no better by the time the session ended. Thoroughly disheartened and totally confused, all she had to say to herself, was *welcome to the world of the mystery shopper.*

Inner Liberation Therapy

Inner Liberation Therapy was developed in the 1970s, after the discovery that verbally focusing on a problem or issue (emotional or physical), while manually stimulating meridians, could bring surprising relief to patients, particularly with regard to fears, phobias and physical responses to stress. ILT was initially patented as Cognitive Restructuring Energy Alignment Method (CREAM), an effective method which is still widely practiced today. However, the complexity of CREAM means it is accessible only to therapists or those willing to make a substantial financial investment in learning the process. It has since been synthesised into a more simplified form, one involving a streamlined meridian system and far less complexity: Inner Liberation Therapy.

ILT has been made available to laypeople via low-cost books and self-help materials. Since that time, it has proliferated steadily beyond traditionally therapeutic circles and taken on added refinements. Despite some rapid evolution in the early years, classic ILT has remained largely unchanged and forms the basis of international training programmes.

16

It had been a fairly shit day. Probably about four out of ten. Kelly had come home on report from school for not having done his homework. Fortunately for Jason, Sharlotte was dealing with that particular problem and he was grateful that they both held a consistent line on it, that this wasn't acceptable. But he was bothered that it kept happening the last few months and he was worried that Kelly was going to go the same way as he did at school, losing interest and not applying himself, when he definitely had the ability. Maybe we shouldn't have named him after a champion surfer, Jason ruminated, because that might have been a self-fulfilling factor in him turning away from anything academic.

At this point, Jason wasn't sure whether he was more troubled by the news about Alexander, or the situation with Mandy, which wouldn't have been complicated by his own lateness, had he not needed to take that rebalancing break before the group. He was seriously pissed off that the day Mandy breached the attendance rules, which he had of course predicted all along, he had unfortunately been late himself. And although Mandy didn't know that, because he had arrived just before her, the rest of the group knew, and he was certain that some of her allies, especially Owen and Paula, would see an apparent unfairness in her being discharged. But just like he and Sharlotte needed to be consistent and firm with Kelly, Jason knew he needed to be the same with the people in the group, probably more so with those who hadn't seemed to learn the importance of commitment, responsibility and self-discipline. He would be doing them no favours by simply giving them more of the same presumably lax boundaries they had experienced so far in their lives. That would just send a message that their wellbeing and transformation was not important to him. This was clearly set out in ZP training and drilled in to both clinicians and patients from the very start of their ZP journeys.

And now, what about ZP itself? Jason had given Sharlotte a very brief account of his shitty day, explaining he needed to take ten minutes to compose an email to Alexander in order to find out more about what was going on. But he'd already been sitting at his laptop for nearly ten minutes and so far, following much stilted typing and deleting, he only had *Hi Alexander* to show for it.

After some considerable huffing and puffing, he eventually settled on a short, friendly but professional email which he decided would have to do.

Hi Alexander
I hope this email finds you well and that the waves are doing their thing for you down there.

I wanted to contact you as I noticed an item on the Apostle discussion list that had somehow escaped my notice up till now, so I didn't know to ask you about it in our recent video call.

I read about the legal case you are pursuing with regards intellectual property theft and, like others on the list, was wondering whether I need to be concerned about the potential outcome. You'll be aware how many of us, as students of ZP, hold you, the founder, in high regard, for having developed this highly effective programme which has transformed the lives of so many. Obviously, we are all keen to continue offering ZP and developing it within our public services and private practices. Indeed, I know you're aware that it has become the psychological therapy of choice for people with personality disorders in public health services and as such it has grown in scale.

So I guess I'm asking you for an idea about what to expect. I realise this is a very sensitive matter and would welcome the chance for a video call as soon as you can manage. I am generally free most evenings but would fit in any time around you.

Hope to speak soon
Kind regards
Jason

Jason was disappointed not to have had a reply after waiting a few days, although over time he had noticed that Alexander's contact with him was more and more sporadic. In the early days of getting to know him, he was always quick to respond to him and enthusiastic about his queries and questions. On reflection, that was the time when Alexander was growing his business and he was in the habit of reaching out to potential trainees and clients to spread the message of ZP. Now that he had got such a firm foothold in the market, he was presumably too busy to personally keep up those early contacts and probably hoped that practitioners could help each other by way of the various discussions lists and forums out in cyberspace. Jason also acknowledged that this legal case was probably taking up a fair bit of Alexander's time, energy and head space, though if anyone was able to deal with such matters in a balanced and productive way, it would be Alexander.

When he still hadn't heard from Alexander by the weekend, Jason checked for any activity on *Apostle* and saw that a brief post had appeared from Alexander.

Hi there fellow ZP practitioners

I am writing this post as I've had a number of people asking about the legal case I am currently involved in, which has been discussed on this list. Due to rules about discussing ongoing legal cases, I am not able to give any details about the case, other than what has already been covered on here. You will be aware that a defamation case was brought against me by Clemmie Service and in response to that, I am now in the process of a counterclaim for intellectual property theft. I am afraid I am not in a position to respond individually to all of you who have contacted me and I am sorry for any uncertainty this creates in your ongoing ZP practice and I can only hope that the case is settled as soon as possible.

Namaste

Alexander McDonald

Jason remembered that it wasn't just in his supervision session with Alexander that he had come across the name, Clemmie

Service. It had cropped up when he had been searching the *Apostle* discussion list for threads on managing suicidality through ZP work. Someone on the list had mentioned how Clemmie Service seemed to be a character in competition with Alexander, that he had built up a substantial business on the back of Alexander's work, seeming not to have any qualms about setting up his own ZP training series and therapy service, which was questionable in itself, but actually diverging significantly from the model, in a way that some had described was dangerous. That fitted in with what Alexander himself had said. So it wasn't so much about the problem with Alexander seeming to want to limit access to ZP, but it was more about him presumably wanting to ensure that ZP was practised in the manner it was intended, and in which the evidence base supported, rather than people going off in their own random directions. He could therefore see now that Alexander's action was essentially about protecting the credibility and purity of ZP, and importantly, protecting clients and patients in the process.

This, at any rate, was useful clarification. If anyone began to ask at work, which he actually doubted would be the case, he would be able to explain the case in the context of this background of the importance of practising ZP in the manner it was developed and according to its associated evidence base. He would actually be able to cite the legal case next time he found himself getting into confrontation with Frances and her unashamedly slap-happy attitude about sticking extra bits in and taking bits out if they didn't fit for her or the patients in her group. Jason expected that Alexander would prevail, on the premise of his compelling case. Feeling reassured by this and having already worked out that they would continue to practice ZP under the guise of *life skills*, he closed the laptop and put it away for the weekend, wanting to be fully present with his family for the rest of it.

Just on time, he heard Sharlotte arrive back with the kids from their swimming session. Everyone seemed in a good mood and Jason felt the day shaping up to be at least an eight out of ten. He went into the kitchen and offered to make eggs and bacon for brunch, an offer which was heartily accepted by all. Sharlotte was pleased to report that the swimming instructor was very impressed with both Kelly and Layne and that they would be moving up into the next group as soon as there was a space. This was welcome news and made Jason feel that maybe he didn't need to be so worried about Kelly not applying himself to anything, that maybe he was just moving in a particular direction. He really wanted to encourage it. Sharlotte handed him the local weekend paper and pointed to an article a few pages in.

'I noticed this, about this woman,' she said furtively, not wanting to draw the kids' attention. 'She's not one of yours, is she?'

There in front of Jason was a picture of Mandy staring out at him. There was a short, repetitive article underneath, with the heading, *Rescue team's thoughts go to the family of Mandy Harper after body found*:

> A team of volunteer rescuers have passed on their thoughts to the family of Mandy Harper. Northbridge Search and Rescue's land search team was called out on Friday as the emergency services continued their efforts to find 38-year-old Mandy who had been missing for three days.
>
> A spokesperson for Northbridge Search & Rescue wrote on social media: "We have some sad news to share with you. "Following on from yesterday's callout (Friday) our land search team located a body, believed to be that of Mandy Harper who has been missing since Tuesday October 10.
>
> "The team were able to perform a respectful and dignified recovery and are getting the support they need. "The thoughts of the team go out to Mandy's family and friends at this difficult time." Mandy was last seen at her home address in Willoughby at 3.30pm on Tuesday October 10. Officers carrying out searches to find her sadly found a body in Lewis Way, Willoughby.
>
> Formal identification is yet to take place however Mandy's family has been informed. Police said there are not believed to be any suspicious circumstances surrounding the death and a report will be prepared for the coroner.

'What?' Sharlotte suddenly looked concerned. 'She *is* one of yours?'

Jason was utterly sick to his stomach, like nothing he'd ever felt before. He could barely speak.

'Oh God.' He was aware the kids were hanging around, in and out of the kitchen and didn't want to draw attention to this horrific news. 'This,' he floundered and lowered his voice, still looking at the photo of Mandy, looking happy in a bar somewhere. 'This,' he said again slowly, 'is the woman I mentioned I had to discharge on Tuesday. Oh God,' he said again.

'Oh Jason, I'm so sorry. This is terrible. Do you want me to take the kids out? We can go to breakfast at McDonalds or something? Or we could all go out together? Or I can cook here. Anything. Just tell me what you need me to do.'

Jason was so grateful for Sharlotte, so appreciative of her immediate understanding, of this thoroughly loyal supporter. He reached for her and hugged her, holding firmly onto her for a good long while, as he tried to get himself together.

'Thanks Shar,' he murmured into her neck. 'I'm completely floored by this. I have no idea what to say or do. I guess maybe the best thing to do right now is to try to carry on as normal, have our weekend with the kids. Maybe we can talk later this evening. Maybe I'll contact Alexander again, though he's not answering emails at the moment due to that legal case. I guess I could contact him and say I've got an urgent issue to discuss, which isn't about the legal case. Look, I'll do that now, if you want to get the bacon and eggs going.'

Jason went back to his laptop and booted it up. He typed the word *urgent* into the subject heading and fired away his message.

Hi Alexander

I'm really sorry to trouble you again at what must be a very difficult time. I have a terrible situation of my own to deal with, having just learned that a patient I discharged from my ZP group on Tuesday, due to breaching the attendance rules, has taken her own life. I'm not sure why there was no contact from emergency services at work, to alert us to the fact that she had gone missing and I have only just found out about this from the local paper. Needless to say I am feeling pretty devastated and would really appreciate some time with you, to talk this through. Any time at all would be great for me – I can fit in with you.

Many thanks
Jason

There was nothing else he could do at this point. Hopefully Alexander would get back to him before the weekend was out. Failing that, he would just have to deal with whatever was coming when he got back to work on Monday.

Internal Selves Structural Therapy

Enabling radical transformation, Internal Selves Structural Therapy (ISST) offers a game-changing way of achieving change for people wounded by this world. ISST views each individual as a structure comprising protective and wounded inner parts, all guided by a Central Self. Embracing the idea that the mind is inherently multiple, and that we are all made of multiple selves, ISST recognises how these inner parts are often pushed into extreme roles within us. The Central Self, an integral aspect of everyone, remains impervious to damage and possesses innate healing capabilities.

In the realm of evidence-based psychotherapy, ISST stands out as a valuable tool facilitating healing by addressing and resolving protective and wounded inner parts. Its effectiveness lies in fostering both internal and external connectivity, guiding individuals to access their Self and subsequently comprehend and heal their various parts, forming a healthy, structural whole.

Importantly, use of ISST is not confined to clinical settings. It offers a comprehensive approach to understanding personal and intimate relationships, encouraging individuals to embrace life BECAUSE these qualities will enable this: Bravery, Empathy, Coherence, Artistry, Unity, Serenity, Esteem. Professionals across diverse fields, including law, education, life coaching and spiritual leadership, can leverage ISST to inform and enhance their work. The expanding array of educational programmes by the ISST Institute seeks to serve not only therapists but also the broader public and professionals in various disciplines.

The overarching mission of the ISST Institute is to promote greater Self Governance in the world.

17

'I'm going to have to put the phone down on you if you continue shouting at me,' the GP practice manager said sternly to Paula on the other end.

Paula didn't think she was shouting. 'Well please can you just explain to me why my blood results aren't up on the online system, when they've been on the last four times,' she tried to lower her voice but was feeling increasingly exasperated.

'It's because they were requested by *us* on the other occasions, rather than by the hospital, so when they come directly back to us we automatically upload them.'

'But that's not true because we used the hospital form on the other occasions, so they were requested by the hospital but still got onto my patient record.'

They were going round in circles and Paula felt unable to control her frustration. She tried to explain how important it was to her, to be able to see her results prior to each chemotherapy treatment. Paula suspected she wouldn't have been getting anywhere near as irate, were it not for the fact that she was on a double dose of steroids, designed to ward off any potential allergic reaction to the chemotherapy, and as usual, it was making her decidedly more animated than she would otherwise have been.

She managed to hold it together and acknowledge to the practice manager that this must unfortunately be a case of the two systems not fitting together properly, which there was nothing either of them could do anything about. As if this all wasn't hard enough, Paula brooded, feeling another pocket of energy slip away from her dwindling internal resources. She worried that she was building a reputation as a difficult and demanding patient, frequently contacting the surgery and the oncology department to check results, chase appointments, query medication and various other things which were not always clear or guaranteed. She wondered what other people did, how other people managed, navigating these confusing processes and potholed pathways between different bits of services. She felt guilty and ashamed for coming across as so infuriated and impatient, and then felt cross that she was feeling bad about herself when it was a problem with these stupid systems. On balance, she thought perhaps it might be a good thing that she was raging her way through all these pitfalls, because maybe it was a sign of *life*, that no matter how much she sometimes felt like just giving in to whatever was going to happen, she was not done yet. She most certainly wasn't that suicidal person who was referred to mental health services, and indeed *had never been* that person. That had been a classic case of people, family, professionals, simply not getting it, hearing some words (*I'd rather die quickly of Covid than a long slow death from cancer*) and taking them to mean something which they couldn't possibly have any real sense of, not being in that situation themselves, no matter how much they might have come across it elsewhere in their lives.

Paula felt guilty about that too, that people close to her were doing their best to do whatever they could to help her get through this most horrendous time, and that she mostly felt irritated with their efforts and their complete inability to understand. Paula's brother would phone every so often, even though she had asked for people not to keep phoning and asking how the treatment was going. He kept saying things like, *you're doing really well, you're amazing*, which Paula felt was kind, but rather misguided, and it made her feel like a child. It also annoyed her because it made it seem like the thing she was doing really well at, or being amazing about, was something like running a marathon, which she had trained for and chosen to do. And of course the awful reality was that she hadn't chosen this fucking cancer and she wasn't *doing really well* or being *amazing*. She had *no fucking choice!* She was exhausted and unbearably anxious and felt very alone. There was nobody who came close to having an understanding of what she was going through. But all she could do at this point was to keep going through with it all. At least, that was how it felt.

After trying to sort out the blood test results, the plan was to do her *Grasp it, Grill it, Ground it* homework. But Paula was in no mood for that and decided to indulge herself with an episode of *Team of One*. There were two contestants, a man and a woman, who looked like they were about ready to call in the team to rescue them. They were struggling to trap any food and seemed dangerously low in weight, which was an added challenge to their situation, making it difficult for them to make sensible decisions and think things through, let alone simply get through their day on little energy. They were both on their hands and knees at times, crawling around, checking their traps and scouring their land for berries and mushrooms. And every so often they would offer some reflection on their dilemma about why they were going to keep going, or why they were close to quitting.

Tom was the first one to go. He had been trying to focus on one day at a time and not think about how long he had been there, or how long he would be able to continue. But after failing to catch any fish or trap any small animals the tenth day in a row, he knew he couldn't continue and called in the team. He tearfully explained his decision to the camera crew, saying how desperate he was not to let his family down and how much he had hoped to win the money to give them a better life. But starving had meant he had little of any reserves to help him through the solitude. He described the vicious circle of trying to stay active, so that the solitude would not be so sharp, but not having the energy to keep moving, meaning that he got lost in all his thoughts, lying in his shelter, trying to keep warm, trying to conserve energy, missing his family so terribly, even though he tried not to think about them.

Just a day later, Belle, who Paula thought had seemed very promising at the start of the series, came to the conclusion that she just wasn't enjoying it and it all felt wrong. Belle had thought she was strong enough for the challenge because she saw herself as ambitious and motivated, but because her body was not getting what it needed, she couldn't perform in the way she expected of herself. And instead of revelling in the beauty and wildlife, she just couldn't find the joy.

Paula could identify with both Tom and Belle. She knew how depleted and poisoned her own body was and how profoundly it affected her will to survive. Usually around the third or fourth day after chemo it was a massive struggle to get washed, to get dressed, to make the trip to the shops for food, to put one foot in front of the other, to keep the show on the road, to perform her life, to not let her family down, to find the joy. And the beauty and wildlife that she loved every bit as much as Belle, she was sure, was something she found retreating from her grasp, overlaid and obscured with a heavy poignancy. The wonderful, life-affirming natural world she had so often cherished, was not giving her enough of what she needed. She wished she could be more like the winner of the first series, enlightened and purposeful and wise. Following his victory, he had said, *I wasn't focused on winning the competition. I was focused solely on my needs, every day. I've never said I'm an expert survivalist and I never will. But what I've found was that I could let my instincts and the land teach me what I needed to know.* But no matter how amazing and inspiring these contestants were, and no matter how brutal and testing their challenge, the fact remained that it was chosen, and they could bail at any point.

Paula's thoughts turned to Mandy and she wondered how on earth Mandy was surviving. It was impossible to imagine something like that happening in her own life, or within her family. Not having children herself made it an experience even further away from her own, though Paula was of course very used to being around young people and often saw her former pupils in town and knew some of their lives were very different from her own. She knew that Mandy's life too had been poles apart from her own. Where Mandy's father had been violent and her mother had abandoned her, Paula's father was like the original new man, doing housework at weekends and amusing the whole family at the dinner table with his ridiculous jokes. Her mother was so supportive and interested it was bordering on intrusive, but far better that than not there at all. And the thought that Gerry would ever cheat on Paula, with some other woman, whether younger or not, was so far from anything she imagined ever likely to happen to her. But how did she know Mandy had not had similar thoughts? And whether it was the sort of thing Mandy could have anticipated herself, or completely beyond the realms of her expectations. Either way, it must have been such a painful and destructive thing. The double blow too, with her daughter turning on her. Mandy's own experience as a child wouldn't have given her any decent model on which to bring up her own child, and yet somehow she had managed this, bringing up Sophie single-handedly, making sure Sophie had the chances Mandy never had herself. Only to be betrayed by her.

She was still very bothered that Mandy had been kicked out of the group and was haunted by Mandy's words, talking about not being able to keep her shit together and how she felt despair. There was almost a sense of a warning signal in what she had said. But Paula had no way of contacting her and whilst she had to reassure herself that Jason was dealing with it, because what else could she do, there was a small part of her that didn't quite trust Jason to handle this properly. She went back and forth in her mind, telling herself that it would be fine, then listing various observations she had made about Jason, which told her that it wouldn't be fine. For starters, she reckoned that Jason simply didn't *get* Mandy, or perhaps more accurately, didn't *get* people in distress generally. That seemed a ridiculous thing for Paula to think about a trained psychological therapist, whose job it was to understand and interpret and make sense and comfort. But so far, in Paula's experience of Jason, he seemed unnaturally stuck to the programme, the structure, the rules, Zen Psyonics, as if it was the holy grail, guaranteed to bring all of them, as keen and compliant group participants, out of misery and into their happily ever after transformed lives.

She also kept thinking of the number of times that Jason seemed to close things down, not even just with Mandy, but whenever anyone in the group diverged into other, often interesting and potentially useful territory. Jason would step in and bring everyone quickly back to the task in hand. He certainly had no time for things like *Team of One* and Jason's irritation was there for everyone to see whenever it had been mentioned. But it also sometimes seemed that Jason didn't even want to hear about misery and despair and other horrible feelings, or at least that they could only be talked about in the context of challenging them and replacing them with nicer things. It wasn't that Paula expected Jason to allow them all to wallow in their deepest distress, but that there should be some level of being able to hear about it, being able to *bear* it, especially when reaching out and being honest about their feelings was presumably so hard for some of them in the group. When Mandy had talked about being desperate and on her own, even though they were in such different situations, Paula felt such deep recognition of those feelings in herself and felt so connected to what Mandy was saying that she was at once both relieved and pained.

She decided she would ask Jason for Mandy's contact details in her half-way meeting which was coming up in a few weeks.

The back door thudded shut and Paula heard Gerry call out. He was back from work early and stuck his head round the door of the lounge.

'Oh dear, you've caught me with my guilty secret!' Paula put on a shamed face. 'It's alright though. I don't mind watching it again with you so you can catch up. *Team of One* was frankly way more appealing than my *Grasp it, Grill it, Ground it* homework.'

'So, do you think Zen Psyonics is all a waste of time then? What about the mindfulness? That must be worth doing, surely? Sean at work was just telling me about some doctor in America who has been using meditation to cure people with cancer and it sounds like there's some good evidence out there.'

'Oh God, don't *you* start, Gerry. What nonsense!' Paula was having none of it.

'I thought there was probably a lot of truth in it. He showed me some videos of these women who had beaten it and from being diagnosed as terminal they were now cancer free. They talked about being in a different place, like it had been a spiritual transformation. I thought you might have some time for that, you know, with you being quite a spiritual person yourself.'

'Okay, Gerry. What did they say about the mechanism for change? Explain to me the scientific process of them having cancer, doing meditation and how that got rid of the cancer.'

'Well obviously, they didn't go into that. They were talking mainly about the meditation and how they chose to move away from mainstream medicine which had given them a death sentence.'

'Obviously', Paula repeated, deadpan.

'What do you mean, obviously, Paula? I'm only trying to be helpful,' Gerry sounded sad.

'You know that carpal tunnel operation you're waiting for? How about you start meditating? If you're very disciplined and you properly commit to morning, noon and night meditation sessions, and if you also start focusing on having healing thoughts towards your hand, and think positively about the state of the world while you're at it, you will probably have cured yourself by the time you get to the top of the waiting list and you won't even need that operation.'

'Obviously your cancer and my carpal tunnel syndrome are two very different things. As far as I'm aware, stress has no role in carpal tunnel syndrome, whereas it sounds like it's clearly correlated with cancer. And you have said yourself that you think stress might have played a role. And you have also said that doing mindful breathing makes you feel better so I'm only taking that a bit further as it could be something helpful.'

'And I have said that I don't want lame suggestions about magical cures with no basis in science or reality and I'm insulted that you haven't seemed to listen to a word I've been saying. Fuck that shit! There is no magic cure. We don't know what caused it. I am not going to become some born-again Buddhist. And the best thing about Zen Psyonics is that another group member persuaded me to watch a reality TV show that I wouldn't otherwise have gone anywhere near, and it's a blessed distraction. But I'm annoyed now. I'm going out for a walk.'

Paula pushed past Gerry and grabbed her coat from the hall,

slamming the back door as she left. There was only about a mile of pavement to cover before she was on the soft, humus paths of the forest and even though she was so upset and her cheeks were still wet from crying, she did feel a little calmer. She climbed the stone steps leading up to the common and at the top took the path to the left, taking her back into the forest. She made her way to one of her favourite trees, a relatively young creature, about two hundred years old, Gerry reckoned. It had plenty of strong branches stretching out at different angles all the way up and a lovely solid, gnarly trunk which Paula couldn't even reach halfway round. It would have been a good tree to climb but the branches didn't start until about fifteen feet up. This had been one of the first trees Paula made friends with and she hadn't noticed initially that it had been bejewelled, presumably without its permission, or perhaps with? How would a tree give its consent? There must have been about one hundred coins, tens and twos mostly, but a few fives and twenties, wedged into the deep grooves of its bark, stuck fast, definitely not coming out. Someone, perhaps more than one, had done this to the tree. But it was probably absolutely fine. Strong enough to withstand the wounds, the toxins, the impress of strangers. She stretched her arms around it and held tighter than usual. She was alone and desperately needed its company, its knowing, its strength, its guarantee that it understood what she needed, even if nobody else did.

Interactive Life Script Analysis

Interactive Life Script Analysis (ILSA) is a systemic theory and method of therapy addressing how social interactions generate life scripts which determine the social role of the actor or patient (whether authoritative, submissive or in balance), and how this in turn is used as a basis for understanding behaviour. In ILSA clients, students and systems are taught how to analyse and alter their social roles as a way to solve patterns of interaction that hinder the achievement of life goals.

Over the past four decades, ILSA has expanded its applications to include counselling, education, organizational development and psychotherapy. Numerous research studies have explored the efficacy of ILSA across various contexts, which has a comprehensive training and certification process.

Professionals opting to specialise in ILSA operate in diverse fields such as social work, healthcare, pastoral work, mediation, change management and humanitarian activities. Interactive Life Script Analysts specializing in organizations are engaged in assessing an organization's developmental processes, challenges and dysfunctional behaviours, using ILSA concepts and techniques.

18

Buddha wasn't coping very well since Alexander broke his ankle. Every day around lunch time, he would wander back and forth between the front door, where his lead was hanging up, and Alexander at his workstation, whining and rubbing his nose into Alexander's thigh, looking up at him with expectant, sad eyes, as if to say, *what's going on? Why aren't we going tatters?* The kneeling chair had been put away in the cupboard under the stairs and whilst Alexander was working, he had his leg pretty much permanently elevated on a stool underneath the desk. It was almost impossible to pick Buddha up from this position, and it wasn't what Buddha wanted anyway. Naturally, Buddha didn't have the benefit of cognitive restructuring and the various techniques of emotional regulation which were second nature to Alexander, so he was finding this change in circumstances somewhat challenging. Alexander knew that if he were to suddenly and miraculously leap up from his chair and fetch Buddha's lead, the mood would switch in an instant and Buddha would smile and bark his delight. Which only went to show how important exercise was for all the world's creatures. And that being the case, Alexander himself wasn't coping very well since his accident either.

There wasn't a time in his memory that Alexander had been laid out in such a disabling way. Surfing had been in his bones from the moment his dad paddled out with him in Caynham Bay on a gentle October day, the weekend of his sixth birthday. He had always loved watching his dad surf and had pleaded for so long to have his own board which he knew would give him much more freedom than the body board he had had to make do with since he was big enough to carry it. Struggling with that little board had at least given him a good sense of timing and how to catch a wave, though he was still a bit on the small size for paddling out. A big set had rolled in and through the lull that followed, Alexander was shouting to his dad that the next one he could see barrelling towards them was *his*. *This one*, he had shouted and his dad duly lined him up and commanded him to paddle, giving him a massive push at the same time. Alexander popped up right on time, as if he had been doing this for years, and pointed his nose towards the shore, feeling like he was king of the waves.

And so flourished his relationship with surfing. He knew his parents were relieved that he had found his *thing*, because whilst he was showing plenty of promise at school, he struggled to fit in. Where most of the other boys were into football, playing in local leagues and trading stickers for their sticker albums, he had no interest in it and was often on the sidelines, even though physically he was as talented as the best of them. It just didn't appeal to him and it was only years later that he realised that he didn't work so well with other people. He was not a team player. So surfing was ideal for him, just him out there, alone on the wave. It had spoken to his little six-year old soul and he couldn't get enough of it. Of course, he couldn't control the ocean and he would get frustrated when the sea was flat for weeks on end, when the only decent rides he got were in the local skate park. It was years later, as he was in the process of launching The Green Room onto the therapy world, that he discovered the coastal paths were not a bad place to run and when he pushed it, not only did he manage to achieve some very respectable times, but he also got hooked on the endorphin high that was not dissimilar to the massive buzz he got from surfing. That turned out to have a pivotal role in the evolution of Zen Psyonics.

But today, and for the last few weeks, and for at least the next few weeks, Alexander was incapacitated and he was finding it far more difficult than usual to focus on his work and to keep his emotions in check. The broken ankle couldn't have come at a worse time, with him being right in the middle of the legal case with Clemmie Service and being bombarded with messages from worried followers on *Couch and Client* and various other discussion lists. He should have been up in Farwater, visiting his folks and shredding the super tide which was forecast.

Instead, he was barely able to leave his house and he felt himself turning into a feeble specimen of a man. Of course, this was precisely Zen Psyonics in action, only in reverse. Healthy body, healthy mind. Get in your SHED. Sleep, Hydrate, Exercise, Diet. Two out of the four of those were not happening at the moment, the sleep not only messed up because of the lack of exercise, but also because of the stress, annoyance and interference of the confounded legal case. In one way, it was reassuring for Alexander to witness first hand that the aspect of ZP which set it apart from the rest, the exercise component, was essential to psychological wellbeing. Certainly in his own case, take out the exercise and he was slowly starting to fall apart. His physical weakness seemed to be fermenting a profound psychological weakness which was alien to him. But at the same time, he was somewhat alarmed to notice that his mental strength was dissipating and that the various techniques of cognitive restructuring and emotional regulation had lost their potency. He would go as far to say that some days, they didn't even work. He did at least have more time to sit and practise deep meditation and thereby try to achieve an inner calm and vitality through that route. But whilst he was convinced by all those brain scan pictures proving enhanced neural connectivity and YouTube videos of people describing their life-changing practices, he knew that for him, exercise had primacy, and without it, nothing else could follow.

Despite being in this sorry state, Alexander was doing his best to respond promptly and fully to any queries coming from Ed Burrell and whilst he was often irritated by the man's demands and the fact that it sometimes felt like he was doing his job for him, he was at least appreciative that Ed seemed to be progressing the case as quickly as possible. So far, they had got nowhere with trying to resolve the dispute without litigation. Clemmie Service was adamant and simply not willing to back down on his use of ZP and he was buoyed by the growing support from *Free ZP*. They were still stuck in the murky business of disclosure and evidence gathering and it wasn't altogether surprising to Alexander that

ZP practitioners from every corner of the globe were emerging from the woodwork in defence of being able to continue running their successful and lucrative practices.

All of this could have taken a different direction were it not for Clemmie's aggressive defamation claim which set the whole thing off. Alexander was sure that there must be loads of therapists out there hawking their mutant variants of ZP and word on the street was that practice was probably most lax in public health services where they had less to gain, in terms of profits. He had been untroubled about turning a blind eye to it as, generally, the more people practising Zen Psyonics, the better. The better for him, the better for the patients, the better for the world. And he felt secure that he would always be at the top of the tree, the person people wanted to consult and return to, to get the pure, unadulterated version of ZP, to become master practitioners. But he wasn't having this imposter, Clemmie Service, passing himself off as the real deal at the same time as having the audacity to make a legal claim for defamation.

As well as the mail from Ed Burrell, there was a much more substantial pile building in Alexander's inbox, from former colleagues, trainees, supervisees and people he knew but had not worked with directly, from the various forums like *Couch and Client* and *Apostle*. Mostly, they were saying similar things, which in effect amounted to them being worried that if Alexander won the case, they would be looking at substantial costs in order to continue practising under the banners Zen Psyonics and ZP. Alexander was in rather uncharted territory. He wasn't aware, and neither was Ed Burrell, of any similar cases in the psychotherapy world, and since being laid up dealing with his compromised physical and psychological state, he simply did not have the capacity to deal with anything too far outside the case itself. He hadn't had the headspace to think about the ramifications of him winning the case and subsequently needing to put structures in place to enforce the judgement. Nor did he have the personal reserves to send a considered, or in fact *any*, reply to each email he had received on the matter, the total of which was nudging three figures and they were still coming. So he composed a brief post which he published on the *Apostle* discussion list, basically letting people know he was not able to reply at this stage. He then created a new email folder called *case closed* and put them all in there, with the intention of replying once the outcome was known and he was in a better position to answer everyone's questions.

It took an age to file all the emails because they were interspersed with his usual ongoing steady stream of contacts about ZP issues which were nothing to do with the legal case. Many queries went direct to his small team of admin staff and they tended to deal with them without bothering Alexander. But there were still plenty of people who had a direct line to him, generally people he had built a closer connection with, through things like training events and conferences, and old students who had been with him in the early days. One of those, who tended to pop up with regularity, was Jason Coriol. He felt some responsibility towards Jason, knowing that he described meeting Alexander as a crucial turning point in his life and he often spoke of Zen Psyonics with evangelical zeal. Jason was a very loyal follower and was decidedly deferential to Alexander, who found this both strange and off-putting. In keeping with the aims and values of Zen Psyonics, it was important that clinicians and patients alike were clear in the powers within themselves and how ultimately they all had the potential to be independent, autonomous human beings who could meet their own needs, deal with their own problems and sort their own shit, without having to go bleating to someone they thought could live their life better than they could themselves. So whenever Jason contacted Alexander, rather than being flattered, he was often irritated by the adulation and found it difficult to keep himself from saying, *man up now Jason, for goodness sake have you not learned anything from all these years of Zen Psyonics? Do you or do you not already have the tools to deal with this yourself?* He had no qualms in charging him the full rate for an hour's consultation either, in the hope that sooner or later Jason might come to his own conclusion that he did indeed have all the necessary tools and no longer needed to pay Alexander to do his thinking for him. Alexander, though, was of course happy to take the money too.

Predictably Jason had emailed about the legal case. Alexander put that one straight in the *case closed* folder. He spent a fraction longer skimming through another of Jason's emails, noticing the word *urgent* in the subject heading. He was moved to hear that one of Jason's patients had taken her own life after he had discharged her from a Zen Psyonics group. Jason was clearly feeling upset as well as worried about whether there might have been something about his own practice which was somehow a factor in the unhappy events. Not only did Jason have the tools to deal with this himself, he was also in a tightly regulated professional situation in a public health service, where he was ensured regular supervision and was presumably surrounded by colleagues who would be able to support him and provide some level of debriefing. He did not need to be bothering Alexander and perhaps now was the time Jason needed to fully realise that and stop reaching out for a hand to hold. Alexander dragged the email to his *routine in-tray* folder, which he had created for non-urgent queries he attended to as and when his schedule allowed. Jason would need to look after himself.

Alexander stretched and lifted his bad leg off the stool and onto the floor. He hoisted himself up with the crutches and went into the kitchen to get some lunch. Switching the radio on to keep himself company, he was immediately drawn in to a pertinent discussion. It was the lunchtime consumer affairs programme and the presenter was in full flow.

'If you've just joined us, we're asking *what is good therapy*? Do you have your own experience of therapy for mental health problems? Was that a good experience? Did it cure you? Or would you like your money back? Or did it actually make you worse than you were before you started? Perhaps you're a therapist? What does good therapy look like from your side of the couch? We'd like to hear from you.'

She then went on to introduce a guest, a professor so and so who was a past president of the General Psychotherapy Council, giving a preamble about the risks of unqualified and unregistered practitioners offering treatment for mental health issues. The professor explained how members of the GPC have ethical and professional standards they're required to meet and emphasised how people should choose a registered therapist. Hear, hear, thought Alexander. It still doesn't deal with the likes of Clemmie Service though.

'You should be able to feel safe and trusting of your therapist so you can open up and explore all the things you need to talk about in therapy. Therapists need to be authentic, grounded and able to offer empathy', the professor went on. 'The training that therapists go through is really rigorous and our main advice is that you should never go to a therapist who is not a member of a professional body. Clients working with unregistered therapists are more at risk of harm, as they've no assurance as to the level of training and proficiency of their therapist. We recommend people choose practitioners from a GPC accredited register, rather than from an unaccredited register or someone who is not registered at all.'

The presenter then went to a call from a therapist who wanted to make the point that even when therapists are regulated, they can still practice all sorts of therapies for which they are not necessarily accredited or they can just do their own versions of various therapies, potentially causing harm to patients. Precisely! Alexander slapped the table and wondered whether Clemmie Service was listening to the programme.

The next caller was a patient who was not so interested in the business of regulation. She spoke quite passionately about how the therapy itself isn't always that helpful. 'So how would regulation help with that? It's just to promote and protect the therapist, not the patient.' Clearly there were people like Clemmie Service out there who were doing some not-very-helpful therapy, but Alexander was also aware of various patients not being able to use therapy properly, often because they were in denial about their problems, and those people simply needed to go away and return when they were ready to do the work.

The presenter picked up on the caller's point and brought the professor back in. 'Our caller Patricia raises an important point here which I would like to put to you, which is the question of *what exactly is psychotherapy?* Because this is something on which its own exponents can't seem to agree. Is it psychoanalysis, is it counselling? Apparently there are over five hundred different psychological therapies. How does a member of the public decide what they need?'

The professor responded with a calm and authoritative voice. 'First, it's important to say that any decent, regulated therapist will be guided by the evidence base and give the client what is appropriate for their diagnosis, but it's also true that there remain different philosophies and clinical approaches which have quite different treatments associated with them and it can indeed make it quite confusing for the public. And it is also the case that you don't need training or qualifications to set up as a psychotherapist, because unlike most other healthcare professionals, psychotherapists are not regulated by law, though the GPC is trying to change that.'

She was, of course, correct, Alexander acknowledged, about many therapists not being members of a professional body and Alexander was pleased that he had made the slog to get his registration once his business started to take off. He was less pleased that people like Clemmie Service also had the badge.

Another guest was introduced, describing herself as both a counsellor and psychotherapist. She was invited to explain the difference between the two. It turned out that she started off as a counsellor but then her membership organisation changed its name to include counselling *and* psychotherapy. 'So magically suddenly we're all psychotherapists', she declared triumphantly.

'I'm not sure *actual* psychotherapists would agree with you there, lady', Alexander said out loud to the radio.

The guest went on. 'For me, counselling is for a specific situation. A bereavement, a break-up of a relationship, being made redundant. It's usually short term and it focuses on the issue at hand. Psychotherapy is a lot more like archaeology, where you're looking at the causes and the roots for what's known in the jargon as psychopathology. The behaviours that you keep repeating over and over and over again that actually get in the way.' After comparing herself to an archaeologist, she then started comparing herself to a car mechanic.

'Dear God!' Alexander shouted this time. 'It's no wonder the public are confused! And it's people like this who are giving the whole industry a bad name!'

Next up was someone who had made a formal complaint about a bad experience with six months of twice-weekly psychoanalytic psychotherapy and ended up having a breakdown. Alexander was not at all surprised to hear this story. In fact, he had heard it a fair few times before.

'There's no solid evidence base,' Alexander told the radio, as the patient continued to tell his story.

'I mean my analyst hadn't done anything unethical. I'd had a very damaging breakdown but he hadn't, in theory, done anything unprofessional or breached his organisation's ethical code. So there was effectively no accountability and there was, as they put it, no case to answer.'

The presenter put it back to the professor, asking whether what was needed, apart from tighter regulation, was a change in attitude.

'Yes, I think so. Being more humble and more open and I think also to acknowledge it's a very high risk endeavour and the damaging effects perhaps are not dealt with very well in the profession and perhaps not even sufficiently well understood. I think maybe the professions needs to be a bit more mature about the whole thing and a bit more genuinely professional in the sense of really caring about the client. It's also worth saying that there's a difference between straightforward bad practice and the nature of therapy itself. There's some evidence to suggest that for some people therapy is very beneficial and for others it can be damaging. As we've been saying, there are a whole range of different kinds of therapies. We're talking about the talking treatments as a whole, so you have psychoanalysis, psychotherapy, counselling and so on and so forth. And there's a big debate going on about how effective they all are.'

'So, everyone's totally flummoxed,' Alexander said to Buddha as the programme ended. 'We should have phoned up to tell them how great Zen Psyonics is. I'm surprised nobody did. At least we're in no doubts about that, Buddha. *Psychoanalytic psychotherapy.* I ask you! People need to move with the times!'

Ishikuma Therapy

Ishikuma Therapy was developed by the Japanese psychologist, Tomoshige Ishikuma, at the turn of the millennium. The aim of Ishikuma Therapy is to foster acceptance of life as it is, with an emphasis on allowing nature to take its course. This therapeutic approach perceives feelings and emotions as inherent aspects of natural laws. Initially developed to address anxiety in patients, Ishikuma Therapy does not seek to eliminate anxiety entirely but rather aims to mitigate its detrimental effects.

Ishikuma Therapy is likened to Response Reformulation Therapy and shares common elements with existential and cognitive-behavioural therapy. The central focus of Ishikuma Therapy is on developing awareness and decentring the self. Mindfulness plays a role in discerning what can be controlled and what cannot, observing situations without attachment to expectations. Acknowledging feelings, even without immediate action, allows individuals to fully engage with the present moment and determine appropriate responses.

The therapeutic goal of Ishikuma is to guide patients in accepting the fluctuations of thoughts and feelings, anchoring their behaviour in reality. Unlike approaches that define cure through the relief of discomfort (which contradicts the philosophy of Ishikuma), success is measured by taking intentional actions in life, free from being dominated by one's emotional state.

19

Working in mental health services for any significant amount of time meant that a worker would be unlikely to go through their career without some sort of involvement in a patient suicide. Frances wasn't sure how many times her colleagues had gone through something like this, but she thought perhaps she had been lucky in her thirty years of service, that she had not had any patients kill themselves whilst she was working with them. She had been involved in the aftermath of three deaths of patients she had previously worked with, but only one of these was due to suicide. That had been a very tragic case of a young man who had been discharged from local services and not picked up by a neighbouring service. Another death had been somebody in hospital with anorexia, who died from starvation. This naturally begged the question as to whether starvation itself was a slow form of suicide, but clinicians tended to agree that despite the obvious logical outcome of prolonged starvation, most people with serious issues around food did not actually want to die. The third death had been put down to physical health issues, but there was a very complicated set of factors in that case, which included many previous attempts by the person to end her life. Frances had wondered about the woman's husband, who it turned out had been out exercising his dogs whilst his wife lay dying. She wondered whether there had been intentional, wilful neglect. She had even mentioned it to the police but they didn't seem interested in that line of enquiry so Frances resigned herself to letting the matter lie.

Unless it was a patient who you were, or had been, directly involved with, you were unlikely to hear about a death through any formal channels and it wasn't unusual to learn about a patient having died some weeks or even months afterwards, often while you were in a team meeting or sitting at a desk in the main office. It was there, amidst the hubbub of people fighting for space, where Frances learned about Mandy Harper. The news had travelled fast on this occasion, as it had only been the previous Friday that Mandy's body had been found. It was young Jess, stationed on the desk next to Frances, who quietly asked if she had seen the papers at the weekend.

'Oh gosh, Jess, that's awful news. What a shock,' Frances said, feeling deeply moved at the same time as being aware of a whole load of other feelings that were in an inexpressible mass. Frances was at least clear about her feeling of duty to Jess. She asked whether she was okay, whether there had been any discussion with Jason or Hayley, whether Jess wanted Frances herself to do anything.

'I think Hayley's planning to meet with us tomorrow, before the group in the afternoon. I've not been in this position before. I can't imagine what we'll say to the rest of the group. I know Jason will take the lead on it but that's not going to be easy for him either. He's really cut up about it. I don't remember ever seeing him like this. He's normally so confident and certain. I'm not sure that he even wants to discuss it with me.'

Frances didn't know Jess very well but she liked her. She liked how thoughtful she was, how bright, how adaptable, how open to trying things she was and how at the heart of her she was so caring, in a way that sometimes older workers had become deficient, jaded by the constant demands of busy public health services which they could never hope to meet. She could sense Jess's compassion for Mandy, for Jason, for the group, for Mandy's family and for any workers who might be affected by the news.

'You know that Jason had just discharged her from the group? She went missing the same day.' Jess stopped there and let that piece of information rest for a while, allowing Frances time to consider it. She was looking straight at her though and seemed to be hoping for Frances to say something which might explain it all, something to say that those two events were not linked.

Frances could only let out a long sigh. Being someone so outspoken and with strong opinions, and whose job relied on language as the tool of her trade, it was rare for her to be lost for words. What if sometimes there is nothing that can be said? But she would feel completely terrible to not say anything. She could hear Jason referring to her, deferring to her on occasion, as a senior clinician. It was her responsibility to find some sort of comforting words for this wonderful young woman sitting next to her, feeling the weight of something so tragic.

Frances let out another long, slow sigh. 'You would think that having been in the job so long, I'd be able to find something helpful or comforting to say about this terrible news. But maybe it doesn't matter how long you've been doing this work, it's always going to be awful hearing something like this. It's always going to be a difficult thing to talk about. And if it wasn't, perhaps there'd be something wrong with us. I'm just so sorry you're seeing this so early in your career, and that you're so close to it, being in the group. We can talk more now, if you need to, or if you want, I can talk to Jason, or Hayley. But I want you to try not worry about whatever you need to say or whatever you're feeling or not feeling. I will just do whatever I can to support anyone who would like me to help.' Frances gave Jess a sad smile and put a hand on her arm.

'Thanks Frances. I appreciate that. I'm okay at the moment. I need to leave for a home visit in ten minutes. I know I could re-arrange but I think I'm just best focusing on keeping the show on the road at the moment. I hope that doesn't sound callous. I just don't want anyone else out there to feel left and on their own, so keeping going seems the most helpful thing I can do right now. But maybe Jason might appreciate it. I'm not sure. I know you two have a lot of differences but that might all seem trivial at a time like this.'

Jess started packing her things away and got up to leave, returning the hand of comfort on Frances's arm as she left.

Jason was nowhere to be seen in the office. Frances pulled up his online diary and could see that he had patients booked in, pretty much back to back and so presumed that he was in a clinic room elsewhere in the building. Hayley's diary had her down for a meeting at HQ so she wasn't around to speak to in person. It didn't feel right to send an email saying she was there to talk if either of them wanted to. She thought that the person possibly most needing comfort or solidarity at the moment would be Jason, so she wrote a short paper note to him, saying she had spoken briefly with Jess about the news this morning and wanted him to know that she was there if he wanted to talk. She left it in an envelope in his pigeon hole, hoping it wouldn't get swamped by a ream of paperwork by the time he got back to the office.

After she had spent a couple of hours finishing writing up clinical notes outstanding from the previous week, her Zen Psyonics session was only about ten minutes away so Frances needed to switch track and get ready for her group. Jess had seen her previous patient and was now back in the building somewhere and, like a trooper, already online.

Frances welcomed the group, all members present and on time, and introduced the mindfulness exercise, which this week was a video narrated by Zen Psyonics master, Alexander McDonald. Frances really wasn't in the mood for him today, though found herself relaxing into the start, watching a loop of breaking waves below a purple sunset, with Alexander's gentle, calming voice telling them to notice their in-breath and their out-breath and any remaining tension. She actually noticed thinking what a relief it was to take a moment of stillness after such a grim morning. But just as it was all going so well, Alexander started explaining how they needed to *unlock themselves* and *embrace the moment*, by repeating five short affirmations.

I welcome this moment
I become present
I open my heart and mind
I unlock my self
I embrace the moment

Then he started talking about *success* and *clarifying your goals* and *becoming your best self*, by which time he had really lost Frances. She wished he had just stayed with the in-breath and out-breath for the whole five minutes and she felt annoyed that he had spoiled something she had been surprisingly hungry for.

She hoped that it was just her and that the rest of the group weren't similarly annoyed by it. She kept an open mind and asked for their reflections afterwards. Someone said they liked watching the waves and the sunset, which others agreed with. Kevin, who seemed to find most things about Zen Psyonics quite challenging, said that the narrator had a good voice for narrating. Nobody said anything about feeling irritated about the affirmations, so Frances was happy to leave it there and concluded that maybe her bullshit register was just way more sensitive than other people's.

Just as she was about to move on, Nick, one of three younger men in the group, spoke up.

'I don't like speaking in groups,' he started, 'but in the spirit of *Grasp it, Grill it, Ground it* I'm trying to ground my unhelpful thoughts about sounding stupid, so I'm just going to go for this. I wanted to say I really didn't like that mindfulness exercise. It was all a bit hippy-dippy for me and I just thought it would have been better if they had just stuck with the mindful breathing. But I seem to find most of the mindfulness exercises a bit irritating, to be honest. I don't want to seem like I'm being difficult but I'm just being honest and like I said, I'm also trying to change my unhelpful thoughts.'

'You're not on your own with that,' someone called Lexie responded. 'If it gets a bit woo-woo I just switch off and go into my own little world until it finishes. Probably not what we're supposed to do but I think you've just got to take what works for you and not pay too much attention to the rest.'

'Thanks both of you,' Frances responded. 'What about others? How is everyone else getting on with the mindfulness practice?' There were various replies, mostly along the lines of it being okay but limited. 'Personally, I tend to approach it in a similar way to Lexie,' Frances shared. 'It's obviously something that most people have heard of these days and is clearly quite popular in many walks of life, but I think it's also worth acknowledging its limitations. I'm not sure whether it's fair to say but I tend to think that unless you're a Buddhist monk who has achieved enlightenment, it's more the sort of thing that for most people can only take the edge off. It's not likely to be magically transformative.'

'What about all the stuff in the handbook that says about the neuroscience behind it?' Nick asked.

Frances could feel herself getting into tricky territory. How much could she allow herself to say what she really thought? It had already been such a difficult day, especially in terms of having to decide on the best things to say. In the end, she found herself inwardly repeating the affirmation, *I unlock myself*, giving herself permission to speak honestly.

'Yes, there are many research papers which make claims about how mindfulness is associated with altered brain structure, but there are also plenty of others which raise doubts about these findings, so in the absence of any cast iron guarantees, I would suggest that you, all of you, might be your own best judge. If it works for you then great. If it doesn't, that's okay, we can try to find something else.' She stopped there, feeling like she hadn't entirely *unlocked* herself, but it had been a reasonable contribution in this particular situation, on a day like today. And Nick seemed satisfied with her answer, she hoped, as he didn't come back in at that point.

They moved on to review their homework. Karrie, who Frances had clocked as having been unusually silent up to that point, was the first to volunteer.

'Well I'm sad to say I think I'm continuing the theme here, after everything I said a few weeks ago about taking responsibility. I was really on a roll with my *Grasp it, Grill it, Ground it* and then I basically hit the wall. I was on day three and had all my examples and had managed to change what I would normally do, then I got wind of a family gathering that my sister was organising but hadn't invited me to. Maybe for some people they would have been able to grill and ground their thoughts about that, but in my case, there wasn't any other way to see this, apart from it being my sister and my mum in cahoots together, deliberately leaving me out. Then as if that wasn't bad enough, the day after that one of my friends, who is another mental health service user with personality disorder, was found dead after taking her own life. Some of you might have read about it in the papers.'

Frances's day just ramped up a notch. For the third time in the space of a few hours, the woman who prided and sometimes chided herself on always having something to say, was temporarily wordless.

'I'm so sorry you've had such a dreadful week, Karrie,' Jess came to the rescue. 'I think you're right about it continuing the theme, but that's no fault of yours or anyone else's. Life just sometimes gets in the way, doesn't it? No matter how hard we try. It just sometimes really...' she paused, trying to find the right word.

'Sucks,' Karrie finished for her.

Yes, that,' Jess agreed. She seemed to wait for Frances to come back in.

'Yes, well said both of you,' Frances nodded to Jess and Karrie. 'We're all only human. We can only do our best and sometimes we can't even do that. We can try and use these tools and techniques and they might work sometimes, but really that's all they are, just tools and techniques. Is there something else we can do instead, right now, that would be helpful, Karrie?' She hoped she hadn't overstepped the mark with Karrie, knowing how important Karrie had said it was to her to actually be finally doing Zen Psyonics, so not wanting to be completely dismissive of it.

'Well, I did write down a pile of unhelpful thoughts, even though I couldn't challenge them or change them. Shall I just tell you them? Most of them were more like questions, so like, is there something wrong with me? Like I mean, wrong with me beyond personality disorder. Am I just really unlucky? Have I brought this on myself? Am I not trying hard enough? But I couldn't come up with any good or helpful answers.' Karrie waited.

'It sounds like you're asking us in the group to come up with some helpful answers, and other people might have some. But I would just like to give you my own. No I don't think there's something wrong with you and yes it does sound like you've been really unlucky and it doesn't sound like you've brought this on yourself. From what you've said, the situation with your mum and sister is something that has been going on for years. And I'm really sorry that you've also now lost your friend. As for trying hard enough, I think from the beginning you've been completely committed to this group and tried as hard as anyone could be expected. But sadly, I think that the sort of world we're in can sometimes lead us to blame ourselves and make us think there is something wrong with *us*, when actually there isn't. Most people who get referred to mental health services have not been dealt the best hand, for one reason or another. But it generally suits those who wield the most power to have us believe that it's ourselves that need to change rather than an unequal and unfair world.'

Gosh, Frances was really unlocking herself now, but she felt it was more important to be authentic and, dare it, *embracing* of herself. In fact, why not go the whole hog, she thought, and carried on.

'I'd like to share a small thought with you. If it's a helpful thought, maybe keep it and use it. If it's not helpful, bin it. It's just a thought after all. When we psychologists do our clinical training, one of the ideas that gets talked about a lot is *insight*. It's essentially the idea that when we're experiencing problems of the sort that lead people to mental health services, a key part of that is because we're not aware of what's going on internally and how that affects our interactions and how we deal with our problems. So if we can develop this awareness of ourselves, this *insight*, we'll be able to deal with our problems. But that way of looking at things is very strongly focused on the idea of *ourselves* being the problem, when in actual fact, there are very likely all sorts of things outside of us that are much more likely to be creating our problems, and if we only focus on ourselves, we might be quite limited in trying to sort things out. So I like to use an alternative idea, called *outsight* to help people think about what they might be able to change about the world around them, or at least *understand* how the world is impacting on them, which might be more effective than trying to change themselves.'

'How does that fit with Zen Psyonics then, Frances?' Karrie asked. 'It sounds like you're saying we shouldn't be doing this *Grasp it, Grill it, Ground it* and we should be going on some mass protest or something. I'm not sure that's very helpful and I'm in danger of being way too confused here. There *is* something wrong with me, which is that I've got a personality disorder and I need to change *me*, not the world. And we can't change the world anyway! Have you tried voting in an election recently? What happens? It all goes to shit. They all say the same thing and nothing ever changes. And what difference would that make to me anyway? I'd like to change my mum and my sister but they're not in this group so they're not going to change either. The only thing I've got a hope in hell of changing is myself!'

Karrie was quite fired up now and Frances worried that she had said too much. 'It makes total sense that you think all that, Karrie and yes, it's all those things happening close to you, in your own life, that are more important than anything further away in the world and they're the things you want to change. But it still doesn't mean that you're the problem, just that's what it feels like because that's where it lands. But I really don't want to confuse you and these are all just ideas and please bin it if that's more helpful.'

'I must say, I'm confused now too, to be honest,' Nick said in a rather apologetic voice.

Frances suggested that maybe they could return to the discussion some other time and instead get back to the homework review because maybe something more helpful would come out of that. It felt like grabbing and clinging on to bits of driftwood, anything floating by that might carry them somewhere safer, but only by chance, not design. She wondered what Jason would have made of her session today. Or Alexander himself? Would he have been appalled by this anarchic diversion? Or would he have simply said, *that's why I have a one hundred percent success rate with my clients and you don't*.

Karuṇā Therapy

Karuṇā is a Sanskrit word for compassion or mercy and is sometimes translated as self-compassion or spiritual longing. It is a significant spiritual concept in the Indic religions of Hinduism, Buddhism, Sikhism and Jainism.

Karuṇā Therapy (KT) is a psychotherapeutic system that integrates cognitive-behavioural therapy techniques with insights from evolutionary psychology, social psychology, developmental psychology, Indic spirituality and neuroscience. A primary focus of KT is cultivating inner warmth, safeness and comforting experiences.

The core therapeutic approach of KT involves training individuals in the skills and attributes of karuṇā, facilitating the transformation of problematic cognitive and emotional patterns related to anxiety, anger and self-criticism. KT draws theoretical support from biological evolution, emphasizing the interconnection of emotional regulation systems with cognitive processes. By incorporating karuṇā, clients can enhance their ability to manage these systems more effectively and respond appropriately to various situations.

KT is particularly suitable for individuals grappling with high levels of shame and self-criticism, struggling to feel warmth and kindness toward themselves or others. The therapy aims to help such individuals develop a greater sense of safeness and warmth in their interactions both with others and within themselves.

20

Time was going both fast and slow. It seemed to be taking an age for people to reply to emails and text messages, yet on the other hand, the next Zen Psyonics group was approaching so fast it felt impossible for Jason to get his house in order. His main concern at the moment was needing to work out how he was going to approach the group, which was happening in just over twenty-four hours. Ordinarily, this would have been something for discussion between co-facilitators but as his co-facilitator was Jess, he felt it was neither appropriate nor fair to put her in the position of thinking through this difficult clinical issue with him, when she was just a support worker. If he was being honest, though, he couldn't get away from the fact that she *knew* what had happened. And he was worried that she would see Mandy's death as his fault.

The news had been going round and round his head all weekend, on a loop, with him accusing himself and then defending himself. *This woman had something terrible happen in her life and she shared this with the group. She just so happened to also have breached the group rules and therefore needed to be discharged. But some discretion should have been exercised, due to the extenuating circumstances. But the rules need to be strictly enforced otherwise it's simply repeating unhelpful patterns which patients have experienced in their lives previously. But a risk assessment should have been carried out at the point of discharging her from the group. But meetings had been set up for the following week. There was nothing to suggest that her being discharged from the group would lead to the event that then occurred. But she had just had something terrible happen in her life and she shared this with the group.* On and on it went. And it was still going on, but now it felt even more urgent and was laced with not only the added factor of seeing it through Jess's eyes but also seeing it through the group's eyes and trying to figure out what on earth to say to them.

There had been no reply from Alexander McDonald and Jason wasn't inclined to keep pestering him. Years ago, he wouldn't have thought twice about it and would have sent a series of messages, getting increasingly cheeky, ending up with things like, *Alexander, are you out there? Show me a sign*, and Alexander would eventually get back to him. But as his empire had grown, the founder and creator of Zen Psyonics had gradually become more distant and a gulf had formed between the two of them, where the shifting sands had never come back together. Jason tried not to dwell on this and instead see it as the natural shaping of life's contours, where relationships forge and move close and drift apart. Besides, he still valued the connection he did have, the fact that he was lucky to be able to get supervision with Alexander every so often, bearing in mind how important and busy the man was. But there was also a part of him that was disappointed with Alexander. Angry even. No, angry was too strong. Disappointed that Alexander hadn't even bothered to reply to his email marked *urgent*. Angry that someone in that line of work, who should pick up certain cues like *urgent*, that someone who knew him quite well, and had almost been a friend, certainly a trusted mentor, did not take seriously his fellow worker's request for help.

With Alexander temporarily stood down from his support network, Jason pondered his limited options. Karen, his clinical supervisor and the lead nurse for the whole team, would have normally been the person to go to, but she was on a rare three week holiday in Mexico. Jason could see why some people, at times of stress, would resort to thinking *someone up there has got it in for me*, as it seemed that so much was against him. Hayley was in theory another person he should have been able to draw support from, but she had no qualifications in psychological therapies and whilst *she* seemed to have respect for *him*, he wasn't really sure what she might have to offer him in this situation. Plus there was already an email from her at the top of his inbox when he got to work that morning, acknowledging the news and calling him to a meeting first thing the next day, to begin the Serious Untoward Incident process. The absence of anything in the email relating to staff support and how anyone might be feeling also suggested that the last thing on Hayley's mind was the Zen Psyonics group who had lost their member.

There were a few people in the main office who he could have approached but none of them were Zen Psyonics facilitators and none of them were the sort he would have had in his *team*, so to speak. Most were pleasant, friendly people and for all he knew, competent at their jobs, but not with the same level of skills as him and certainly not possessing the ability to deal with this tragic and difficult situation. The only person vaguely fitting that bill, though frankly the last person he would want to discuss it all with, was Frances Fisher, who, as it happened, had left a handwritten note in his pigeon-hole. She must have only recently put it there as he had cleared his pigeon hole first thing, but she wasn't around in the office, much to his relief actually, as he had no intention of baring his soul to her of all people. He could just imagine her being all superior and whilst she might refrain from actually saying *I told you so*, she would definitely hold forth about all the things that were wrong with Zen Psyonics and how if it didn't have such silly, strict rules, there wouldn't be such tragic outcomes.

Okay Jason, you're on your own now. Time to step up, he told himself, realising he would have to decide what to do about the group himself. He thought about cancelling it and buying himself more time. He would at least then be able to discuss it fully in Covision. But he quickly dismissed that idea because it would be making a terrible situation even more confusing, bearing in mind the very thing which had set this all off. It was unheard of to cancel Zen Psyonics sessions. It would go against everything recommended in the therapy itself, the strict rules on attendance and any absences being targeted as a focus for therapy. He would also be deviating once again from the protocol himself, as he had already done in the previous session by being late. It was absolutely not an option to cancel.

He never imagined that he would be in this position of having to discuss the loss of a group member due to suicide, the very behaviour that Zen Psyonics was supposed to address. He decided that he would have to open the next session by informing the group about what had happened, which was of course information already in the public domain. He felt he needed to prepare though for the possibility that some of them might ask him about whether he thought Mandy's death was related to being discharged from the group and they might well want to express their sense of unfairness and anger. Jason decided he needed to write something down and rehearse it, so that he was ready to respond to whatever came up. He wanted to say something about Mandy having shared her story about her boyfriend and daughter and that perhaps it was more likely that she was devastated by those events rather than being discharged from the group. But another voice was telling him, *but that was the final straw, her being discharged from the group. She had friends in this group and you took her away from them. You left her in a Team of One!*

Jason had visions of the whole session raging out of control and it causing even more turmoil and upset. In the end, he decided that he would first say that he, too, was devastated but that it was simply not possible to know precisely about Mandy's decision, and that it was understandable that they might feel angry about the fact she was discharged from the group. He would explain that he wanted them to be able to discuss the feelings that were coming up for them and was happy to book individual sessions with them for that purpose, but that it was important to also limit discussion about Mandy in the group as it would not be conducive to their wellbeing, as they were working incredibly hard to manage their own feelings and behaviours and needed to continue following the group programme to help them further develop their skills. He would emphasise once again the importance of maintaining structure, and remind them of the need to learn coping skills for getting through the greatest challenges. He also thought of the sailing metaphor he sometimes mentioned in Covision, when trying to persuade colleagues who were trying to persuade patients about the essential requirement of keeping up with the skills. He might use that again.

Jason suffered the meeting with Hayley the next morning. She had her laptop with her and launched into explaining the Serious Untoward Incident procedure. Jason found himself surprised to be thinking, hang on a minute, shouldn't we be doing a *pulse check* first? Shouldn't you be asking about the wellbeing of your employees before we get into anything else? He was acutely aware that he had not yet had chance to properly speak to Jess after thinking through the strategy for the group later and he had no idea how she was faring, or what she was thinking about his role in the events.

Hayley was keen to point out that the SUI investigation was not to hold any individual, or the organisation, to account, just in case Jason and Jess were worrying about that. Jason couldn't tell whether Hayley assumed he *was* worrying about that, but the fact that she went on to say that other processes exist for holding people to account wasn't exactly reassuring.

'We must advocate justifiable accountability and a zero tolerance for inappropriate blame,' she added, reading from something on her laptop. 'So you know, this is about understanding what went wrong, how it went wrong and what can be done to prevent similar incidents occurring again.'

Jason nodded but stayed silent, waiting for Hayley to carry on. Jess sat motionless.

'So, we're not going to complete all this today, but I need to get the basics at this point. Obviously I'm now aware that Mandy went missing last Tuesday and was found by the police at her home on Friday, having hanged herself.'

Jason hadn't known that detail and judging by the look of Jess, she hadn't either. Jason felt the shift in the atmosphere but it must have gone past Hayley who carried on.

'I'm also aware that Mandy was discharged from the group the same day she went missing, but the police aren't clear yet of the timing of her taking her own life. Can you just fill me in on the details of what happened in the group and why she was discharged?' Hayley had her fingers at the ready and typed rapidly on her keyboard as Jason told her about the group that day. It felt strange speaking about it with Hayley looking at her laptop instead of him. He felt less scrutinised without her looking at him, but at the same time he couldn't help thinking that it was terribly inappropriate.

Jason stopped talking and Hayley stopped typing and looked up again. 'I can understand that you might be worried, you Jason in particular, about the sequence of events, but I want you to know that we've got your back here and to remind you that we can't be responsible for everything that goes on in people's lives outside of our services. I can see that you took all the necessary precautions and booked in the discharge planning appointment with Mandy and short of sorting out her family situation, I can't see what else you could have done. It looks like you did everything according to the book.'

'Thanks,' Jason said. It was all he could manage.

'Is there anything you want to add, Jess?' Hayley was ready with her fingers again.

'No, I think Jason's covered it,' Jess said. It was impossible to tell what was going through her head.

'We just need to do a quick pulse check.'

Shouldn't you have started with that? Jason thought but had no intention of saying.

Hayley rattled off a series of questions, to Jason and Jess in turn and then thanked them, saying they could get in touch with her any time if they needed to talk things through or wanted more support. She hurried off to another meeting, whilst Jason and Jess remained seated, in a momentary awkward silence. Jason felt stunned.

'Are you okay, Jason?' Jess asked with such gentleness and compassion that he almost felt moved to tears.

'Thanks for asking, Jess. I think I'm okay, just a bit stunned. Are *you* okay? I was worried that I didn't give you any time yesterday, in case you wanted to talk, and I've no idea how all of this is affecting you. But also, I wanted to talk to you about what I've planned for the group.'

'Yes, I'm okay. Frances was around yesterday so I didn't feel left on my own. I also assumed we'd be able to talk a bit more when we have Covision. But yes, I've been wondering about the session today and what we'll say.'

Jason told her what he had decided was the best way of approaching the group, giving them time at the beginning but then sticking to the format, arguing that it was at times like this that it was most important to keep going with the structure and the skills practice. He skirted over the bit about anticipating their questions and their expressions of anger and unfairness because that would have meant a longer conversation with Jess about his role in the sequence of events, and he was just not ready for that right now.

Jess didn't allow him the luxury of time though and boldly brought the subject up. 'I was thinking that some of them, Owen and Paula maybe, might say something about you and Mandy both being late and seeing an unfairness in her being discharged when there was no consequence for you. But please don't think I'm criticising you in any way for that. I'm sure you had good reason for being late and these things happen. It's just that I sometimes struggle with the rigidity of the rules, but I'm only a support worker and I have such little experience and you've been doing this for years so I guess it's probably me just not always understanding everything.'

Jason was unsettled by her directness. He hoped that Frances Fisher hadn't been feeding her all sorts of unhelpful ideas in their contact yesterday.

'Yes, it's a tricky balance sometimes and I'm anticipating some of them bringing up some of those concerns too, but I'm ready for them, so hopefully it will all be okay.' He thought he probably sounded more confident than he actually was.

By the time the group started, Jason was feeling even less confident and couldn't remember a time when he had so dreaded running a group session. Even in the early days of his CBT training he had felt excitement rather than anxiety at the prospect of performing an assessment or intervention session in front of a supervisor, keen to show his knowledge and competence. But they hadn't role-played a situation like this in his training, and performing in front of Jess, with her knowing all that had happened, seemed far more of a challenge than following some protocol in front of a superior.

Everyone was on time, early in fact. They went straight into the mindfulness exercise which just so happened to be one of Alexander McDonald's narrated videos. Jason had been so wrapped up in figuring out what he was going to say to the group that he hadn't noticed the session content and the fact that Alexander would feature today and he didn't find it entirely welcome. Still, he made every effort to focus on the waves and the sunset and calm his breathing to help prepare for whatever came next.

'I've got some very sad news,' Jason went straight in at the end of the video clip, without even asking how people found the mindfulness exercise. 'Some of you may already have heard from local news that Mandy was found dead at home by police last week, having taken her own life after going missing.' He saw some people nodding. 'I know that some of you really enjoyed Mandy's presence in the group and felt quite connected to her. Obviously she had been discharged last week so she was no longer in the group anyway, but to hear now what has happened to her is very shocking and may mean that today's session is very difficult for you. I want to allow a few moments if any of you want to say anything about any feelings that might be coming up for you and I'm happy to book individual sessions for that purpose, but it's also important that we continue to follow the programme for today's session because it's at times like this that you need to use the new coping skills that you're hopefully beginning to develop.'

Jason paused. It was difficult to tell from the screen whether any of them were hearing this for the first time. Nobody spoke. Jason waited. Sometimes it took a while for people to formulate what they wanted to say, even in normal times. The anticipated barrage of outrage had not yet transpired. After about a minute, still nobody had spoken so Jason continued.

'I appreciate this may be a horrible shock and you might not be able to put it into words at the moment, or might not feel comfortable talking about this in the group. So I want to repeat that if any of you do decide you want to speak with me more about Mandy, please use the Zen Psyonics email address and I will get back to you with an appointment. I also thought it might be helpful to share a thought with you about sticking with the programme, even though it might seem like the last thing you feel like doing. I sometimes use the metaphor of sailing a boat in the ocean, where the weather conditions require us to adjust our sailing skills. Some days will be smooth sailing and it's easy to use our skills. Other days we need to draw on more skills to adapt to the conditions. And when we're hit with a big storm, we don't jump ship and give up. It's then that we need to remain upright and sailing in the direction we want to go. We need to use all our skills with determination and perseverance, until the storm has eventually passed and the waves have settled.'

Again, there was silence. Jason had no way of knowing whether this was because people were stunned by the news or whether some of them were furious and in their heightened emotional state, simply unable to speak. He suspected a mixture of the two, possibly along with other reasons, and as he had already underlined and elaborated the fact that they needed to focus on today's session he was keen to move on and considered the discussion space closed.

Mehta Meridian Touch Technique

Achieve immediate relief from anxiety, stress, fear, worry and trauma within the comfort of your home through the Mehta Meridian Touch Technique® (MMTT®).

Developed in the late 1980s by Zara Mehta, a Licensed Acupuncturist in Sidney, Australia, MMTT is a swift and uncomplicated transformational process. Utilised by hundreds of thousands of people across more than 80 countries, this technique has gained global popularity.

Research indicates that MMTT can effectively address stress, anxiety, depression, trauma, PTSD and eating disorders, and is increasingly employed to alleviate political fear. The MMTT process involves a combination of stimulating meridian systems and progressing through a series of six statements, taking approximately 20 minutes to complete.

Whether through MMTT video recordings, webinars, workshops, or private sessions, you will be systematically guided through this user-friendly technique. As you engage in the process, you will also acquire an understanding of the MMTT process.

21

Some people apparently couldn't resist telling Paula where she was up to in her treatment schedule, as if she needed to be reminded. *Well over half way now*, her brother had commented when he phoned for a progress report a few weeks ago. *Bet you can see the light at the end of the tunnel now*, her assistant head teacher had said at a recent keeping-in-touch meeting. And in the last treatment review, the oncologist concluded the appointment with *in the home straight now, just the final hurdle*. Paula hated the language around the whole ordeal. It seemed so misguided and inappropriate, and a million miles away from her experience. In her head she had started a little mental game, something she came up with to try to disconnect from her intense irritation every time someone came up with another ridiculous, lame comment or suggestion. If the comment got her back up but was otherwise only momentarily irritating and was from someone she couldn't really care less about, she filed it under *kind but stupid*. When a neighbour went on and on about what a lovely hat she was wearing (a twenty-year old tatty thing she had dug out to keep her bald head warm), that went into the *kind but stupid* category. Then there was the *really fucking irritating* file, which contained a surprising number of very similar comments, things like, *we're all dying*. But the difference, you fuckwit, is that you're not looking into the jaws of your own hell. And finally, far from empty, the pinnacle for thoughtless, insensitive and upsetting shit people said, was the box of delights labelled *should know better and should be utterly ashamed of themselves*. These probably amassed at the rate of about one each week. The most recent addition was Paula's brother's girlfriend, herself a nurse in a hospice, phoning to see whether Paula and Gerry wanted to go to watch a film about a man creating a prize winning forest garden after the death of his wife from breast cancer. *One, how many times have they been told that I'm avoiding public places at the moment to reduce the risk of infection?* Paula had shouted at Gerry after the phone call. *And two, why the absolute fuck would I want to go and watch a film about a man whose wife has just died of cancer?* Paula appreciated that at least Gerry didn't argue with her on this one.

But even Gerry couldn't help himself sometimes. He'd let a *nearly there now* slip out after the oncology review. Paula could tell he was getting excited about a time when normal service would be resumed. All of this just compounded Paula's sense of loneliness, knowing that normal service would never be resumed. Even if she could have had extra radiotherapy to eradicate that troublesome area of her brain which was reminding her of the ever present cancer cells hiding in plain sight, it was going to take many months for her body to recover to the extent that she *looked* vaguely normal. Who knew how long it would take for her red, ravaged, blotched and swollen face to recover? *Even a year* would not give her enough hair regrowth to look anything like she had before this stroke of fate slayed her and robbed her of her identity, which she sometimes needed to remind people, was not about a superficial attitude towards beauty. It was simply about not wanting to be seen as the cancer patient. So it was likely that everyone else would be enjoying themselves in the pub in six months' time, waiting for her, not being able to understand why she was still sitting alone at home. By which time, who knew, maybe the cancer would have already made its return known. So no, normal service was a thing of the past. When even her husband didn't get it, after the hours she had complained and explained and pained him with her fears and worries, then who was there left on her team?

Paula didn't mind the topic of where she was up to in her *other* treatment, even though it was arguably every bit as personal and something others might want to keep private. She had almost completed the cognitive restructuring module, which was the second of the four modules. And now she was faced with a dilemma. Unlike the cancer treatment, which she felt she had little choice about other than to go with the experts, she could drop out of the Zen Psyonics group at any time. She probably wouldn't have even been grappling with this dilemma were it not for two significant and slightly related factors. The first was that she would soon be starting radiotherapy and the timing of this meant that it clashed with the Zen Psyonics group. There was no way she could therefore carry on attending the group, but she was under the impression that it might be possible to transfer to another group, something one of the other group members did in the first few weeks due to having a new job. However, she was also aware that radiotherapy treatment was reliably *running late*, often by an hour or so, as displayed by the wipe board in the centre of the waiting room every time she went for chemotherapy. This could mean that even if she joined another group, she might not be able to guarantee her timely attendance and as recent events had proved, two absences or significant late shows, meant discharge from the group. Therein lay the second factor in her dilemma. The death of Mandy Harper.

Paula had been angry enough about Mandy having to leave the group and she had been all ready to make her grievance known to Jason, though she was going to spare him the shame of raising it in the group. And then came the utter shock of hearing Jason tell the group that Mandy had killed herself. It looked like some of the other people in the group already knew and Paula suspected that Owen was one of those. But she couldn't bring herself to speak, to ask whether anyone knew any more, to find out whether there was any note, to say that she thought Mandy shouldn't have been discharged from the group. She had hoped that in her own mute state, Owen might step in and say something, but maybe like her, he just couldn't find the words, and nobody else said anything either. She couldn't believe how yet again, even in *these* circumstances, Jason had kept to his lesson plan after sharing some derisory metaphor about *sailing in bad weather*.

Had things unfolded differently, with Paula's cancer treatment not getting in the way and Mandy still being alive and her wonderful self in the group, Paula would have happily carried on to the end, even despite Jason's frankly strange and rigid style. But with all this, this unimaginably tragic juncture, Paula couldn't see

Zen Psyonics as anything other than harmful quackery and she wondered how it had come to be so ubiquitous in mental health services. It was probably this, her astonishment and incredulity, which in the end led to her decision to email Jason to request a transfer to a different group. There she would be able to see how it was run by somebody else and whether the problem was Zen Psyonics itself or just Jason Coriol. And she would also raise her concerns about what had happened to Mandy. She owed that to Mandy. She wished that she had been able to tell her that she hadn't been on her own and that she, Paula, was in her team, even if that meant there were only two of them.

Paula was surprised to get a prompt response from Jason saying the team had discussed her situation and she was welcome to join a different group, though he emphasised that reliable attendance would still be necessary and if her cancer treatment was likely to get in the way of this, then perhaps now was not the right time for her with Zen Psyonics. She thought Jason was probably relieved to get rid of her because it meant one less person challenging him about what had happened to Mandy. She was mildly comforted on receiving a letter a few days later offering her a half-way review appointment with Frances Fisher, the psychologist who assessed her when she was first referred to mental health services. She remembered being surprised by the woman, that she asked and said things she had not expected, and that she had been disappointed that she was going to be passed on to someone else and wouldn't be seeing her again. But now here she was, waiting to be admitted into the virtual room.

Frances appeared on the screen in the sudden way that always happened in video calls. Paula immediately felt comforted on seeing her welcoming face and thought it strange how it seemed like she was with an old friend she had known for years.

They both spoke at the same time and then both stopped and smiled. Paula let Frances go next.

'So we got to see each other again after all,' she said. 'I imagine you might have a lot to talk about. So I'll just get my bit out of the way. Obviously this is your Zen Psyonics half-way review that you would have had with Jason, but since you're coming into my group now it seemed more sensible for you to meet with me and then I'll get a sense of how you're finding it and any problems you're having with the skills practice and the materials. But we've got fifty minutes. I do a fifty minute hour, by the way, so I've got time to write up the notes before the next appointment. So hopefully that will be enough to get through everything we need to, but we can always book another appointment if it seems like we haven't finished. We're not strictly supposed to arrange extra appointments outside of the ones prescribed by Zen Psyonics but well,' Frances paused, appearing to choose her words carefully, 'I like to think of myself as a higher authority than Zen Psyonics. I think my many years of experience and training qualifies me to make my own decisions and override accepted protocols if necessary.'

That introduction was a lot for Paula to take in. The fifty minute hour thing immediately made her think of Jason and his rules and structures. It was rather ominous, if anything. And yet it didn't really fit with Paula's gut feeling about Frances, plus she had then gone on to say that she would basically bend the rules if she wanted to. Paula also wondered if this was an oblique reference to what had happened in Jason's group and the tragic consequences that can unfold if you stick too rigidly to any rules. She wasn't sure about whether she should pick up right from there and say how shocked and upset she was about Mandy and how it raised serious questions about Zen Psyonics, or at least, the way it was being practiced in *her* group.

'Obviously I'm aware that you might want to talk about Mandy,' Frances said, as if reading her mind, 'as you would have had the opportunity to talk with Jason about it, had you stayed in his group.'

At that invitation, it all came tumbling out. How she had really bonded with Mandy and knew that others had too. How she admired her frankness when she talked about difficulties with the homework. How Mandy had given her the gift of *Team of One*, which she would never have watched if Mandy had not persuaded her, and how that in itself had been probably *the* most helpful thing anyone had suggested, in helping her endure the assault, exposure and isolation of cancer and its treatment. She said that when Mandy had talked about trying to survive and how brutal and lonely that sometimes was for her, it made her recognise how she herself was feeling and through that unexpected connection, it helped her feel less alone.

'And then, she was late for that last session. Jason himself had been late but Mandy didn't know that. Yet Mandy was sanctioned with being made to leave the group. And that was just after she had shared a devastating story about her boyfriend having slept with her daughter. She had been betrayed by the two people she should have been able to count on. And I can only think that being chucked out of the group was the final straw. We might have been the only people left that she felt cared about her, and she was taken away from us. She might still be here now. I'm so angry and so upset for her. I couldn't even contact her because the rules don't allow us to have contact outside of the group. I might have been able to do something. So I don't know if this is Zen Psyonics, if this is what it's supposed to be like, or if this is more about Jason and some problem he has with having to stick to rules, but either way, it's not very therapeutic. I'd go as far to say possibly dangerous. And I was thinking of dropping out, seeing as my radiotherapy has got in the way now, but I thought I owed it to Mandy to at least say how terribly I think she was treated. And I guess I wanted to see whether it was Zen Psyonics or Jason, and whether in a different group it would be different.'

Paula stopped and there was a respectful silence, which Frances eventually broke.

'I'm very sorry,' she said in her warm, gravelly voice. 'You would hope, wouldn't you, that coming to a mental health service would be more healing than harming. It's completely understandable that you're so angry and upset. It's such a terrible thing when someone gets so desperate that they can see no way of carrying on and it may very well be that was the final straw for Mandy, though I don't think we'll ever be able to say. The police have said that they didn't find a note, not that a note would necessarily make things clear either. There will of course be an investigation on our side, and I will make sure that you're able to give your own account of what happened so at least it gets heard. I never met Mandy myself but it sounds like she was someone I would have liked. Someone who speaks their mind and truth to power. We need more people like that in the world. It's very sad she couldn't hold on.'

There was space again. It seemed that neither of them felt compelled to fill it. Paula felt comfortable and found it calming to sit there for a moment, both of them having time to notice all the different jumbled up thoughts, memories, feelings, about Mandy, about health services, about life and death, about unfairness, about power.

'I appreciate you're in a difficult position and I don't want to challenge your duty to your colleagues, but going back to what you said at the beginning, about bending the rules,' Paula wasn't sure how to put the next bit.

'Would I have discharged Mandy for breaching the rules?' Paula nodded.

'No, I wouldn't. Like I said at the beginning, I think I get paid enough to make my own decisions. Rules sit below judgement and values in my hierarchy. That may simply be because I'm a bit of a rebel and I don't like being told what to do and it has got me into trouble on occasion. So it's not to say that my way is better than somebody else's way, but maybe in this particular case it would have been. Other times, maybe sticking to the rules would have been better. Maybe if you're a rule keeper, life is simpler because you don't have to make a judgement each time there's a dilemma. You just stick to the rules. You're a teacher yourself, though. You've probably got bags of experience with rules.'

'Yes absolutely. And I guess that's another reason why I'm so angry about this. I'm in those sorts of dilemmas day in, day out and I know how important it is to have rules but also how sometimes you need a bit of flexibility and it can make all the difference. I'm like you, I think. What you said about judgement and values trumping the rules. But in my work, sticking to the rules isn't usually a matter of life and death, or at least it hasn't been so far.'

'But you'd agree that it can be a tricky judgement, whether to obey the rule or override it? It always presents a dilemma and it can be difficult to predict the outcome or know whether we've made the right judgement. And so that even though you and I might have done something different, Jason was only doing what he thought best by sticking to the rules.' She paused then added, 'I'm not defending Jason by the way. Just saying how there are different ways of seeing things and at the end of the day, we're all human and all fallible and we can only do what we can do. You'd probably also know from your own job, too, how much we're shaped by the system ourselves. We might not even question things that should be questioned because we're products of a toxic system which has caused such a lot of harm in the first place. We're forced into making decisions about limited resources, like anyone referred to secondary mental health services is offered a choice between Zen Psyonics or nothing,' Frances trailed off.

'Yes!' Paula agreed. 'It wasn't just the rules around punctuality and reliability. It was the whole programme. How we had to stick to the topic, how it seemed like there was something wrong with us if we couldn't get to grips with the homework, how we weren't allowed to contact each other outside of sessions, how the mindfulness not working was simply because we needed more practice. All of that. But from what I can see in the handbook, that's what Zen Psyonics is. Jason was only delivering it as it was intended. But surely it has to be better than that? It's practically the only thing on offer here!' Paula was reminded of the next possible phase of her cancer treatment. 'You know I find it staggering but it's not even much better in physical healthcare. Once I've finished the radiotherapy, they recommend I take this type of drug to stop the cancer coming back. The thing is, I'm fortunate enough to have had a decent education and know how to work my way through complex information. And it turns out that this drug only reduces the chances of cancer coming back by two percent, and that's only reducing the cancer coming back in the bones, not the brain, liver or lungs, the other three places it's likely to come back. But at the same time as that, it significantly increases the chances of you getting a serious condition that causes bone cells in your jawbone to die and your jawbone to poke through an opening in your gums. And there's nothing you can do about that. But they recommend the treatment anyway! Tax payers' money being spent on treatments which destroy you!'

Frances sighed. 'I know. It's a minefield out there. And with mental health being so nebulous, there are far greater problems with psychological research. And there are of course all sorts of different therapies out there in the big wide world, but do you know what? Regardless of what type of therapy you do, all the evidence suggests that what it comes down to in the end is the therapeutic relationship. So it's basically quite random, a lottery in fact, as to whether you get to meet with someone you connect with. And in a group, that can be challenging, as the facilitator needs to connect with however many different people attending the group, and we, none of us, can be all things to all people. But again, you'd understand that from teaching. There's a lot of parallels I'm sure.'

'So maybe it's just that I was never going to click with Jason,' Paula reflected.

'Maybe,' Frances agreed. 'But then other people might click well with Jason and not with me. I try to adapt and mould myself according to the person I'm with but I don't always get it right. I'm only human after all. But I've learned to be okay with myself. This is me. Take it or leave it.'

'You know, you remind me of Mandy. Her fierce determination to be okay with herself. How she was able to see that there wasn't something wrong with her, but actually how she was being treated. I'll always remember in one of the sessions when one of the other group members was saying how he was such a failure because all the CBT he'd done hadn't worked, and Mandy said maybe it was the fact that CBT was no good, or the therapists had been no good. The awful irony of it now. Zen Psyonics was no good for her. I guess she had just had it with the world being so cruel to her. Maybe she was still defiant in her decision. Maybe she was saying *I'm not taking this anymore.* I wish I could be more like both of you. Defiantly me. I worry that I've turned into something nasty since this cancer monster. I want to be okay with myself. If I can get some of that from you in these last two modules, then maybe that's some sort of tribute to Mandy.'

Neurolocation Processing and Release

Neurolocation Processing and Release (NPR) is a potent and targeted therapeutic approach designed to identify, process and alleviate core neurophysiological origins of emotional and physical pain, trauma, dissociation and various challenging symptoms. NPR operates as a dual-function method, serving both as a diagnostic tool and a treatment modality, enriched by bilateral sound for a profound yet focused and contained impact.

While NPR serves as a neurobiological instrument to bolster the clinical healing relationship, it emphasises the irreplaceable role of a mature and nurturing therapeutic presence. This involves engaging with individuals who are undergoing suffering in a secure and trusting environment where they feel heard, accepted and understood.

Within this clinical relationship, NPR provides a tool to neurobiologically pinpoint, process and release experiences and symptoms that often elude the conscious mind and its cognitive and linguistic capacities. By working directly with the deep brain and the body, NPR accesses the autonomic and limbic systems within the central nervous system. Consequently, NPR functions not only as a physiological tool or treatment but also elicits profound psychological, emotional and physical healing.

22

Even though the five bar gate had been almost permanently shut the last few weeks, Buddha was still easily managing to escape through gaps in the hedges and shrubs that lined the front garden and screened off the lane going past Samling Stead. In normal times, Buddha would very occasionally slip under the wooden fence at the back of the house, into the fields beyond, usually in pursuit of a rabbit or similarly interesting creature. He never tended to go out the front, where the tarmac started and any potential furry companions were unlikely to be roaming. But with Alexander severely incapacitated by his broken ankle, Buddha had taken to widening his zone of exploration, possibly knowing that the lane was the route to the beach and the beach was always a good place to meet other dogs. It was becoming rather a headache though for Alexander. Buddha clearly had a good nose for direction so he wasn't worried that the dog was going to get lost and not be able to find his way home, but more worried about him getting himself into bother, probably with another bigger dog, or causing trouble himself. At the moment, Alexander couldn't even drive him to the beach to let him run around off the lead, so both were confined to their spot on the hill and nice though it was, there was not enough there to keep Buddha both exercised and entertained. Buddha of course was only confined by the limits of his imagination, which was not restrictive in the slightest.

It had been over six weeks now since the accident and Alexander had only yesterday had his first physio appointment. He had been hoping to be told that he would be back running and surfing in a matter of weeks if he followed the programme and did all his exercises, being the committed and compliant patient that he was. But the physiotherapist had seemed strangely keen on holding him back, emphasising what a bad break it had been and how a compound fracture can take far longer to heal.

She even got the x-rays up on the screen, pointing to the metal rake that was now holding his ankle and foot together, saying *remember this is what we're dealing with*. He was certain that he was likely to go fairly crazy having to exist solely on dumbbell workouts, which not only did nothing for his legs or cardio, but had no effect whatsoever on his mood, clearly not getting close to generating an endorphin high, or in fact any endorphins at all. He was also feeling decidedly flabby and floppy and certainly not the best for the upcoming court appearance. At least it was going to be heard remotely, which was one small piece of good news amongst the larger pile of shit Alexander felt he was swimming in.

Because he had far too much time to think these days, and no opportunities to exercise his way to more positive thoughts, he found himself doing an inordinate amount of stewing over Clemmie Service and the whole defamation nonsense which had kicked off this inconvenient court case. He reminded himself that Clemmie Service had been going off at all sorts of tangents in his practice of Zen Psyonics, that people in *Couch and Client* had described how he was adding bits and taking bits away and being lax about boundaries and rules. There was also the very real evidence from some patient discussion forums of complaints that Zen Psyonics felt unsafe and that someone had in fact taken their own life whilst in treatment with Clemmie. *This is what I am fighting for. His name and his business should not be associated with my name and my business in any way, shape or form*, he railed against the spectre of Clemmie Service.

He could just about see the light at the end of the tunnel now, though, with the date for the court case now set and all evidence gathered and neatly filed, ready for the decisive onslaught. The whole process had so far been intensely irritating and Alexander suspected that he would only have been mildly less annoyed if he had been fully functioning physically, able to work it all away with surfing and running. Ed Burrell had explained that they would be pursuing a *multi-track* claim, rather than the *small claims track*, as the value of the claim was likely to be well over ten thousand pounds and the complexity of the case, involving knotty psychological concepts, necessitated this. Fortunately, and amazingly to Alexander, Clemmie Service was complying with the process and meeting deadlines well within the statutory limits, so at least it was progressing at pace.

Whilst proceedings around trademark infringements were sometimes fairly uncomplicated, in the case of psychological therapies Ed Burrell pointed out the slippery nature of intangible things and how difficult it was to pin these products down, being as they were, essentially, *talking*. At times, Alexander found himself frustrated with Ed, because he didn't seem to *get* the nature of talking therapies and sometimes it felt like Ed was putting him, Alexander, in the dock. In a recent meeting when they were preparing their opening submission for the trial, Ed had ventured, *I know you've explained how exercise is a key component in Zen Psyonics which marks it out as different from things like HCT, but please can you explain to the court how you, Alexander McDonald, have the exclusive rights to exercise as therapy?* When Alexander answered him, clearly exasperated as he had explained all this before more than once, Ed held his open palms in front of chest and said, *hey, don't shoot me, I'm just preparing you for the fight.* It bothered Alexander that Ed seemed to be going over and over similar points, because even though Ed had been very clear about his good chances of winning this case, and even though Burrell Bond Solicitors had a great track record in intellectual property cases, along with great reviews on Lawdirect, he just wasn't convinced about Ed's ability to grasp the nuances of psychological therapies and the industry it had become. They both knew that Clemmie's defence was that ZP had become a generic, descriptive term for the psychological therapy Alexander had created, and that there were thousands of therapists, researchers, professors, trainers and other professionals and organizations who were now routinely using the words Zen Psyonics in their work. Still, Alexander had done all he could in furnishing Ed with the clear evidence that Clemmie Service was operating a business under the guise of Zen Psyonics but not adhering to the programmes, format nor standards set out in the formal practice manual and treatment handbooks. He therefore should not be referring to his practice as Zen Psyonics, nor should he be profiting from doing so.

It occurred to Alexander that the apparent disconnect between himself and Ed Burrell hinged on the different worlds they inhabited, where a similar language might be spoken and sound the same, when in actual fact certain words had noticeably distinct meanings. Take the word *evidence*, for example. Alexander and Ed had had many conversations about evidence over the last few months and, being experts in their fields, it might have been fair to assume that these were productive conversations and helped them both make headway in preparing the legal claim. But it often wasn't like that at all and it was more common for them both to be at loggerheads, as if they were each talking in their own obscure, primitive tongue and neither had a hope of understanding the other. Ed had suggested that Alexander might want to book onto a courtroom skills training course, where he would learn more about how to refine and enhance his skills in presenting evidence in court, as he concluded in the end that the difference between evidence in the legal profession and evidence in the psychological professions was the degree to which it was taken as *absolute*, with the former being *fixed*, and the latter being, well, rather a wishy-washy matter of opinion. They had almost come to blows when Ed had challenged Alexander on the claims that Clemmie's practice was so negligent that it had led to *actual* patient harm. When Alexander pointed once again to the material he had gathered from *Couch and Client*, alongside, crucially, *real* patient accounts, Ed simply responded that saying that something *was* the case, as in saying that somebody had made you feel suicidal, wasn't the same as *proving* that the one thing had led to the other. And if the legal system relied *solely* on what people *said*, it would be not much more than a kangaroo court.

Not everyone in Alexander's professional network seemed to have such a problem seeing the world from these different viewpoints. Alexander made the mistake of raising the issue in the

Couch and Client coffee meeting which ended up making him far more nervous about the impending court attendance. Although it was a small, select group of people, since he made sure he was only in trusted company at the moment, there were a couple of psychologists in private practice, who attended regularly, and they would sometimes take the conversation off into territory Alexander was not so familiar with, especially when it teetered on the realms of philosophy and psychoanalysis. But he had always felt he was on safe ground when it came to ZP research and its evidence base.

One of the psychologists, Collette, had a very successful private practice, and as well as being an active ZP trainer and practitioner (trained and accredited by Alexander himself), she also had a successful medico-legal arm of her business, and was making vast sums of money as an expert witness. Collette explained that she knew from her extensive legal experience that the *level* of evidence needed in a court of law was far more stringent than the supposed evidence amassed in psychological research. She said she could understand why Alexander was confused by the proceedings but as far as his lawyer would be concerned, the onus was on them to prove that the defendant was selling a product which exclusively resembled Alexander's product and therefore not his to sell. She could see that was a tricky case for any lawyer. Phil, the other psychologist in the group took up from where she left off, saying how it was a little acknowledged fact that most players in the psy industry were rather relaxed about the clinical evidence, or actual lack thereof, for the majority of therapies. A few people, including Alexander, looked confused at this point, and he imagined they were probably frantically rewriting their websites to amend their claims about the compelling research for the therapies they were offering. Phil acknowledged their surprised faces and said that even in the national clinical guidelines, where various therapies were recommended, the conclusion was that the evidence was poor for many of them, and wasn't even that great for CBT, the daddy of them all. But whoever had written the guidelines (and it was always panels of experts in the field), considered the evidence *good enough* to make their recommendations, in the absence of anything better. Phil added that he himself was not really worried as nobody really paid much attention to these detailed and unwieldy documents, and he was more guided by his *sense* that ZP was helpful, and his *conviction* that it was what his clients needed, even though his website was clear about him being guided by the evidence base. Just when Alexander thought Phil was finished sharing his rather unhelpful reflections, he casually posed the question, *who's to say that any of our practice doesn't diverge sometimes from pure ZP? I mean, we're not robots, right? You can't standardise how a therapist behaves in a therapy session and you can't reduce the truth to some numbers and a line on a graph.*

Whilst he felt he had fallen into a deep black hole with all this scrutiny of the meaning of evidence, Alexander was not stupid. He was beginning to understand how a judge might see the claim as something which could not be substantiated, and it being in the eyes of the law all rather nebulous. He had also found this normally lovely coffee morning chat alarmingly reminiscent of the consumer affairs programme he had heard a few weeks previously. That professor had confidently said there was a *big debate* going on about how effective all the different therapies were, so clearly she wasn't taking the evidence base too seriously either.

Alexander stretched in his seat and returned to the present moment with some in breaths and out breaths, becoming aware that Buddha was whining and scratching in the porch, so he hobbled on his crutches to the front door and set him free, on the proviso that he was allowed to go off into the back field and chase any passing rabbits but not allowed to squeeze through the gaps in the fence and head off to the beach. He shuffled back into the kitchen and sat on the bench to do his round of physio exercises. He tried gently flexing his foot towards his body and was disheartened that it seemed no easier at all than the first time he tried it yesterday. It was actually really painful and the physio had told him to ease off if it was too painful, but at this rate he'd be still using crutches three months from now and he wasn't sure he could keep his shit together for that long, without his surf therapy. He had been determined to defy expectations and be back on his board well before the twelve weeks predicted by the orthopaedic surgeon, who had also warned him that his was one of the more extreme breaks he had worked on and therefore the timescale for his recovery was likely to be longer than average. Feeling doubly disheartened now, from the discussion in the coffee morning and the pain from his ankle exercises, he gave up and decided to make coffee instead. The bench scraped across the floor tiles as he levered himself up with the crutches and almost in unison he heard the squeal of car breaks in the lane outside. The engine momentarily revved slower before pulling away again sharply. Probably a local boy racer rushing to nowhere in particular and certainly going too fast down the country lanes. Then Alexander was hit with another thought. Where was Buddha?

    He lumbered like the disabled person he was, as fast as possible to the front door and called urgently for Buddha. He couldn't see the whole of the garden from the doorway, but there didn't seem to be any sign of him from what he could see. He called again, more desperately this time, shouting *tatters* as a sure fire way to lure the little dog back to him, with the promise of a run on the beach. But that didn't bring him back either. Alexander started towards the five bar gate, staggering through the pebble gravel on the driveway, which made his movements even more precarious than when he was stumbling about the house. The gate proved a testing obstacle, as it was difficult to unhitch it from the lock whilst holding onto his crutches. When he eventually made it out into the lane, the gate swinging behind him, he was immediately reacquainted with Buddha, who lay still, in a small bundle, on the tarmac. There was no blood, no exposed flesh, no whimpering, no life left in the adorable little creature. Alexander threw his crutches aside and dropped to the ground, cradling Buddha close to his chest, whispering his name as tears flowed gently into the dog's fur. He had never felt so alone in the world.

Outcome Based Brief Therapy

Outcome Based Brief Therapy (OBBT) is a goal-focused therapeutic approach that directs attention towards desired outcomes rather than the issues prompting individuals to seek therapy. Rooted in positive psychology principles, OBBT facilitates change by envisioning and constructing preferred futures rather than dwelling on problems.

In OBBT, practitioners initiate the goal-setting process by creating a detailed vision of how a client's life will differ once the problem is resolved or their situation reaches a satisfactory conclusion. Collaboratively, the therapist and client explore the client's life experiences and behavioural repertoire to identify resources necessary for co-constructing a practical and sustainable outcome. This often involves examining past 'anomalies' — instances when the client effectively coped with or addressed previous challenges.

The practicality of OBBT is attributed in part to its inductive development in community mental health service settings, where clients were accepted without prior screening. The approach was refined through extensive observation of therapy sessions, noting questions, statements and behaviours that correlated with positive therapeutic outcomes. These observations were then integrated into the OBBT approach.

OBBT's popularity has grown due to its effectiveness and brevity, now making it one of the prominent schools of psychotherapy globally.

23

How so much had changed in the last few months, Jason pondered as he waited for the clock to reach the hour before entering the Covision meeting. He was haunted by the Covision session they had had back then, after some of them had just started with new groups, and he was trying to manage the disruptive dynamics of having Mandy and Paula in the group. He remembered how he had said very clearly, predicted in fact, that he was foreseeing problems with his group, due to having two inappropriate referrals. This was something he planned to raise with Hayley in the SUI process and he was at least relieved that it had been documented in the minutes. But he also remembered how the discussion progressed into an argument between him and Frances about reward versus punishment, ending with Frances pointing out that Jason had Mandy down to fail before she even started the course. He recalled her words, *you've already predicted that Mandy is going to drop out or get thrown out*. He knew very well that he had said as much, that he was *fully expecting* it in fact, and this troubled him at least as much as the other details, that he had also been late to Mandy's last session himself, and that Mandy was potentially in a more vulnerable state due to what had happened with her boyfriend and daughter. He was worried that he would be seen as vindictive for not giving Mandy a fair chance with the group, that it would be obvious he was taking out his annoyance about the referrals on Mandy herself, and that he was more bothered about proving he was right than doing what was best for Mandy. Whilst Hayley had said very clearly, if not very compassionately, that she had *got his back*, he was fully expecting the wrath of Frances, and having given up on being able to talk it through with Alexander McDonald, he felt completely unprepared. He didn't want to discuss it at all, though knew he would never be able to get away with that.

After the mindfulness exercise that they always started

with, the next item on the agenda was the *ZP accord*, where they discussed one of five elements of practice around delivering the groups. It just so happened that today's *accord* was *validation*, which required them to be open to and accepting of the views of others, however much those might differ from their own. The meeting required them to reflect on this and discuss how far they were achieving it, as a group of ZP facilitators. Jason could see how this could be a salve to him, in his vulnerable state, possibly encouraging Frances to be gentle with him, more validating and less challenging. But he could also see how it could be used against him, highlighting the glaring lack of compassion and validation he had shown to Mandy. Whilst he was normally the team member to do the most talking, he decided that the best he could do today was to keep quiet and perhaps then at least people would get the message that he was not feeling robust enough to defend himself.

It was Vicky's turn to chair the meeting and she seemed inclined to gloss over the obvious material for discussion with today's *accord*. Jason was really grateful and to his surprise, Frances didn't weigh in. But then they got to the bit on group *traffic*, where they discussed people who were being discharged and new people joining, and it was simply not possible for Vicky to gloss over this. To his relief, Vicky just said that the group were aware of what had happened in Jason's group and there was no need to discuss this at the moment if he didn't want to. It seemed that Frances had other ideas though.

'I can understand that some of you might find it better if we do leave these discussions for another less painful time, and I will go along with that too, if that's the majority decision. You know me, I think some things are left well alone. But I also think we all know enough about human beings that it's very easy to torment ourselves about what others are thinking and saying, even about what we ourselves are thinking and saying, and that can be a very lonely place. So I just wanted to say something and then I'll shut up. I'm really sorry about what happened to Mandy, Jason. I don't want to begin to presume what you're thinking about it all, but

I think the situation is an example of just how difficult our jobs are, how we're pulled in so many different directions, how we are all trying to do our best with very limited resources, how we're so busy chasing around trying to find rooms and sort out tech issues that we barely have time to think, let alone have discussions with colleagues. What happened could have happened to any of us. Maybe we would have made different decisions and maybe the same would have happened. We can't ever know. I just think it's important that you don't feel like you're on your own with all this.'

That certainly wasn't what Jason had been expecting. He felt compelled to respond but he found himself wordless.

'Thanks, Frances,' Vicky filled the silence. 'I'm sorry if it seemed I was being a bossy chair. I'm not wanting to close anything down. I maybe should have checked it out with people before the meeting. It might be worth reminding each other about the other accords, especially the ones about being non-judgemental and accepting uncertainty. I guess myself as chair and Frances just now, we're both saying that we are committed to this being a safe space and don't want anyone to feel that there's things they can't say. But at the same time, don't want anyone to feel pressured either.'

'Thanks both of you,' Jason eventually managed. 'There *will* be a time. I will come back to this. But my head is really jumbled at the moment and I'm not sure I can string a proper sentence together so I will leave it there at the moment.' He completely surprised himself with what came out of his mouth next. 'But I would appreciate if you and I could make time to discuss this further, Frances, outside of Covision, if that's okay?'

There were no rooms available later that afternoon when Jason and Frances had agreed to meet. So it was that they found themselves wandering along the footpath by the river at the back of the health centre, the very same path Jason had been on weeks earlier when he got muddy and soaked and ended up late to the group. It was a bright and crisp late autumn day this time and Jason found himself telling Frances how different it was to last time and how events unfolded as they did, his own lateness occurring the very same day as Mandy's, and how he had justified the discharge to himself, thinking about boundaries and consistency. Frances said that she already knew about him having been late, as Paula had told her in their half-way review meeting.

'I knew Paula would be aggrieved by it. I'm sure there are others too. I'm pretty sure Jess thinks it was a terrible decision too, even though she was very diplomatic about it to me. And what about you? I can't believe we're even out here together talking about this. How come you've not said *I told you so* yet? What is this? Keep your friends close and your enemies closer?'

'It's a lot easier outside, isn't it?' Frances said. 'Something about looking at the river and the gold leaves and not eyeballing each other. Maybe we should have brought life jackets though, in case one of us gets pushed into the river.' She winked at him.

For the first time since that awful Saturday, Jason felt a lightening, an easing, a blast of oxygen, like he could actually breathe properly again, and this was not the situation he expected to find such comfort.

'What *do* you think then?' Jason decided he may as well get the wrath of Frances over with, if it was destined to come at some point.

'I said the bones of what I think back in the meeting earlier. It's a difficult job. Awful things like this sometimes happen. I'm sure if someone told you that discharging Mandy would lead to her killing herself, you wouldn't have discharged her. I wouldn't have discharged her, but that's more about me having a different relationship with rules, than me being able to predict the future.'

'But she had just told the group about her boyfriend having slept with her daughter. She was devastated. It seems so obvious now.'

'Clearly you didn't think that would lead to what it led to. I guess you saw her as more robust than she was.'

They walked along in silence for a while.

'Have I ever told you about my quadrant?' Frances asked.

'No,' Jason said, realising he didn't really know much about how Frances worked, other than not like him.

'So you know how in sailing a quadrant is something sailors used to work out where they were by measuring the angle of the sun? Well I've got my own kind of word version for working out where I am in a conversation with someone. It's just a way I have of talking about talking, and a way of thinking about whether things might be helpful or unhelpful.'

It all sounded a bit fuzzy to Jason and he wasn't sure whether he wanted to hear more but clearly Frances was going to tell him anyway.

'Basically you've got difficulties and opportunities at opposite ends of the vertical axis and assets and obstacles at opposite ends of the horizontal.' She drew the model out in the air. 'So the talking about talking bit is thinking with people about whether they would find it more helpful to focus on the opportunities and solutions to their problems, and the assets and obstacles which help or hinder that, or whether they would prefer to speak more about their difficulties and problems and how they keep stuck in them.'

Jason couldn't see why she was telling him about all this. It didn't seem remotely relevant.

'Anyway, that's just one way of using it. But another way is when you put an idea in the middle and think about how, depending on how you relate to that idea, it can be helpful or unhelpful. It can open up new opportunities or it can pull you back into more difficulties. It's important to add that we're not just working with ideas but the very real material conditions of people's lives, so their ability to do something about their difficulties will depend very much on the resources or assets they have available to them, not just how they think about reality. An example I often like to use to explain it, is the idea of punctuality. So you and I, right, I think we both place a lot of importance on punctuality, which is one reason why you're so upset about what happened, because you didn't meet your own standards, plus it seemed like double standards. We tend to operate as if punctuality is always a good thing, that it always helps us move towards new opportunities and being punctual never creates difficulties for us. But the thing is, that's not always the case. I've got a very dear colleague, retired now, but when I used to supervise him he was always late for our supervision and it used to irritate the hell out of me. I thought it was disrespectful and undisciplined. But sometimes his lateness was because he was attending to the needs of a patient, so he would run over time in their session because it was more important to him that he helped sort out what needed to be sorted out, than getting to his supervision on time. And who knows, maybe the fact that he was more flexible than me might have prevented some horrible thing occurring as a result of him sticking to time. The thing is, we'll never know. But the point is, these are all just ideas and they can be helpful or unhelpful, depending on the circumstances, and keeping this model in mind can sometimes help make more sense of things. You can put anything in the middle. Rules, consistency, love, money. Once you start putting things in there you can see how a thing can sometimes be an asset, which you have at the top of the quadrant, leading us to new opportunities or sometimes an obstacle, at the bottom of the quadrant, which pulls us back into difficulties. Or an obstacle can actually lead us to new opportunities and vice versa. I'll always remember a patient of mine saying how her arthritis was an obstacle that had led her to new opportunities as it meant she took up cycling, as recommended by her orthopaedic surgeon, and she ended up travelling all over the world on her bike and would never have had that were it not for the arthritis.'

'So basically this is your way of kindly saying that me sticking to the rules might be helpful in some situations but in this particular one it was most definitely not.'

'That's one thing you could take from what I'm saying. But it was more that I was trying to both give you something you might use in similar situations in future, at the same time as saying perhaps be kind to yourself. You did what you did because you thought that was the most helpful thing at the time, plus with the resources available to you. You were late. You were frazzled. You couldn't find a blasted room. Maybe our working conditions fry your own patience just like mine sometimes and Mandy was on the receiving end of that.'

'But remember you said that I had predicted Mandy would breach the rules and therefore get discharged. So you could say it wasn't even about me following the rules but just proving that I was right. Having some stupid battle of wills with a patient. And now look.'

'It *is* awful and I know that you would turn back the clock if you could. I know it feels terrible. But congratulations, for it proves you're a human being and not a robot. And maybe you'll be a bit different with rules from here on.'

Jason badly needed to unburden himself. Nobody but he and Mandy knew what had been said between them in the group break.

'You're aware I'm going to have to discharge you from the group, Mandy?' Jason had been direct from the off. 'You were more than fifteen minutes late today, as well as not having done the homework last time, so that means automatic discharge, not just from the group but from the service, but we can set up your discharge planning meeting to make sure you have all the necessary supports in place.'

Unusually for Mandy, she hadn't come back shouting and swearing, saying how useless Jason was and how shit the whole team was. Instead she had politely asked to be allowed to stay in the group.

'I *know* I've broken the rules, Jason. I wouldn't have been late today. I had everything ready, everything prepared. I'd done the homework and everything. But my daughter decided to come back to the house to get some of her stuff. I had no idea she was coming. It was just before the group started.' Mandy had looked close to tears.

'I'm sorry this is upsetting and comes at a difficult time for you, but you must acknowledge that this is a pattern with you. There's always an excuse about why you can't commit to treatment. I honestly don't think our service has got anything more we can offer you.' Jason had tried to say it gently, but clearly not gently enough for Mandy who had started protesting.

'It's not an excuse, Jason. She actually threw my laptop across the room and the screen detached from it. She said I was a mental waste of space and was never going to be normal. I told her to get out and then tried to log on with my old tablet but it took me ages to find the links and passwords to get into the session.' Mandy had looked like she was trying to choke back her tears. 'It wasn't an excuse, Jason,' she had said again, desperately.

'Look, I'll get admin to send you an appointment for your discharge planning meeting, but I can't spend any more time on this now as I've got to get back to the group.' Jason had known they would have just gone round and round in circles if he had allowed the conversation to continue and that wouldn't have been helpful for anyone.

'Please don't discharge me, Jason,' Mandy had carried on. 'I need to stay in this group. It's the only lifeline I have at the moment. I've never felt this bad.'

'Mandy,' Jason had said firmly. 'I know, and you know, you've said many times before that you've *never felt this bad*, and we both know from experience that whilst it's painful right now, it doesn't last and you bounce back. You're resilient. You're a survivor. It will be the same this time, I assure you. And now I need to get back to the group. I'll see you in your discharge meeting.' Jason had quickly clicked the button to end the call.

Frances listened without interrupting Jason and didn't jump in when he had finished telling the awful truth of his conversation with Mandy.

'So it's not just about rules, is it, Frances? What about compassion and validation? Surely you think I could have done better for Mandy considering what she had told the group about her boyfriend and daughter? Surely you'd judge me more harshly than passing it off as me simply being inflexible?'

'Well, yes, one judgement would be that it was rather callous to have Mandy leave the group at that point. But I come back to the fact that you're fallible, just like the rest of us. Your judgement was clouded by the system. In an ideal world, all of us workers would be able to set a good example of simple decency and caring, of *taking care* of each other. Our patients should be able to expect that. But sometimes we're hardly more powerful or enlightened than the people we're trying to help. Our own emotional resources are often depleted and we don't always have the capacity to keep our hearts open. Plus we get sucked in to the rotten machine which obscures the important things like caring and patience and humility and tolerance. We get sold a line about being an expert practitioner and how the latest fancy therapy will be able to solve a whole host of problems, completely missing the facts that some people have led such terrible lives, have had so few opportunities and have so little access to the assets and resources that are more freely available to the rest of us. That's where we're all going wrong, Jason!'

'But sometimes people have had such terrible lives that they can't engage with our programmes. I can only work with people who can engage with us,' Jason said rather desperately. He was acutely aware though how he was contradicting an earlier position he had argued in the group, when Paula and Mandy had been complaining about being unable to do the homework. *It's probably even more effective with people with more severe difficulties because they have got the most to gain*, he had said. *So I don't think it's helpful to go down the road of this can't possibly work for me because my difficulties are too severe.* Jason was sure Frances must have heard him say things like this too, in his frequent defence of Zen Psyonics.

'Well, that's a very popular narrative these days, Jason, that *people need to be ready*, they need to be committed and able to *do the work*, as if they somehow haven't been doing the work of survival up to this point. I think it's an excuse on the part of services, a way of them managing their own limited resources. In the past engagement would be an important part of the work itself. It's a slippery slope when we start talking about only working with people who can engage. They're the ones who could probably sort themselves out without us. I mean, are we in some sort of war zone where only the people who look worth saving get saved? Plus it's not a case of moral fibre, whether people can engage or not. It's generally a case of resources they have available to them.'

Frances was railing against the system, as usual, but Jason knew it was not directed at him. It still sounded all a bit vague and uncontained but he had no compulsion to argue with her. If anything he felt a lot more open to simply talking to her and it seemed like a good time to mention Alexander's court case, although that no longer seemed so important since Mandy's death had overshadowed everything.

'There is something else I should mention seeing as we're here,' he started. 'Have you heard about the Zen Psyonics court case?'

'No?' Frances sounded intrigued.

'Basically, someone called Clemmie Service was suing Alexander McDonald for defamation because Alexander had allegedly been running him down on one of the practitioner discussion forums, saying that his practice was dangerous and that he was not delivering ZP like it should be delivered. I don't know if maybe that was a factor in making me stick even tighter to the rules. But after all that, I end up like Clemmie Service. *I'm* the dangerous one, but for the opposite reasons!'

'There you see,' said Frances triumphantly. 'That's a perfect example of what I was just talking about with the quadrant!'

'I *think* I can see what you mean,' said Jason, though he still wasn't entirely sure. 'But anyway, the whole thing mushroomed from there and now Alexander McDonald has filed a counter-claim for intellectual property theft, saying that Clemmie Service is passing off his own work as Zen Psyonics and that he has no right to use that term to describe his work and should not be profiting from it.'

'Oh dear, I fear this is going to be the bit where you push me into the river!' Frances turned to look at him and smiled before she continued. 'It just seems completely crazy that we've got a situation where there's a legal case to stop someone basically copying what he does, when the same person makes a vast amount of money from precisely that, trying to get people to copy what he does, and some people try really hard to copy him and bad things happen, and others don't copy him too well at all and more bad things happen. Who's to say that what he was doing in the first place was worth copying anyway? Not to mention the fact that there are loads of other people out there doing similar things, that he probably copied himself!' Frances stopped in tracks and held up her hands. 'The mistake is to think we're so powerful or that ZP is so powerful, when it's actually what happens in the world and people's lives which is powerful. What happened with Mandy proves this. I don't think ZP would have saved her. But compassion and solidarity might.'

Redetherapy

Redetherapy is dedicated to reshaping the entirety of one's environment to establish a more harmonious connection between individuals and every facet of an individual's interaction with their surroundings.

In the realm of mental health, Redetherapy introduces a novel concept. While conventional wisdom has long held that with human effort, determination, and some scientific advancements, we could address all disabilities and handicaps associated with psychiatric disorders, it appears we have exceeded our capabilities. Numerous mental disorders are classified as 'chronic,' with limited impact from health professionals on their symptoms and course. Redetherapy proves beneficial for many, particularly those with personality disorders who have become entrenched in the mental health system. These individuals may have been misled by the notion of 'recovery,' believing that more of the same treatments that have failed will miraculously lead to complete improvement. In Redetherapy, the focus shifts to modifying the environment to achieve the best fit for an individual's personality, thereby mitigating the problems contributing to their disorder.

While the mental health field acknowledges the role of the environment, Redetherapy advocates for a more systematic analysis and personalised alteration of the environment. Instead of viewing the environment as an external force that simply happens, Redetherapy encourages embracing and nurturing it as a companion and guide. By making the right environmental adjustments, all aspects of mental health can witness improvement.

24

People who didn't know Frances well, were sometimes surprised by her gym habit. She was so outspoken in her loathing of the wellness industry and the idea that keeping healthy and making healthy decisions was now seen as some kind of moral virtue, that her daily commitment to an hour in the gym before work (with weekends off) seemed like some kind of strange aberration from her stance of *absolutely not* doing what the wellness police (an arm of the government) were apparently mandating. But people who did know Frances well, knew that she delighted in that muscle pump and deeply euphoric state that clearly motivated the gym rats half her age.

She had almost accidentally found herself in the alien environment of Freedom Leisure centre after her friend who needed to lose weight had persuaded Frances to keep her company. The friend would have had no chance ordinarily, but the request had coincided with Frances being visited by a week long bout of back pain and at the age of fifty-two, having lost faith in conventional medicine and being of the opinion that alternative medicine was mostly hokum, she decided she was probably better off taking matters into her own hands. She also quite liked the idea of challenging the fitness freak stereotype, although on that front, she was disappointed by the amount of gym worshippers who appeared not only more overweight and unfit than herself, but many of whom were substantially older. She very quickly began to enjoy the routine as a powerful antidote to the sedentary but stressful time she was about to endure each day at work. A daily hour of mindless obedience to her personally tailored workout seemed almost like freedom, fun even. Her friend ultimately didn't stick with it and joined a local group of ramblers, deciding the outdoors and social aspect of their rambles was more conducive to weight loss than brutal workouts in a sweaty gym. She lost weight too and found a new husband, so it was a result all round. But for Frances, there were predictable rewards to be earned in the gym and she enjoyed keeping an up to date log of reps and sets and amounts lifted, as a kind of proof that she was achieving what she had set out to do, namely staving off the inevitable physical decline that comes with age. And she had cured her back pain, so it was validation for her shunning both traditional and alternative healthcare.

Much as she liked to tell people that she worked out because she enjoyed it, particularly the feeling afterwards, she was also aware that it appealed to her inherent work ethic and that in the gym she was like the perfect employee, monitoring her own performance and putting herself through ever more demanding tests. Years ago, this recognition of her being a good citizen and *getting with the programme* would have bothered her, such was its acquiescence with the doctrine of individual responsibility. But she was more relaxed about how she lived her life these days and if something *felt* good and wasn't hurting anyone else, she didn't feel the need to rebel against it, even if it might look like she had swallowed her employer's latest self-improvement circular.

So with this backdrop of her existing gym habit, Frances was hoping that the exercise module would probably be the least annoying part of facilitating the Zen Psyonics group. The first session was a gentle introduction and Frances and Jess thought it had gone well. They watched a short video of Alexander McDonald cherry picking his way through the research on exercise and mental health. With her intimate knowledge of clinical guidelines, Frances was able to temper this with counter claims, for example, that not everyone found exercise beneficial to their psychological wellbeing, and that exhorting people to do things they didn't believe in, or worse, that caused them physical or psychological pain, was not likely to get them the promised results or improvements. No group of hers was going to turn exercise into a moral imperative, no matter how much she enjoyed it herself.

Possibly because surfing had been dropped from the programme to make it more accessible, Alexander only spoke briefly about it and its role in the foundation of Zen Psyonics, but in this part he was more circumspect and, Frances thought, potentially more helpful. He said how it was difficult to separate all the variables in exercise research. It was therefore difficult to know whether psychological benefits were coming from the exercise itself, or from the environment in which it took place, with the sea being an obviously powerful setting. Or perhaps benefits were coming from the social context of the activity. Some surfers found great value in their sense of identity as a surfer and their sense of belonging to a surf community.

Frances was glad that the initial psychoeducation seemed to give people confidence in talking about their own exercise history, which turned up a few more gym goers along with a fair few people who had been put off exercise at school, never to return. They spent the remainder of that first session identifying a suitably bearable exercise activity that they would engage in for homework, ready for reporting back next time.

When week two came Frances was genuinely keen to know how people had got on with their exercise *experiments*, as she preferred to call them, trying to emphasise curiosity and learning over self-improvement and achievement.

Karrie was clearly pleased with herself. She explained how she had settled on the goal last time of going to her local gym but it turned out that it was eight pounds per session, even with a GP referral. There was just no way she could afford that, even going just once a week, which would not fulfil the ZP requirements of daily exercise anyway. She had got into an argument with the leisure centre receptionist about the costs being prohibitive and asked how people like herself, who were genuinely trying to improve their mental and physical wellbeing and better themselves, were ever going to pull themselves out of the big hole they were stuck in, if everything was too expensive? But an hour or so later, she decided she wasn't going to be beaten by her lack of funds and she was going to stop raging about how unfair everything always was. She resolutely decided she would instead get stuck into the exercise coaching freely available on

YouTube and damn well get fit for free. She proceeded to give a run down on what she considered were the best and worst fitness instructors currently offering free online classes.

'That's impressive, Karrie. So you overcame that barrier to your plan and did your homework as well as providing our group with a whole lot of useful information about online fitness classes,' Jess congratulated her. 'And did you get anything from the exercise itself?'

'If I'm honest, Jess, the biggest reward for me was knowing that I didn't let the gym cost get in the way of what I needed to achieve. The gain from that is worth more to me than any fitness, at the moment anyway. I can't say I got that endorphin rush or anything and I can't say it feels any easier physically after a week of classes. But I'm determined to continue with it, so I consider that a result.'

'Good for you, Karrie,' Frances joined in. 'You're completely right about the unfairness of the prohibitive costs and whilst that receptionist couldn't do anything about it, I think it's important for these things to be talked about and known about. It's a good example of the outsight I was talking about a few sessions ago. It's a well-established fact that people with less money have poorer physical and mental health and then they have less resources available to them to do something about it. And yet if you believed some of the things in some papers and on various TV programmes, you'd think their poorer health was down to their own fecklessness, rather than their lives actually being harder. But like yourself, Karrie, many people whose lives are difficult and filled with hardship are possibly more resourceful than the general population and in fact could teach us all a thing or two about survival.'

To probably most people's surprise, Nick, who didn't like talking in front of a group, went next. Just over half way in to the Zen Psyonics programme, it definitely seemed that he was growing in confidence. Even though they were all mainly heads on screens, the group knew that Nick was fairly overweight, from his chubby face and thick neck, plus he had put it out there the previous week, saying this module was going to be a challenge for him. It turned out though that like Karrie, he too was pleased with himself. For a considerably smaller sum than the cost of Karrie's gym sessions, he had joined his local ManVFat football group. He had already said last time how he had been planning to try the group out for months but it just felt like far too much of a challenge, mingling with strangers and trying to heave his bulk around a football pitch. But having to find something for his ZP homework, as well as the encouragement from the group proved enough to get him to the pitch, even overcoming a panic attack in the car on the way there. He had been pleasantly surprised at how welcoming the group was and he even managed to chat with an old acquaintance from school as they were leaving the ground at the end of the match.

'Fantastic!' Frances exclaimed, 'and very interesting. It sounds like a really great initiative and I'm looking forward to hearing more about it in the coming weeks. So how about the exercise? Did you notice any psychological benefits?'

'Not yet. A bit like Karrie, I was more pleased with myself for just taking that step, rather than there being any feel-good factor from the exercise. But I've got over the first hurdle and maybe the benefits will come later. I did lose a pound in weight though,' he added and then joked, 'but maybe that was all the sleepless nights leading up to it and the nervous energy from the panic attack.'

'Go Nick!' Karrie applauded and Nick beamed back at the screen of smiling faces.

There was a short pause and then Kevin took his turn. 'I don't want to be a party-pooper, everyone, but I don't really have my own success story unfortunately. I know you always say to look at these exercises as an experiment, though, Frances, and I did at least complete the experiment.'

'Absolutely,' Frances confirmed. 'Remember we're human beings, not robots! And who knows? Maybe you're not on your own in not having a success story.'

Kevin's plan had been to take up running. He had a few friends and family members who had caught the running bug and it often seemed they were part of this wonderful club, connected by the joy and pain of running and racing, sometimes travelling all over the country to take part in running events. Nevertheless, he was rather ambivalent about signing up to something he didn't expect to make much of an impact on him, since despite making a genuine effort with the whole Zen Psyonics programme so far, he really felt it was missing the target and unlikely to change him much. He was still of the firm opinion that he needed to sit down and talk with a suitable expert in order to get to the route of his problems and only then would transformation be possible. As that was not on offer, he was going along with the group, with as much good faith as he could muster.

The running went well to start with. He actually managed three miles straight off and his friend, a keen runner, suggested he was probably one of these genetic freaks that had an Olympic athlete inside of him, waiting to burst out. He was pleased with that initial performance and managed to increase the distance and reduce the time the next few days. Unlike Karrie and Nick, he definitely noticed a psychological benefit. He felt energised rather than tired *at the end* of the first run and he noticed an unfamiliar sense of positivity.

What he hadn't been expecting was how transformative the run would be on managing his emotions. He had had a row on the phone with his girlfriend the day after his first run and where he might previously have sent an angry text to her after listing all the ways she had made him angry, he instead decided to go out for his run. By the time he got back he was amazed at how much calmer he was, how the inventory of hurts he had compiled in his head had reduced to an irritation and something he was able to pass off as really not important in the scheme of things.

And then fate struck a blow. On the fifth day, he was doing nothing particularly different to previous days, not unduly pushing himself and paying attention to the pavement beneath him when with no warning, his foot landed awkwardly, causing his ankle to twist abruptly. The pain was immediate and excruciating and even limping along was an agonizing challenge. It did ease off as he walked on it and by the time he got home he was walking more normally than in the immediate aftermath. But there was no way he would be running on it for at least a few days. This was more than an unfortunate sporting setback. In that short space of time, those five days of homework, he had become hopeful that he had finally found a very reliable way of disempowering his unhelpful emotions and even better, generating some positive ones. So what now? Back to his pit of despair?

'So I was obviously very gutted about all that and I have just resorted to walking instead. But what I want to say is what I learned from the experiment. It's all very well using this exercise and enjoying the endorphin rush and the post-exercise glow and all that, but then what do you do if you're physically disabled, if you can't get that hit? And more to the point, you, I, haven't actually achieved anything to manage my compulsive and destructive outbursts. I've simply worked out that exercise can be a good distraction. But I'm not dealing with the underlying issues am I? I'm not really changing anything about myself.'

'I'm really sorry to hear about your ankle, Kevin and it's not going to do anything to physically heal you, but for what it's worth, I'm grateful for your thoughtful contribution to the group as you've raised some really important issues, not least how any of us at any time might be faced with having to contend with the fragility of the human body. And even though accidents and illness can happen whatever the size of your pay check, going back to what I was saying before, it's likely that you'll have far more resources to deal with those setbacks if you happen to be on the wealthier side of life,' Frances waited, wondering if she was sliding in too many lessons from the gospel of Frances, 'though remind me to tell you the Chinese fable of the lost horse. But I also wanted to pick up on your point about distraction, as opposed to change. And that was just to say, all the *evidence*, and I use that word lightly because it can be so problematic, all the evidence suggests that it's actually really hard to change ourselves as human beings. We can tweak things around the edges and that might make a difference, but it's very difficult to change our fundamental nature, our characters. It's a bit like the weather. We have a climate and there is a range within that climate but we're not going to radically affect our climate. If we're hot and fiery, we're not going to transform ourselves into the cold, slow, arctic. And so maybe sometimes distraction is all we have. It's a perfectly valid way of achieving damage limitation.'

'So what are we all doing here, then?' Karrie took issue. 'I'm doing this therapy so that I can change myself. I cannot carry on living my life like I have been doing. And I don't think I'm the only one here who thinks that.'

'Well I can't speak for everyone, you can all speak for yourselves, but the way I see it, is as a rather more modest aim. We're trying to find ways of managing our lives better. That might involve all sorts of things, including ourselves doing things a bit differently, and so that might help you, Karrie, to live your life less like you have been doing, but it's not about you radically changing yourself.'

'Is it okay if I share *my* homework?' Paula interrupted. 'I think it's similar in some ways to Kevin's experience. I'm another person faced with the fragility of the human body, the cancer that decided to make its appearance and has completely floored me. I've been a committed walker for as long as I can remember. It's something my mum got me into. I must have notched up thousands of miles over the decades and I swear I would go mad if I couldn't get my daily fix. So this exercise module, well it's preaching to the converted really with me. But now, suddenly I find myself in the terrible situation of my medicine being taken away from me, or at least, the dosage reduced when I need it most. For me, I don't really get the endorphin high because my walking doesn't really get my heart rate high enough, even though I do get hot and sweaty and out of breath. But I get another kind of bliss, from being out there amongst the trees, communing with nature or whatever you want to call it. I *am* still going out walking and all the patient information leaflets and websites go on about how helpful exercise is. But the last few rounds of chemo seem to have generated this horrendous side effect where every beat of my heart sends a painful electric current through my whole trunk, and weirdly, this seems to be greatly magnified if I shout because I'm upset. So I feel like a bit of a wreck, really, like an addict going through cold turkey and chemo at the same time. And there's not a lot I can do about that. So that's my homework. The fact that I couldn't do my homework, even though I normally do the homework when it's not even homework. And so I can't say I learned anything but I would like to say that I've really appreciated listening to all of you talking about yours. It's kind of a reminder that this is real life, not a fairy tale. At least we're struggling together, even if we can't possibly know what each other is going through...' Paula trailed off.

'It's knowing people are taking you seriously that's important, and that you're not on your own,' Nick concluded for her.

Relational Interpretive Therapy

Relational Interpretive Therapy (RIT) is a collaborative program designed to examine an individual's thoughts, emotions, actions and the underlying events and relationships shaping these experiences, often rooted in childhood or earlier phases of life. This therapy integrates concepts and insights from various therapeutic approaches into a cohesive and accessible framework.

Tailored to meet the unique needs and manageable goals of each individual, RIT is a time-limited therapy, typically spanning between 6 and 32 weeks, with an average duration of 12 weeks. Widely available in public health services, private RIT therapists also practice globally.

At its core, RIT fosters an empathic relationship between the client and therapist within established therapeutic boundaries. The primary objective is to assist the client in comprehending their situation and devising strategies for positive change. RIT seeks to explore the origins of problems rooted in past relationships and experiences, enhancing awareness and facilitating change. Its effectiveness lies in its ability to analyse how problems manifest in everyday life, including the dynamic between therapist and client.

25

The light in late autumn had a soulful, wistful beauty that was far more captivating than anything summer could produce and though spring was probably Paula's favourite season, the patterns of nature closing down for winter always invited Paula to stop and wallow in it. Not in a maudlin way like listening to sad songs in times of distress, but more *basking* in it, quietly revelling in nature taking its natural course. Some things would be renewed and bloom again next spring. Others, leaves, petals, stems, would meld into the ground beneath them and provide food for whoever was coming next. The sky, too, had that look about it, a kind of brooding tiredness, heaviness, panels of grey streaked with strips of light and the promise of more warmth and energy out there somewhere, beyond reach until the earth tilted on its axis and let the light in again.

All this death and decay might have been inclined to make Paula feel even more miserable than she already was, but it was actually strangely comforting, a rare element of the universe that was in tune with her, alongside her, not constantly jarring her to be upbeat and happy, or expecting her to get ready to celebrate the end of treatment. No, this wonderful globe was turning at its own speed, doing its own thing, completely outside the jurisdiction of misguided human demands. But it was hard to fully enjoy it, fully immerse herself in it as she did in normal times, simply because her wrecked and ruined body was a constant draw on her attention, the burning sensation here, the ache there, the gnawing in her bones, the dog-tiredness when climbing the steps she was used to skipping up.

As her daily walking medicine became harder and harder to swallow, Paula was grateful for the solace of the Zen Psyonics group. She never for a moment imagined being in the position of appreciating the group where she started out as a mystery shopper a few months ago. And she had been ready to completely write it off after Mandy died. Maybe she would have done if her radiotherapy hadn't got in the way and she had still been in Jason's group. She missed Mandy, even though she barely knew her, and she missed Owen too. But there were other lovely characters in Frances's group, including Frances herself who was a breath of fresh air.

When Paula introduced *Team of One* into the group, instead of seeing it as an interference or threat, Frances welcomed it as a useful addition to the group reflections. Paula had brought it up when Karrie had told her story of being unable to afford gym membership and Frances had suggested that people with little means were sometimes adept at surviving simply because they had had so much practice, with so much adversity in their lives. Paula immediately thought of the very rudimentary resources available to the contestants on *Team of One* and asked if anyone else was watching it. Frances actually encouraged Paula to explain more about the show. She told them how many of the people on it came from poor backgrounds and were clearly used to making do with very little and were masters of survival. But the one thing they couldn't reap through foraging or trapping or fishing, the one thing the land didn't provide on top of the materials to build some impressive shelters, was other people, and this was the undoing of so many of them. Even Karrie didn't seem to mind the divergence from ZP.

'I talked about that show with Mandy but never watched it,' Karrie said. 'We both wondered whether we would get on better on our own because other people always disappoint us so much and our personality disorders mean that we can't bear being abandoned. So if there was nobody around to abandon us, maybe we'd be better off. But we reckoned we wouldn't be better off at all because we desperately want to be with people, just our relationships don't ever seem to work out. Maybe that's what finishes those people on the show though. Maybe it gives them a taste of what it's like to have a personality disorder and be totally on your own.'

'I don't want to get into an argument, Karrie,' Kevin said

cautiously, 'but you know I've said before how I don't buy the whole personality disorder thing, even though that's a label that's been slapped on me. But I agree with you about feeling desperate for other people and then sometimes being so desperate that ends up messing up the relationship.'

'That's what happens when you've got a personality disorder, Kevin!' Karrie said playfully.

Kevin laughed. 'Paula hasn't got a personality disorder though. She's got cancer. Not wanting to speak for you, Paula, but from what you've said it sounds like you sometimes feel just like the rest of us. And those people on the show presumably haven't got a personality disorder either. Well actually, nobody has as far as I'm concerned. But it sounds like they feel desperate too, being on their own, even if it's for different reasons.'

'That's the thing though,' Karrie clearly felt she wasn't getting her point across. 'They're feeling desperate because they've put themselves in that situation and they weren't expecting to feel so alone because they've never been in that situation before. We're all here feeling desperate because we keep doing things that put us in that situation, where we annoy people and push people away. It's our *selves* which are the problem, whereas for them, it's the situation.'

'I thought you said last time though about your mum and sister, how they'd left you out. That's what *they* did, what they keep doing, not what *you're* doing,' Kevin argued.

'But they leave me out because I'm *me*. If I was different, if I was a nicer person to be around, they might not leave me out.'

'It's easy to think that it's *us* that's the problem, isn't it?' Paula joined in gently. 'Maybe it's just that the one who's most vulnerable gets the blame pinned on them, and when you feel crap about yourself, you're going to blame yourself. I know that's what I do. And nobody's given me that personality disorder label yet, although they might do by the time I get to the end of this round of cancer treatment!' Paula drew a few smiles.

'It sounds to me that you're all talking about universal aspects of the human condition,' Frances reflected. 'This is what it's like to be human and it's worse for some than others, just out of luck more than anything else. I agree that any one of us might get into unhelpful patterns in relationships, where we keep on doing the same things and messing up in the same way, but again, that's what being human is. And also, there's always at least two people in a relationship so it's likely to be something about the space between, what happens between them, rather than just all about what happens inside one individual. Take this group as an example if you want. Some of you have real differences of opinion, but you're respectful, you listen to each other, you're even able to joke about your disagreements. That's pretty good if we're talking about relationships.' Frances wasn't finished and had clearly been lured by the discussion of *Team of One*. 'If I'm understanding it right, and I haven't watched the show myself, the thing they're dealing with which seems to connect with the experiences people are talking about here, is that terrible sense of being on their own, with nobody there to comfort them, nobody to tell them it's going to be okay, nobody to tell them it's totally understandable that they're feeling lonely, frightened, weak, hopeless. And feeling like that could make any of us do desperate things. But for them in the show, that's when they call for rescue. Who do we call to the rescue in *real* life? It's not so easy. Especially if it seems there's nobody out there, or at least nobody around who understands what we're going through. Maybe we don't like calling for rescue either. Maybe we might have that in common with those contestants.'

Paula thought they had made a lot of sense together as a group, and far from being the mystery shopper and misplaced cancer patient without a personality disorder label, she felt she definitely had a rightful place in the group because what they described fitted really well with so much of what she was feeling. But even though that provided some comfort, she was left with a sense of hopelessness. Were they just consigned to their lots then? Was that it? They just had to get on with it, because those were the hands they had been dealt with.

'It all feels a bit hopeless,' a young woman called Lexie seemed to speak Paula's mind. 'We're on our own. We keep doing the same things. Nobody really understands. We're just playing a game of survival and probably the more of a psychopath you are, and the less you care about other people and what they think of you, the more likely you are to win.'

'Ah, but that's assuming you're all in a *Team of One*,' Frances said with surprising confidence. 'The way of the world, the messages we get from our TVs, newspapers, social media and so on, tend to be about our*selves*, what we need to do to be successful, autonomous, good citizens and all of that. I had a wonderful colleague who used to run courses called *Psychology in Real Life* and instead of bringing people together because they had a shared problem or diagnosis, he brought people together who had a shared interest, like wanting to come off medication, and wanting to better understand toxic mental environments, and wanting to understand human behaviour. One of the sessions he used to do was called *How come so many people don't like themselves?* And the point was that it suits big business for us to think there's something wrong with ourselves that needs improving, so that we spend vast amounts of money trying to rectify ourselves! Just think for a moment about all the adverts on TV for beauty products. And we have a similar thing in the therapy industry, only for things like our behaviours and relationships and performance in the workplace. All of this is about what we should be doing to make ourselves better people, and whilst we might be able to do some of that if we try really hard, it moves our gaze away from what we might do together, from what's going on in the *world* that needs changing, like greater equality so that people like Karrie can afford to go to the gym if she wants to, like Kevin being able to have an appointment to talk with someone about whatever his difficulties are, instead of being shunted into the only option, a group. Though, I have to say, that brings me back to my point. Look at this group! What a great bunch of thoughtful, respectful, committed people you are. It's maybe not what you want to hear, but trying to find like-minded people, who understand you and want to support you, and vice versa, that's where you're more likely to find the comfort and encouragement that you so desperately need in order to carry on. Not everyone is a psychopath, Lexie. There are some lovely people out there, and you lot are proof of that. That's probably the best thing about being in a group like this. But I appreciate, it's not easy once you go back out into the big wide world.'

'How do we have a virtual group hug?' Karrie joked.

'Just like that, Karrie, I suppose. I think you just hugged us all!' Jess smiled back.

'You said we should remind you to tell us about the lost horse,' Nick said.

It occurred to Paula that they were now well and truly off-piste and exploring whatever terrain took their fancy. She thought about that notion of *therapy interfering behaviours* and wondered whether they might have diverged too far from what they were supposed to be doing. But she also had in her head some lovely memories of lessons at school, where the plan was all laid out and it was important that they stick to it, in order to cover the whole syllabus in the tight timescale they had. But occasionally something came up, a philosophical idea one of the pupils had, or an emerging debate, or a film or book that did a particularly good job, and she would shove the lesson plan aside so that they could talk and share and clarify. She would come away with the sense that they all knew the world better for it. That it had been much more valuable and enriching than the curriculum that someone somewhere else had decided they needed to learn.

'I can tell you about the lost horse, but,' Frances seemed to put the brakes on faintly, 'are you all clear about your homework for the coming week? I think we need to make sure we strike a balance between our very interesting and constructive conversations and completing our Zen Psyonics tasks. Also I don't want Karrie to feel short-changed by the time we get to the end of the programme!' She waited briefly. 'Please say now if you're *not* clear about the homework.' Everyone was apparently clear. 'Okay then. I hope this doesn't disappoint. I sometimes get a bit carried away with my little stories and anecdotes and it might be more about them appealing to me than anyone else. So like I say about most things, if you like it and think it's a helpful idea, keep it in your medicine bundle for those times when you might need it. If you think it's a load of nonsense, simply chuck it out!'

Frances proceeded to read them the story of the lost horse.

An old farmer lived in a small village on the northern frontier of China. One day, his only horse ran away to the nomads across the border. The villagers expressed their sympathy for his misfortune, but the old man remained calm and replied, 'Maybe it's a blessing, maybe it's a curse. Who knows?' A few days later, the lost horse returned, bringing with it a splendid nomad stallion. The villagers rejoiced at the old man's sudden good fortune, but he remained composed and said, 'Maybe it's a blessing, maybe it's a curse. Who knows?' The old farmer's son decided to tame the stallion. During the process, he was thrown off and broke his leg. The villagers expressed their sorrow for the family's misfortune, but the old man stayed serene and said, 'Maybe it's a blessing, maybe it's a curse. Who knows?' Soon after, the nomads came in force across the border and all able-bodied young men were conscripted to fight. The Chinese frontiersmen lost nine of every ten men. Only because the son was lame did he and the farmer survive to take care of each other. The villagers realised the wisdom of the old man's words: 'Maybe it's a blessing, maybe it's a curse. Who knows?'

'It was Kevin's ankle that reminded me of the lost horse. That awful experience of just when you think you're on track, cooking on gas, finally able to handle the world, and something smashes into you and wipes you off track. Apart from it feeling grossly unfair, and maybe that you get more than your fair share of bad luck, you can't possibly imagine getting back on your feet again, so you feel like giving up. But here's the thing. *You never know what's around the corner.* So much of life is about luck. The country where you are born, the family you're born into, the area you live in, the genes you carry which shape your looks, strength, intellect, health, the events in your life, whether you're in a benign or toxic cohort in school, and so on. Politicians know this. That's why they often get away with some scandal or other because they know that random lady luck will be just round the corner with another story which trumps their own and soon their scandal will just be yesterday's news. And luck, like the weather, can change. That's where the solidarity comes in, where we need other people to weather the storm, because we might not have been born with the strength to withstand it on our own. Solidarity and luck. Today's life lessons.' Frances ended boldly.

Response Reformulation Therapy

Response Reformulation Therapy (RRT) is as an innovative iteration of cognitive-behavioural therapy, devised as an action-oriented strategy for managing dysfunctional cognitive, emotional and behavioural patterns.

According to RRT, disturbances in emotions and behaviours are largely influenced by our interpretations of events. Emphasizing the present moment, individuals are guided in examining and challenging dysfunctional thoughts that contribute to emotional dysregulation and self-defeating behaviours.

As a practical approach, RTT aids individuals in navigating adversity, reformulating unproductive responses and improving life satisfaction. With a focus on the present, RRT addresses attitudes, unhealthy emotions (such as anger, depression, anxiety, guilt), and maladaptive behaviours (like substance abuse, aggression and eating disorders) that impact overall well-being. RRT practitioners collaborate closely with individuals to identify their unique set of beliefs—attitudes, expectations and personal rules—that often lead to emotional distress.

RRT guides individuals in developing a philosophy and approach to living that enhances their effectiveness and satisfaction across various aspects of life, including work, relationships, citizenship, environmental stewardship and personal emotional well-being.

26

It was a long time since Alexander had felt nervous. He couldn't remember the last occasion. It must have been years ago. He used to get a bit anxious in the days he first started presenting at conferences, but by the time he was flying to international destinations he had come to love it and really enjoyed his time up on stage, usually received by admiring audiences. He was also completely comfortable with remote working, and well-practiced in resolving various tech issues which were in fact hardly ever a problem for him. But today he felt like he had regressed more than ten years and was back in psychotherapy college having to perform a perfect CBT session in front of peers and tutors. It didn't help that Ed Burrell seemed increasingly equivocal about the case over their course of preparing for it and even though Ed attempted to reassure Alexander that they were just making their arguments watertight, Alexander wasn't convinced. He suspected that Ed had never quite been won over by his arguments about evidence in the psychological therapy industry and how it was different to legal evidence which took a much more absolute line.

He was all set up, having tested the required software, and was just waiting for Ed Burrell to call him in. He was stationed on his kneeling chair, no longer having to rest and elevate his ankle which was at last slowly improving. The house was quiet and empty though without Buddha snuffling and wriggling below the desk, or wandering into the kitchen from time to time, keeping Alexander company when he went to get his coffee. It was times like this, when he was waiting nervously, that he would have really appreciated being able to chat to Buddha, tell him what was going on and cuddle up with him for some comfort, also knowing that stroking pets was a scientifically well-established method for people to get their heart rates down. Into the bargain, Buddha enjoyed the cuddles, the routines, the food, the beach and the pride of being the best, or probably the only surfing dog in the locality. At least Alexander inferred that particular pride to Buddha, seeing him stand so upright, so confidently and smiling his head off on the board whenever given half the chance. But this lovely memory, now so painful and poignant, was not helping him at all in getting into the right head set for the trial so he instead decided to listen to some mindfulness bells and simply breathe until Ed called him in.

That time came soon enough and after an introduction by the judge, confirming various details and the adaptations for video conferencing, Alexander was being sworn in. Then very quickly it seemed proceedings were under way and Ed was giving their opening statement.

'Ladies and gentlemen of the court, today, we come before you to address a matter of utmost importance that pertains to the very core of our legal system: the protection of intellectual property, the safeguarding of consumers' rights, and the preservation of honest and transparent commerce. The plaintiff, in this case, brings forth three grave allegations against the defendant, and we seek to shed light on their unlawful actions.

'On count one, trademark Infringement: the plaintiff alleges, unequivocally, that the defendant has engaged in trademark infringement of his cherished and meticulously cultivated brands, Zen Psyonics and ZP. These trademarks represent not just products and services, but also countless hours of innovation, dedication and commitment to excellence. The defendant, by his actions, has flagrantly disregarded the plaintiff's rights as the rightful owner of these marks. He has exploited the plaintiff's intellectual property for his own gain, thereby diminishing the distinctive value that he has laboured to establish. We contend that the defendant continues to infringe upon these trademarks, undermining the plaintiff's ability to offer his services and causing irreparable harm.

'On count two, false endorsement: our second grievance centres on the defendant's unauthorised use of the plaintiff's name, which has had a profound and detrimental impact. By appropriating his identity without his consent, the defendant has created confusion amongst consumers, who have been led to believe that there exists an affiliation or endorsement that is simply non-existent. This false endorsement tarnishes the plaintiff's reputation and causes significant damage to the goodwill that he has worked so hard to foster.

'On count three, violation of consumer protection: the plaintiff asserts that the defendant's use of the trademarks Zen Psyonics and ZP to describe his services is not only misleading but also deceptive. This deception has been perpetuated to the detriment of unsuspecting consumers who have been tricked into believing they are receiving services or products directly affiliated with the plaintiff's esteemed brand. Such deceptive practices not only harm the plaintiff's reputation but also betray the trust of consumers who deserve honesty and transparency in the marketplace. Our claim of violation of the Trade Descriptions Act is not merely a matter of monetary damages; it is a quest for justice and the safeguarding of the rights of individuals who rely on accurate information to make informed choices. Moreover, it is a quest for transparency and safeguarding in mental healthcare which for some people can be a matter of life and death.

'Your Honour, esteemed members of the court, the plaintiff enters this virtual courtroom with the weight of these three charges to seek redress for the wrongs committed by the defendant. We stand firmly in the pursuit of justice, the preservation of intellectual property rights, the protection of consumers and the defence of our integrity as a trusted brand. We urge you to consider the evidence carefully and impartially, for the case before you holds significant implications for the very essence of our legal and healthcare systems and the principles of fairness, evidence and truth that underpin it. Thank you for your attention, and we look forward to presenting our case in full detail during the proceedings.'

At the invitation of the judge, the solicitor for Clemmie Service proceeded to give the opening statement for the defence. She was a good decade younger than Ed Burrell, though also a partner, albeit in a smaller law firm. Alexander had researched her credentials and background on the internet and hoped that Ed's comparative gravitas would bode well for them in the eventual ruling.

'Your Honour, esteemed members of the court and opposing counsel, today, as representatives of the defendant, we stand before you in response to the claims brought forth by the plaintiff. We also assert our own counterclaims, which we believe are fundamental to achieving justice in this matter.

'On counterclaim one, cancellation of the ZP Trademark: first and foremost, we challenge the validity of the plaintiff's ZP trademark registration. We contend that this mark has become generic over time and is merely descriptive of the services offered in the psychological therapies industry. The mark ZP fails to serve as a distinct source identifier, as it is widely used to describe common practices in the field. Furthermore, we believe that the plaintiff's actions, or lack thereof, have led to the abandonment of this mark, thereby rendering its registration null and void.

'On counterclaim two, opposition to the registration of Zen Psyonics: we vehemently oppose the plaintiff's pursuit of the Zen Psyonics mark. We argue that this mark is generic and merely descriptive of the very services provided in the healthcare market. Moreover, we contend that the mark has been abandoned and thus its registration should be denied.

'On counterclaim three, declaration of non-infringement with respect to ZP: in response to the plaintiff's claims of trademark infringement, we maintain that our use of the mark ZP does not infringe on the plaintiff's rights. We assert that there is no likelihood of confusion between our services and those offered by the plaintiff, as our use of the mark serves the purpose of identifying the practice of ZP within the business CentreFlow, which has a large and well-established consumer base of its own.

'On counterclaim four, abuse of process: lastly, we assert the claim of abuse of process, arguing that the plaintiff's pursuit of legal action in this matter is motivated by ulterior motives and intended to stifle competition rather than protect genuine trademark rights. We believe that the plaintiff has engaged in an improper use of the legal system, and we seek redress for the harm caused by their actions, not just to ourselves but to mental healthcare patients worldwide.

'Your Honour, we firmly believe that our counterclaims are not only valid but essential in achieving a just resolution in this case. We look forward to presenting the evidence and arguments that support our position. We request that you consider our counterclaims alongside the plaintiff's claims, as we are committed to upholding the principles of fairness, accuracy, and truth in the legal process.

'Thank you for your attention, and we trust that the court will carefully consider all the facts and arguments presented during these proceedings.'

When Alexander took to the stand himself he confidently reiterated the arguments he had rehearsed in the prep meetings with Ed, being rock solid about the distinctiveness of Zen Psyonics, the therapeutic elements that made it different from the range of other new-wave cognitive-behavioural therapies on the market, and the unique role of exercise in ZP. It seemed to go much more quickly than he had been expecting and in no time he was thanked and told to step down.

And then they were off into the next witnesses. With his considerable standing and popularity in the psychological therapies industry, Alexander had had no problems enlisting people to help fight his case. Some were loyal colleagues who had been with him at the beginning, as he developed the ZP brand. They felt part of a family that they wanted to protect. Others were more newcomers who had trained in and wanted to be associated with the pure, unadulterated version of ZP. They wholeheartedly believed in fidelity to the model and that messing with the finely honed product challenged the very evidence base which supported it, as well as potentially being detrimental to patients.

Alexander's first witness was Gabriella Diya, a clinical psychologist with a very successful and well-respected private practice and one of the people who had been with Alexander from the outset. When questioned for the plaintiff, she argued that the Zen Psyonics mark had become synonymous with her business's high-quality therapy programmes and allowed them to distinguish their services in a crowded market, playing a crucial role in establishing trust and recognition among their clients and consumers. She reported her observation that the defendant used the Zen Psyonics mark in connection with their services, which led to confusion among consumers who initially sought their services but ended up with the defendant's instead.

So far, so good, Alexander thought. It seemed to get a little sticky when she was asked by the defence to define Zen Psyonics. She talked about how it was a unique blend of practices which had also gained distinctiveness through the long-standing use and development by practitioners aligned with the founder, Alexander McDonald. She could have been much more robust in her answer, Alexander thought, but reassured himself that the picture would be completed by other eminent witnesses to follow.

He was feeling quietly confident by the time all his witnesses had been called and sent a quick text to Ed to ask how he thought it was going. *So so*, Ed replied, which was not the sort of response he had been hoping for. Still, all he could do at this point was sit tight.

When it came to Clemmie Service's turn, Alexander thought the man was decidedly and surprisingly bullish. When asked to describe the nature of services provided by his business, CentreFlow, he emphasised his years of experience in the market and extensive, unashamed use of ZP and still had the gall to say that CentreFlow had never claimed any affiliation or endorsement by the plaintiff and that their use of the ZP mark was entirely distinct and unrelated to the plaintiff's Zen Psyonics.

Clemmie's first supporting witness was Alex Reynolds, founder and CEO of ZenBody Psychotherapy, who claimed to represent the practice of a *unique* blend of behavioural and meditation techniques for their clients to achieve holistic wellbeing. He argued that ZenBody's use of ZP was genuinely representative of its services, and that they had no intention to deceive consumers or infringe on the plaintiff's marks, respecting their rights as much as they asserted their own. He was then challenged by Ed Burrell that his use of ZP bore a strong resemblance to Alexander McDonald's Zen Psyonics. He conceded that both incorporated the term Zen in their names but that their usage was significantly different. He reported having experienced no instances of confusion amongst consumers, as ZenBody had always been clear about the distinction between its offerings, and those of Zen Psyonics and other third wave CBTs.

As several witnesses presented their evidence, both prosecution and defence laboured points on the distinctions between the different therapies, with both sides arguing that their particular products were indeed distinct and backed by a compelling evidence base. One of Clemmie's witnesses, Lily Parmer, whose practice specialised in trauma resolution, got into what seemed a very protracted discussion about *how human beings function*. Her argument was that whilst manuals might exist for all sorts of different branded therapies, in the end it's not possible to truly standardise a psychological therapy or standardise the way a therapist behaves in a session, because *human beings don't work like that*. She said that if all ZP practitioners were to be videoed doing their sessions, they would all be doing different things, some rather miniscule differences and others more obvious. A lengthy discussion then ensued about a large body of evidence showing that differences in outcomes are due to what individual practitioners do, rather than the particular techniques of various therapies.

By the time they had finished with the witnesses, Alexander was in a fog about what had actually been established and amidst all the emphatic statements from supporters of ZP, the thing that was most going round his head was the Columbo guy back at that conference years ago. *I find it difficult to tease out the differences between the different therapies, with there being so many on the market now...It makes it quite a challenge for us practitioners...And it does genuinely make me wonder about industry regulation...the development of psychotherapies has reflected the efforts of practitioners to market* their skills, rather than it being a result of scientific advancement... I'd go as far as to say that the third-wave therapies have a deliberate mysteriousness about them, when in reality there's nothing mysterious about the world being a cruel and damaging place.' Ed Burrell was also in the back of his head, challenging him: *I know you've explained how exercise is a key component in Zen Psyonics which marks it out as different from things like HCT, but please can you explain to the court how you, Alexander McDonald, have the exclusive rights to exercise as therapy?*

Both parties made their closing arguments and the judge declared the case adjourned, summoning them to reconvene for the verdict at two o'clock the following afternoon. Alexander wasn't sure whether he should be pleased, surprised, dismayed or what, that the verdict was going to be the very next day. When he spoke to Ed after they had all left the virtual courtroom, Ed was sanguine and said he thought it could go either way, but *fingers crossed*. Alexander had the sense that Ed had been slowly distancing himself from the case and certainly didn't feel like the man had got his back. Was that normal? Was Ed just *dabbling*? Was it because it was a rather unusual case of intellectual property theft, psychotherapy not yet generally providing substantial fodder in legal cases? Why would he take on a case he thought he wasn't going to win? Why would he risk his own and his firm's reputation? He surely must have believed they would win it, when Alexander first approached him. Did he have a change of heart as they started gathering evidence and was that when he started to withdraw?

After a fretful and sleepless night, with no Buddha to curl up to, Alexander struggled along the beach for his morning walk and was grateful for the fact that he could now drive to the beach and get some fresh air, exercise and vitamin D, even if there was no endorphin high at the end of it. He could at least begin to imagine there would be a day when he was recovered and back stronger than ever, even though the prospect of the afternoon's verdict didn't fill him with strength. It seemed particularly cruel that the surf was up and he could see some familiar boards and bodies out ripping up the waves. There was Regan in the distance, sauntering along the sand towards him, looking like he was finished for the day.

'Alright, Alex, how's it going?' Regan asked as they approached each other. 'Was real sorry to hear about Buddha. Mate, that sucks after your accident as well. How long's it gonna be till you're back on the board?'

'Not long now, hopefully, thanks for asking, Regan. You're right it's been a total fucker and on top of that, don't know if you heard but I've got this bloody legal case going on with my business. Someone was trying to do me for defamation so I came back with intellectual property theft. The verdict's this afternoon.'

'Yeah mate, I *did* hear about that. It's way over my head though. I never really understood that, how you could make surfing into an actual therapy. I mean, don't we all just need to go out and surf? It's just the simplicity I love, just living in that moment! I don't get how we need all this therapy talk around it, complicating it. But that's just me I guess. Each to their own and all that. Well look, I know you're not up to shredding any time soon, but if you fancy a smoke down at my place to take the edge off, depending on your verdict, just give me a shout, mate.'

'Thanks Regan, I appreciate that,' Alexander said politely, though of course he had no intention of going to get high with Regan. He had his own tools. But he didn't want to lose any more support from the local surfing community and Regan being a key player, it was important to keep in with him. 'I might take you up on that. I'll probably just wait and look forward to when I'm next out back with you, but thanks though. It means a lot to have your support.'

Two o'clock came round so soon. Although he wasn't required to perform today, Alexander was probably more nervous than yesterday as this was going to be the moment of truth. Not since he first started practising mindfulness had he felt it to be so weak and futile in managing his inner workings. He tried to settle himself by focusing on his breathing but he felt as though he was being ridiculed by the comments of novice practitioners he had tutored over the years, with their common complaints about mindfulness. *I just found it impossible to stay in the present moment... My worries kept intruding... My physical pain was getting in the way... My inner critic was just too loud today.* Of course he had many well-rehearsed arguments to help them get back on track, but he was finding it so difficult to apply them himself today. It was almost a relief when the proceedings started again and the judge finally prepared to deliver.

Alexander heard the formal, legal language used by the judge, repeating back the claims and counterclaims. He noticed himself getting hung up on various phrases which seemed to get stuck in his head and ring around his ears, meaning he lost track of what the judge said next. *I find the arguments and evidence presented by the defendant in their counterclaims to be compelling and persuasive.* One by one, the blows landed.

The plaintiff's ZP trademark is, in fact, a generic and descriptive term that should not be entitled to trademark protection.

The plaintiff has not adequately demonstrated distinctiveness in the mark.

There is no likelihood of confusion between the services offered by the plaintiff and the defendant. It appears that the plaintiff's actions may have been motivated by motives other than the protection of legitimate trademark rights.

In no time, the judge was summing up.

'Based on the evidence and the arguments presented, I find in favour of the defendants on all counts. They have successfully defended their position and the court finds that they have not engaged in trademark infringement, false endorsement or consumer protection violations. The plaintiff's actions did not meet the burden of proof necessary to support their claims. This case is hereby closed, and the parties are free to pursue any appropriate legal remedies or resolutions outside of this courtroom. Thank you all for your participation in this matter.'

Alexander was stunned. The part where the judge said about his motives felt like a sting in the tail. But then even more unpleasant was the financial blow. He wouldn't be paying Ed

Burrell any money, due to the no-win-no-fee agreement, but he was going to be shelling out a painful amount in court costs. He was at least grateful that the judge had not imposed any additional financial sanctions on him. As he was mulling it all over with a heavy heart, he received a text from Ed asking if he wanted ten minutes debriefing. He sent a quick message back, lying that he had to get to another meeting and he would catch up with him the next day.

In the weeks that followed, a few people got in touch with Alexander to commiserate with him, although on the whole the airwaves were quiet. He wondered what the relative silence meant and whether people were largely in agreement with the judgement, or whether it was simply of little consequence to them. But he did notice a rather scathing piece on the court case, by Jamie Gallagher, the man who had interviewed Alexander months back, for the article in *The Outdoor Cure* magazine. Even though the original article had been favourable, it turned out that Jamie was clearly in that camp of surfers who thought Alexander was commodifying something that wasn't his to sell. He had obviously known all about the court case when he asked Alexander for the interview and he had just published the first article as a ruse, fully intending to put out his real piece once the judgement had been made. Jamie had recycled some of the quotes and used them to make Alexander sound like someone who corrupted surfing and had now been struck by karma. *Prior to this court case, Alexander McDonald was in no doubt about his currency*, the concluding paragraph started. *His defence is that we're all striving to support ourselves, and every commodity holds a value. So, why settle for less when you can maximize the worth of your product or service? With a rather large bill for court costs following his defeat, I wonder if he might be thinking twice now about making claims on life's riches which are not, and never have been, for sale.*

Self Integration Therapy

Self Integration Therapy (SIT) is a psychotherapeutic approach that places a strong emphasis on personal responsibility and centres on the individual's current experiences, the therapist-client relationship, the environmental and social contexts and the self-regulating adjustments individuals make in response to their overall situation. Two core principles underpin SIT: the belief that the most beneficial focus in psychotherapy is on the experiential present moment, and the understanding that knowledge of oneself is intricately tied to one's relationships with others.

SIT prioritises the process of therapy, emphasizing what is happening in the present moment over the specific content of discussions. It operates as an awareness practice, akin to mindfulness in other clinical domains, where perception, feeling and action are considered essential for interpretation, explanation and clarification. Throughout the therapeutic process, the distinction between direct experience and indirect or secondary interpretation is elucidated, enabling clients to develop an awareness of their actions and fostering the ability to initiate shifts or changes.

The ultimate goal of Self Integration Therapy is to empower clients to achieve a more complete and creative integration, liberating them from blocks and unresolved matters that may impede satisfaction, fulfilment and personal growth. Through SIT, clients are encouraged to experiment with new ways of being, enhancing their capacity for positive change.

27

There was hardly any noise coming from the lounge where Kelly and Layne were tucking into pizza and enjoying a Friday night film. Sharlotte was out with her girlfriends and Jason had been planning to catch up with various bits of admin until he saw all the activity on the *Apostle* discussion list, where people were picking through the outcome of the Zen Psyonics legal case. The first part that Jason needed to get his head round was that Alexander had *lost* the case. *What the fuck? No way!* Jason was totally shocked. He had definitely not seen that coming. Much space was taken up on *Apostle* with people generally arguing one of two positions. Either the outcome wasn't surprising and it meant more people would be able to access ZP and the help they needed, or, in line with Jason's own thinking, the ruling was a travesty and had serious implications for the regulation of the industry, not to mention the financial state of their private practices. There were the odd few who said they could see it both ways and had got into long and convoluted arguments about the inherent problems with psychological therapies research. Jason could imagine Frances Fisher at the end of the keyboard inputting similar comments, only he knew that she would never spend precious time outside of work repeating the same objections she spent most team meetings vocalising yet knowing it so often fell on deaf ears.

Jason began to realise how sad he felt, as well as disorientated. For the whole time he had been working in mental health services, he had admired, respected and valued Alexander McDonald, and felt indebted to him for his essential role in helping him get to where he was today, living a cherished life with purpose and meaning, and having become someone his parents were truly proud of. He thought of all those early conversations with Alexander and how Zen Psyonics had made such sense to him, and then how blindsided he was on hearing about the legal case which had revealed a different side of Alexander, one apparently driven by ambition and a desire for personal gain. It just didn't fit with the spiritual foundation of the therapy he had created. Jason understood the lure of greed and ambition, knowing it to be not a million miles away from the lure of drugs and alcohol that both he and Alexander understood only too well from their work in that field. He felt naïve for failing to see how even someone as successful and *together* as Alexander, could still be led astray by the trappings of wealth. He had seen Alexander as someone *other*, someone who was so clear and sure-footed on his path in life, that he wouldn't possibly be the sort of person to pursue a fight about *ownership*, about the rights to help people build better lives. He had felt so certain and confident that both he and Alexander were *on the same team*. But now it all seemed to be unravelling.

What he was most bothered about though, was all the mess of contradictions which had been exposed by the court case itself and the questions it raised about Jason's own practice. On the one hand, Alexander had fought the case on a clear line about his unique brand of therapy and how Clemmie Service had caused confusion to consumers in touting his own version of ZP and therefore potentially engaging in unsafe practice. When Jason first heard about the case, the argument about keeping consumers safe had been the main thrust of it, in Jason's mind, and he was able to go along with the idea that Alexander was trying to protect the public. That all might have been fine, had Alexander won the case. But not only had he lost the case, the premise of that argument was shaky to say the least. Jason himself had followed ZP protocols to the letter. He had stuck rigidly to the rules, the format, the spirit of Zen Psyonics and in doing so, it was Mandy, one of *his own patients* who died. Add to that the fact that the case had been lost largely due to presentation of the evidence base which persuaded the judge that Zen Psyonics was actually not that much different from a whole host of products out there on the market, and more to the point, it was very unlikely that people were practising pure ZP in a uniform and standardised way, then the whole thing started to resemble a house of cards.

The term Zen Psyonics was *generic and merely descriptive*, as far as the judge was concerned.

As well as feeling very sad and disorientated, Jason was also both grateful and annoyed, with Frances Fisher. Instead of claiming that Mandy's death had proved her right, and trotting out all her usual arguments about the overselling of psychological therapies and the poor evidence base and how we needed to help people cultivate *outsight*, she had taken a rather different line and actually come out in support of Jason. She had gone on about being human and suggested Jason needed to be kind to himself. He appreciated that she refrained from crushing him at his most vulnerable. But he wondered now whether that had been her cunning way of getting him to open up to her and he regretted that he had got sucked in and told her about wanting to prove himself right and suggesting this meant he was to blame for what happened to Mandy. He was also irritated with Frances because of the way she talked about the lessons that could be learned from it all. She wasn't solely singling him out for the learning, but it felt like she was very firmly positioning herself as the more experienced, skilful, master practitioner in the situation, when for so long she was just this burnt out lady near retirement who was long past making a mark on her profession. He had seen her as the opposite of him and even though she had been so friendly and apparently supportive when they had walked along the river together after Covision, he could see now that it may well have been her strategy to get him to confess the errors of his professional ways and in doing so regain the upper hand for herself.

Jason was still up, though the kids had long since gone to bed, when Sharlotte got back from town. She appeared in the study with a half-empty bottle of wine and two glasses and settled into the armchair by the side of Jason's desk. She nattered on about her evening and then listened to Jason as he tried to articulate all his turmoil about Alexander's legal case and Mandy's death. Sharlotte listened earnestly and offered words of comfort and agreement every so often. He wasn't sure if it was the wine doing its thing at that late hour, or whether it was simply the balm of the company of a wonderful woman who he knew, without any doubts, loved him dearly and understood who he was and what was most important to him, but he suddenly felt *better*.

'It's easy to get the whole filing cabinet out, isn't it, J?' she said sympathetically, using one of Jason's own therapy phrases. 'It's totally understandable that your head's in such a mess. God, I really don't envy you your job. I wouldn't last five minutes. But I'm proud of you and I'm lucky to have you in my life and so are our kids. It'll all work out in the end. Don't you worry about that SUI meeting next week. Hayley will just twizzle her hair and read a load of questions from her laptop and then it will all be forgotten about. And don't you worry about that Frances Fisher either. She sounds like a harmless lady, even if she's a bit of a loony leftie. She's not about to bring you down, J. She'd soon realise she's got Team Coriol to reckon with!'

Jason refilled their glasses and clinked his with hers. 'Here's to Team Coriol!' he toasted.

'You know,' Sharlotte smiled, 'the girls were talking about holiday plans this evening and I think it's about time we had a family holiday ourselves. Maybe we should head off to Portugal for some warmer weather and waves and have a bit of a refresh! I reckon we need to have some fun and enjoy the moment and spend time with the kids and give ourselves a break. We've all deserved it!'

'That's not actually a bad idea at all,' Jason agreed. 'We could use it as a little leverage with the kids too. But is this just the drink talking, Shar?'

'Yeah probably! So you better find something and book it quick, before I change my mind!'

With his balance restored and his self-confidence back intact after a wonderful weekend with the family and a last-minute surfing holiday booked for the end of the month, Jason was ready for the SUI meeting with Hayley when it came round. Although Frances had offered to attend with him, for moral support,

Jason politely declined her offer, wanting instead to assert his reawakened independence and professional authority. He explained to Frances that he'd managed to get some clarity over the weekend and was confident that Hayley would understand the terrible event for what it was, an unavoidable outcome in a case of despair and desperation, which, no matter how competent the practitioner, unfortunately could not have been averted by mental health services.

Fortunately never having been called to a Serious and Untoward Incident investigation before, Jason didn't know what to expect. It seemed like Hayley had played it down but he wondered whether in fact this might all be new to her too, bearing in mind she only qualified a few years ago. Not enough time for something drastic to happen. The meeting was being chaired by one of Jason's old colleagues from his drug and alcohol days. Cathy Faulkner was doing well for herself. She had recently been promoted to the position of Quality and Governance Lead across the whole organisation and she was wearing a nice suit to go with the role. She was still her friendly self though, thank goodness, and she made an effort to put both Jason and Hayley at ease, although Hayley appeared comfortable enough already. Jason had had only vague dealings with the Care Group service manager, Curtis Bowers, who was, as usual, immaculately presented. With Hayley in her own swish skirt suit and powerful navy heels, Jason, in his chinos and sweater, felt the odd one out and was annoyed with himself for not thinking to dress for the occasion.

Cathy went through the facts of the case and Hayley explained the changes they had made to the pathway, in order to manage the increasing referrals and growing waiting lists. She then passed over to Jason to describe the Zen Psyonics group programme. Jason explained how Mandy had been repeatedly referred and discharged from the service and how each time, she had failed to engage with what the service was offering. They all acknowledged that this was very common in secondary mental healthcare and that if patients didn't feel able to meet the expectations of the pathway, they would be discharged from the service but always welcome to return as soon as they were willing to fulfil the commitment required of them. Hayley produced a patient information leaflet stating exactly that. Curtis wanted to know about the specifics of Mandy's situation. He asked Jason whether he could have met with Mandy for her discharge meeting the same day, after the Zen Psyonics session, but Jason explained that he was fully booked and therefore unable to. He added that although he didn't complete a risk assessment that day, Mandy was well known to him and there was nothing about her presentation that day which suggested what she was about to go on and do. Of course, if there had been, he would have updated the risk assessment, re-arranged his schedule, and invited her in for the discharge meeting. The other three acknowledged that this was reasonable and that nobody, unfortunately, had a crystal ball.

Jason was beginning to relax, sensing that the meeting was coming to a conclusion, when Cathy pulled a piece of folded paper from an envelope.

'This will be part of a separate conversation,' Cathy said, 'but this letter came through only yesterday so we thought we'd take the opportunity to ask you about it today, in case it adds anything to our report. It's a complaint from someone called Paula Vale, another patient in the same Zen Psyonics group as Mandy. I appreciate you weren't necessarily expecting this, so please don't feel like you need to respond right now,' she stalled and handed the paper to Jason, giving him the nod to go ahead and read it.

Dear sir/madam,
Complaint regarding Zen Psyonics group programme and associated death of patient, Mandy Harper
I am writing to express my serious concerns about the Zen Psyonics programme currently being offered in the secondary mental healthcare pathway. I myself was offered a place on the group programme after being referred by oncology services, due to suicidal feelings related to my recent cancer diagnosis and treatment. Whilst I was not sure that

this programme was suitable for me, with it being largely for people who have been given a diagnosis of personality disorder, I decided to take up the offer as I was told there was nothing else available.

I am still attending the group programme, although I had to change groups halfway through, due to the session times clashing with my radiotherapy treatment. I would therefore like to emphasise that my complaint is about Zen Psyonics as practiced in the first group I attended, which was facilitated by Jason Coriol.

I was present at the session where Mandy was discharged due to having been more than fifteen minutes late. Whilst I appreciate the need for commitment, for patients to get the most out of the programme, I am firmly of the opinion that there should be a degree of flexibility when interpreting the rules. To do otherwise is not only lacking in compassion but actually dangerous. I believe that Mandy being discharged was a factor in her suicide which occurred later that day.

I would also like to draw attention to the fact that Jason Coriol himself, as group facilitator, was over ten minutes late to the session that same day. He gave no explanation to us as a group of patients, nor, it seems, was he required to. It would appear that there is one rule for patients and another for clinicians, and that patients, who arguably are having a far more challenging time in their lives, are required to meet higher standards of engagement than clinicians. I also find it very contradictory that a group programme which is trying to teach people skills in flexibility of thought, and counteract black and white thinking, has a facilitator who doesn't appear to have any capacity of flexible thinking himself.

Finally, I would like to raise the issue of the Zen Psyonics group programme being the only therapy available to patients referred to the pathway. Zen Psyonics might be helpful for some, but not everybody. I am aware that the evidence base for Zen Psyonics is poor and that in fact, the most compelling evidence for a therapy being helpful is when there is a good therapeutic alliance. From my experience in Jason Coriol's group, I would say that his alliance with Mandy Harper was sadly lacking and I wonder whether, had he shown more compassion and more warmth to someone who was in crisis and feeling very alone, Mandy might be still with us today.

I look forward to your response.
Yours truly
Paula Vale

Jason passed the letter to Hayley.

'You're lucky if you've managed to escape letters like that so far in your career, Jason,' Cathy said gently. 'This woman's obviously very upset but personally I don't think there's anything extra in there that would make a difference to our report and recommendations.'

'Yeah, I agree,' Hayley said, even though she couldn't possibly have finished reading the letter yet, unless she was a super-fast skim reader. 'That therapeutic alliance thing gets trotted out, doesn't it? But it's just random luck whether you're going to get on with the person you're seeing. We can't match patients up with clinicians as if we're a dating agency. I think what happened here is that Mandy and Paula joined forces and they had it in for Jason anyway. Neither of them were ever going to be satisfied with what was on offer. They shouldn't even have been referred. And it's really clear that Mandy's death was about what was going on in her own life, nothing to do with Zen Psyonics. What group is Paula in now, Jason?'

'Frances Fisher's.'

There were a few eye rolls. 'Ah, Frances,' Curtis said. 'Hasn't she retired yet? You'd think she would have been long gone, the way she's always complaining about how we do things in mental health services. Some people just like to always have something to complain about, I suppose. She might have even been feeding all this stuff to Paula, for all we know.'

From wanting to be vaporised into an alternate universe, Jason felt almost miraculously recovered, in the space of just a few minutes, finding it quite hard to believe how he had been given this implicit vote of confidence. He hadn't needed a suit after all. His colleagues respected him whatever he was wearing.

Somatic Mind Body Therapy

Somatic Mind Body Therapy (SMBT) is a therapeutic method tailored for addressing trauma and attachment difficulties. It embraces the body as a crucial source of information, guiding the process of resourcing, accessing and processing challenging, traumatic and developmental experiences. SMBT adopts a comprehensive approach that encompasses somatic, emotional and cognitive dimensions for processing and integration.

Within SMBT, clients can identify and transform ingrained physical and psychological patterns that hinder optimal functioning and overall well-being. SMBT proves beneficial in addressing dysregulated emotions and behaviours and the various impacts of trauma, as well as the constraining belief systems associated with developmental issues.

An essential aspect of SMBT is assisting clients in nurturing their strengths while introducing sufficient challenges to stimulate growth, fostering enduring change and promoting overall well-being.

SMBT is underpinned by research in physiology, neuroscience, psychology and sociology. It has a strong evidence base and is a well-developed approach with decades of success in the treatment of a range of mental health problems.

28

In the final episode of the most recent series of *Team of One*, conditions were getting really tough. Paula had eked the show out for as long as possible, using it as a kind of time-off from the grim reality of her situation, as advised by Jose, the winner of series two, in the book he wrote on wilderness survival. The long term aspect was important. Jose's winning approach had been to eschew all ideas of being rescued and settle in to the challenge as if it was going to be for the rest of his life. This is what Paula identified with. The fact that he was asking, *what if you can't escape? What if you have to carry on? What if there's no way out, other than death itself?* Paula was at the point now where her body was clearly beginning to break down. The final dose of chemotherapy had delivered such horrendous effects where her hands and feet were so sore she struggled to do most practical tasks with her hands and she certainly could no longer go for her restorative walks in the forest as her feet were so painful. It seemed the only respite left was *Team of One*.

With each series, as the number of people remaining dwindled to three or four, Paula would find herself wanting them all to win. After more than two months out there, and with winter set in and not enough food, the three contestants left in series nine were all tired. Paula was fascinated by how they commented on their physical decline, how they were getting weaker every day, but how in their *heads*, they had more push to keep going. The last woman standing still had the energy to *play* and filmed herself having a snowball fight, with herself. Half way in to the episode, the first of the three, Johnny, radioed to be rescued. From this point on, Paula pretty much wept her way through, beyond the closing credits. She was deeply affected by so many of their observations, having thought and said and asked similar to herself over the last long nine months. *How many days can this go on?...I'm doing everything I can to address everything I can...I'm frickin exhausted. It's too much... How much is enough?* They were all ravaged by the contest and so was she by her own. There was comfort to be had in that, but she also felt sorry for herself, seeing their quest for survival as a trial entirely different to her own. They all had a firm eye on an imagined, wonderful future, be it enriched by the prize money or not. Either way they had more big dreams and bold plans. *I have a long life ahead of me and now I have such clarity in who I am and what I'm meant to do on this earth and who I want by my side,* Johnny shared in his exit interview. *My body has reached a limit and this is how I want my story to end.* Lucky you, Johnny, Paula thought sadly. *I did my dream here and now I'm ready for the next dream,* Michelle, the last woman standing, joyously said to the camera. Lucky you too, Michelle. She shared with them of course, the undeniable fact that neither she nor they knew what was going to happen next in their lives, but for Paula there was the very real statistical probability of the cancer coming back.

Paula sobbed for Mandy too, in the parts where the three contestants enthused movingly about the people in their lives. It occurred to Paula that even though these people were absolutely on their own for however long they could stand during the series, along with most other contestants, the three carried with them a whole team of people in their hearts, people they would return to just as soon as they left the show. Johnny declared his reason for leaving, that *life is just better being surrounded by people who love you*, and he decided to choose that over the prize money. *It's time for me to just be there for the people that need me, my friends and my family,* Michelle said. It was Jose who really captured it, when he explained that *being in survival mode amplifies the need for family and friends. When you're isolated, all your longing for your family and friends just intensifies so much.* They all seemed to have people back home who loved and cared about them. How would any of them have fared, if they, like Mandy, had no-one left in their hearts to sustain them? If even the most precarious of connections had been brutally ripped from their souls?

A shoddy and frankly inadequate response had been sent to Paula following her complaint. It was the briefest of letters and in no way did any justice whatsoever to the seriousness of the matter. A few lines told her that her complaint had been investigated and that the team had *added some learning events for staff in future to prevent it happening again.* It said absolutely nothing to address her points about there being nothing else other than Zen Psyonics available for people referred to the pathway, that the rules for patients were unduly strict and for clinicians non-existent, and that the use of Zen Psyonics itself was questionable. Everything had just been brushed under the carpet, and all this said to Paula was that the organisation privileged its reputation over the care of patients, and that the delivery of psychological therapies was nothing more than a charade.

The letter was the first thing Paula talked about in her discharge meeting with Frances a few weeks later. She was in the strange position of both the Zen Psyonics group coming to an end and her cancer treatment also, *for now,* nearly finished. They were actually in a real room together, as it would have been impossible for Paula to get back home from her radiotherapy appointment in time to log on to a virtual meeting, whereas the trip from the hospital to the health centre only took ten minutes. Frances was solidly the same, no different from her virtual self. Paula wasn't surprised. She felt this woman was so authentic and genuine that she could imagine putting her in any environment and she would be the same. Like Theseus's ship, she might even have all her parts replaced, piece by piece, and she would still be the same solid vessel.

Frances held the letter, along with Paula's complaint, and took time to read them both.

'I applaud you for making the complaint in the first place. It must be quite difficult for you to muster up the energy for anything much, with all you've been through, though I can see that your compassion and concern for Mandy compelled you to write it, energy or no energy,' Frances approved. 'I'm sorry it's such a meagre response. Is there anything you'd like me to do? Could I support you in pursuing it further? Do you want to take it to the health service ombudsman?'

'No, it's okay,' Paula sighed. 'I know we talked about all this last time. I don't imagine it would change anything. Maybe that's defeatist but I don't think I've got more energy for this and maybe there are other ways for me to honour Mandy.'

Paula thought about how she had sobbed for Mandy. 'You know I cried my way through the last episode of *Team of One* thinking of her. Just the stark contrast of those contestants going back to loving friends and families. It's not just that though. It made me think about how much easier it might be when they're actually there, isolated in the wilderness, when there isn't someone watching their every move and criticising them. They film what they want to film. They select what gets performed and judged. They know the parameters of what they've got and it's just them and the beasts and the land and the weather. But back in real life, there's a whole load of shit affecting our choices and resources. A whole load of shit telling us what to think and how to feel. I just think Jason didn't *accept* her and who knows? Maybe that was the story of her life. Never to be accepted. And my main takeaway from Zen Psyonics, and the whole therapy industry for all I know, is *you are not acceptable in your current form and we will help you make yourself into an acceptable human being.* Social fucking control. As if schools aren't bad enough!'

Paula shook her head, threw up her hands and rolled her eyes and noticed that Frances was smiling at her, whereupon she frowned back.

'There's so much in what you've said. I agree with a lot of it, not that it matters whether I agree or not. Some of it I've been saying myself for years, not that anyone has listened much. I think you're spot on about the therapy industry. It *is* a form of social control, in my eyes, anyway.'

'So what on earth are you doing working in it then, if you don't want to be in the business of social control?' Paula asked, having fully riled herself up now.

Frances took a long while before she responded. 'Well, that's a question I have asked myself many times over the years. And the answer is complicated and changeable and I wouldn't want to bore you with a performance on the soap box of Frances Fisher. But I guess the briefest way I can explain it is that I never trained as a therapist. I'm a psychologist. And my job is to help people work out what's going wrong in their lives and to see if there's something they can do about it, which will depend on the powers and resources available to them. It's nothing fancy. There is no jargon. It's about three things really. Providing comfort, clarification and encouragement. The clarification part might be where being a psychologist is put to most use, the bit about working out what's going wrong in someone's life. To develop *outsight*, to realise that much of what is going wrong in someone's life is not to do with something inside of them, but things which are out there in the world. But there are a lot of psychologists and therapists who are more likely to focus on the individual, like you said about making someone into an acceptable human being. And you know, the comfort and encouragement, *that* comes from all sorts of places. That's why it doesn't challenge my integrity too much to run the Zen Psyonics groups, because I know that the people in the group will give comfort and encouragement to each other. Which is another reason why what happened to Mandy is so sad and so tragic. The way I see it, we suffer pain because we do damage to each other, and we'll carry on suffering pain as long as we continue to do the damage. The way to reduce distress is for us to take care of the world and the other people in it, not to *treat* them.'

Paula was overcome with sadness, for Mandy mainly, though also for the world, and for herself, and all people everywhere feeling alone and scared and deficient and unacceptable.

'God, do you think there's something wrong with me? Do you think I was an appropriate referral after all?' Paula cried, sniffing back her runny nose and wiping her eyes.

'There's absolutely nothing wrong with you! Rejoice for you are human!' Frances declared. 'But you know, it is important to make sure you try to surround yourself by like-minded people, to at least take the edge off feeling so alone. I forgot to say that. The fourth ingredient for getting by in life. The importance of solidarity. But I probably already said it in the group, didn't I?' Paula nodded. 'It reminds me, all that talk of *Team of One* and the idea that those contestants weren't on their own after all, because they had internalised others along with them for the ride. That's something I talk about sometimes with people who are referred to me, often at the end, when they're going to be discharged. I explain how many people referred to mental health services have been on the receiving end of an *abuse team*. They've sadly experienced many people in their lives who have been horribly abusive to them and struggle to recall any exceptions to that. But hopefully, through our conversations we *do* uncover some important exceptions and we spend a bit of time at the end building a *supporting team* that the person can take with them back out into the world after they've been discharged. So it's a bit like how you described what the contestants on Team of One were doing. They were carrying those people with them. I mean in this context, you might just think that's disingenuous sugaring of the pill but people do seem to appreciate it. They can have anyone on the team, dead people, alive people, celebrities, old teachers, fictional characters, anyone they want. Nobody's ever had a tree before, but you could have a tree, I guess, if that seemed like a good idea!'

Paula smiled at the suggestion. 'Yes, I'd definitely have a tree. I know exactly the one I'd have and it wouldn't require me to be anything other than myself! And I'd have Mandy too.'

'What role would Mandy perform? What qualifies her to be on the team?' Frances asked.

'Because she would have good suggestions about what to do to feel better. She would feed me the best TV programmes to watch when I'm totally wiped out and she would hold up a sign saying *permission to be you* every time I told someone to fuck off for saying stupid insensitive things!' *Hmmm, a tree and a dead person*, Paula pondered. 'Mmmm, I can see how it *might* be helpful to some people,' she said politely, but unconvinced.

'If it's not, chuck it out!' Frances said. 'Maybe it's too much of a stretch for some people and they need to actually have that real team around them, holding the hope that they can get through this. Maybe it wouldn't have worked for Mandy either. I remember going to a talk with a famous Buddhist monk years ago. At the end, questions were invited from the audience. The woman next to me got up and talked about how she found mindfulness helpful and she practised daily. But she said that when she was at her most low, the time she needed it most, it was no use to her. She just couldn't do it. The monk replied with an analogy, explaining how if you throw a stone in the water, it will sink. But if you throw a stone in a boat which is floating on the water, the stone will float too. So you need the boat, or Sangha, which is their word for community. When you're at your most vulnerable, you need the community in order to survive. Someone who's feeling stronger can hold the hope and carry the load. And I guess we all take it in turns, whenever we can. It's just another story about solidarity.'

'What about you?' Paula asked.

'What about me?'

'I think I'd have you on my nurturing team. To hold the hope, keep the boat afloat, walk alongside me, stop me looking too far down into the abyss, tell me stories I can chuck away.'

'I think you're cured!' Frances joked.

Thought Void Therapy

TVT® - Thought Void Therapy® - introduces a novel model of psychological therapy that seamlessly aligns with contemporary understanding in neuroscience. This approach is not only swift, efficient and typically permanent but also doesn't necessitate clients to engage in sensorimotor activities. It simply works.

Grounded in neuroscience research, TVT recognises the absence of conscious control over impulses due to a 'thought void,' where the brain initiates a response before conscious awareness. Unlike conventional therapies that aim to access the anxiety-triggering amygdala through conscious processes, TVT operates from the early stages of the brain, intervening before the amygdala even receives the message.

Widely adopted across the globe, TVT is employed by psychologists, hypnotherapists, medical practitioners, psychiatrists, counsellors and various other professionals. The only challenge associated with TVT is its seemingly too-good-to-be-true nature, particularly for those with extensive experience in psychology. The notion that altering thought patterns in the brain requires a substantial amount of time, if at all possible, used to be true. However, this was primarily because older therapies focused on changing thoughts at the 'thinking end,' where TVT changes thoughts at the point they are generated, offering a more direct and efficient approach to instigating lasting change in thought patterns.

29

All eight of them were sitting round the boardroom table, some eating their lunch, others helping themselves to the remains of the tea or coffee left over from the previous team's meeting. Hayley had not appeared yet but nobody seemed in any hurry to go and find her. It was such a treat to have a few moments of down time. Vicky, Jess, Sophie and Steve were chatting passionately about *Team of One*, exchanging opinions on which were their favourite series and who were their favourite contestants. Jason was either pretending, or actually was engrossed in something else on his phone. Frances, Sharon and Bob were sharing their plans for Christmas.

Hayley breezed in, clutching a bunch of papers and her laptop, apologising for keeping everyone waiting. She plugged in and logged on, and after a quick sup on her water bottle, immediately got down to business.

'Who would've thought we'd be this far along? Well done team!' she praised everyone, nodding at the graph she had projected onto the wall, showing the number of people having completed the latest round of groups. 'One hundred people completing an evidence-based therapy and discharged in under six months. That's an achievement to be proud of!' she beamed.

'Except it wasn't actually a hundred, was it?' Frances pointed to the graph. 'Twenty four of those, or nearly a quarter, either didn't ever show or dropped out.'

'But that's normal with any therapy, isn't it? And look at how it compares with the figures for the last two years,' Hayley argued.

'Yes, I think average drop-out rates are around thirty per cent for psychological therapies generally, so you could say we've done better than average, if we're just looking at the completion rate,' said Frances. 'But I was just pointing out that it wasn't a hundred people who completed an evidence-based therapy. And of course, what does that actually mean in real terms? Are those people cured now, never to return? And what about the twenty-four. How are *they* now?'

'Obviously there's all sorts of extra data that we can gather but the purpose of *this* meeting,' Hayley had the manner of a cat raising its spine, ready for a fight, 'is to celebrate what we've achieved and look at what we need to do next.'

Frances held off further comments for the time being, knowing it was prudent to allow Hayley to use some of her huge reserves of energy by announcing her plans for the future. In all likelihood, she would at some point tire herself out.

The next graph showed in stark terms how even functioning at the rate they were, the waiting list was building, due in part to the fact that referrals were outpacing the movement of people through the groups. But referrals were also increasing. It was almost as if clinicians in the team had decided that they themselves were useless and had nothing to offer to people in distress, not even listening, and so the only place to direct people was towards Zen Psyonics. Hayley showed the basic maths that if the team carried on as they were, they would be back in the same position, or possibly an even worse position than they were when they agreed to the larger roll out of the groups.

'So, it's precisely as I predicted, Hayley, back in that meeting six months ago. I said this wasn't going to help waiting times. That much was obvious. There's also the equally important question of whether the groups have actually helped people feel any better. I imagine you've got some more nice graphs there showing how people's scores have improved.'

'I have actually, Frances, right here,' Hayley said, bringing up her next graph. 'And you can see that there's been a significant improvement for the vast majority of those who attended our groups.'

'Well I'm not going to go over old ground about outcome measures with you again, Hayley, but I'd caution against setting too much store by those results. We'd at least need follow-up data in a year's time to make a better judgement on how much ZP makes a difference to people's lives. Because if even half the people who completed the programme are getting referred back to our service a year or even two years afterwards, then we're going to be needing a whole load of extra groups for all those people coming back!'

Frances could see that Hayley was beginning to lose her patience. She imagined the switch being flipped and Hayley suddenly shouting, *why don't you just fuck off and retire, you silly old bag!* But Hayley had some useful skills, one being composure, which was probably how she had got to where she was in such a short space of time. Most people who had worked in the health service for even just a few years were likely to have blown their stack at least once over something or someone, after one stress too many tipped them over the edge.

'What do you suggest then, Frances?' Hayley confronted her. 'I'm getting really tired of your constant negativity, your criticising, nit-picking, lording it over everyone as if you know better than the rest of us! We're supposed to be a team! We're supposed to be supporting each other, helping each other out. You're just constantly rubbishing everything we're trying to achieve.' She looked close to tears.

Frances realised that it was she herself who was the cat, arching her back. A cheetah in fact. And that whilst she might not be as fast as this young springbok, her guile was enough. Hayley had clearly tired herself out and Frances was within easy reach of the kill if she wanted. She felt slightly ashamed thinking that. Where were the adults in the room? Everyone else was silent.

'I at least agree with you on one thing, Hayley. Yes, we *are* supposed to be a team. But quite honestly, it's been a very very long time since I've felt part of this team. *Your* team. You rarely give me any positive feedback. The only time you say anything remotely encouraging is when you're trying to get me on side, to get me to do what you want me to do. You don't even try to listen to what I have to say. Believe me, I don't say any of it simply because I want to be difficult. I say it because I'm fed up with the lies and the nonsense that gets trotted out in the name of patient care and being told to do things by people who have no idea what they're talking about. I'm fed up of people either believing, or pretending they believe that psychological therapies are these powerful things that transform people's lives, or that if we only train up in the latest product, we'll make the necessary breakthroughs, because the old ways were obviously faulty. All that jargon. All those models. People who love all that might have qualities that make them great technicians, but those are the same qualities which make them lousy with human beings. I'm fed up of watching people being given an illusion of a cure, when in fact there's a revolving door. And I'm fed up of people being seen as sick and in need of treatment, when the reality is that the world is sick and needs diagnosing. This *organisation* is sick and needs diagnosing! Whatever happened to providing comfort pure and simple? But as far as I'm aware, with the exception of a few kind souls, there's barely anyone here who seems to take any of this seriously, so I'm on my own. I don't *feel* part of this team. I'm in a bloody team of one!'

Both Frances and Hayley were very red-faced now. Hayley was probably fine and would bounce back up in a few seconds but Frances knew she would need considerably longer to recover from almost giving herself a heart attack.

'I'm sorry you've felt like that, Frances,' Vicky eventually broke the silence. 'I often don't understand a lot of what you're talking about, but I've always valued you being in the team. And you do make me think about things differently sometimes. I've even stolen a few of your tricks to use in my own work and I appreciate how you give us all permission to do things our own way if somebody else's way doesn't work. I've been around a while myself, like you, and I know what you mean about getting tired of it all. I had no idea you were feeling so isolated. Obviously I hear you talking about all your ideas but you always come across as so strong. Like you could easily be in *Team of One* and win that show! Which, by the way, I know it annoys you Jason, but I really do recommend you watch it. Maybe you two should apply to the show and pit yourselves against each other. You too for that matter, Hayley!'

The tension in the room lifted. 'Thank God for you, Vicky, lightening the mood,' Frances said.

'I'll put my application in for the show if Frances and Hayley agree to come for some healing and bonding surfing with me,' Jason joked.

'Can we all come?' Jess piped up. 'It might do us all the world of good. I actually mean that!' Jason looked pleased as Jess continued. 'I'd like to say my bit, if that's okay. It's great if we can still joke with each other but is there a danger that we brush some really important things under the carpet? I don't want to reignite the fire but I also don't want to ignore what's been said.' Everyone was listening intently to her, more so because she herself tended to listen more and talk less, so when she did say something, it was often unexpected. Also, being one of only two support workers in the group of ZP facilitators, she didn't have that authority of a professional background, but she certainly had the clarity and confidence to hold her own. 'I've only been here less than a year and even *I* sometimes get ground down by it all. I'm pleased to be involved in delivering the ZP groups because I'm learning such a lot. But even though I don't have all that knowledge about psychology and statistics and all that, I know just from working with people and *being with* people that something like ZP isn't always going to work and that it's a case of working out with each person what's going to be helpful. I genuinely think that going surfing with some of the people on my caseload *would* be helpful! Some of them have so little fun in their lives, no money to go for a day trip, let alone a holiday! And we think ZP is going to fix them? And I also don't think it's right to have such strict rules. I'm not wanting you to feel blamed about Mandy, Jason. It might not have made a difference anyway, but I think it works better when we make our own judgements instead of following somebody else's rules.' Jess stopped and glanced around the room, waiting for a response. Frances smiled her warmest, heartiest smile, closing her eyes momentarily to fully enjoy the solace she was feeling in her heart. She wanted to hug her. 'By the way,' Jess continued. 'I don't have any suggestions for what we do about the waiting lists, Hayley. It's just really difficult, isn't it? But can't we just say that? Isn't that more honest?'

Frances wasn't sure what might have been going through people's minds, but it seemed that all the energy had gone from the room, especially her own, and feeling that she'd definitely said her piece, and that Jess in fact had said it even better, she decided not to comment further. Hayley too was sitting twizzling her hair, surveying the room as if waiting for others to speak. Bob, the other support worker, stood up, looking like he was about to creep through a pile of dead bodies, and quietly gave his apologies, saying he needed to leave early for a patient visit.

Finally Vicky spoke up. 'Would it be helpful if we all reconvened in a couple of weeks after we've had time to digest the data and have a think about things? We could also talk about it a bit more in our Covision meetings.'

Apparently relived, everyone agreed.

The obituary was published in Frances's in-house professional journal. It was brief and written by her dear colleague, Margaret, who had retired only six months previously. It told the story of how Frances had always been fascinated by human beings and nurtured her passion initially through her undergraduate degree in anthropology, completing her thesis on the rise of spirituality in relation to the rise of neoliberalism, drawing on Foucault's *technologies of the self*. She had spent the early part of her career working as a research assistant in the national Alcohol, Drugs, Gambling and Addiction Research Group. She had then gone on to train in clinical psychology and was an honorary lecturer at four universities, teaching courses on research methodology and social materialist psychology. Margaret wrote about Frances' legacy of more than fifty publications in the form of book chapters and peer-reviewed articles, as well as countless students, colleagues and patients who benefited from her expertise and gentle, supportive mentoring. There was the familiar obituary style of the final paragraph, stating that: Frances died suddenly of a heart attack, whilst at work. She leaves behind her husband,

David, son Ben and daughter Rosa, extended family and many friends. Margaret concluded, I am very grateful to have had her friendship for almost 20 years and will really miss that familiar twinkle in her eye.

At the funeral, David and Margaret embraced and cried and said how they felt they had been robbed. How unfair life was, just as Frances could see the door leading to retirement getting ever closer. But they were also able to smile at their memory of her.

'You know, David,' Margaret held his arm. 'If she was somehow able to be here, if her spirit were to visit us, she would be telling us that story about the lost horse. She would be smirking at us saying, aren't I the lucky one? A quick, relatively painless discharge from this planet. I won't ever know the pain of arthritis or immobility, the inconsolable loss of loved ones, the gruelling slog of cancer treatment or the simple, slow, shrinking of the world through old age or dementia. I won't ever have to see any more fires burn out of control or homes being washed away or horrific wars being fought. I've had a lucky escape, she would say, David.'

Zen Psyonics

Zen Psyonics (ZP) was originally developed as a treatment for people with substance abuse issues and initially included immersive surf therapy experiences which aimed to engage and energise clients, thus enabling them to be more open and receptive to the other aspects of behaviour change practices, including mindfulness and CBT. Zen Psyonics therefore offered a far more holistic approach to human wellbeing and crucially addressed the need to integrate mind and body, along with science and fun.

Zen Psyonics was subsequently honed and refined to incorporate other mind-body practices, meaning that many different forms of exercise could be substituted for surfing, making it more accessible to wider populations and a wide range of mental health problems.

Zen Psyonics is the distillation of various therapeutic practices and is increasingly delivered in group formats. A typical ninety minute ZP session involves a careful blending of four elements: Zen meditational practice, communications exercises, physical activity and selected thought restructuring exercises drawn from cognitive therapy.

ZP is grounded in evidence-based therapy, built on the latest neuroscience and bio-feedback techniques and is practiced widely throughout the world.

Epilogue

The tide was at its lowest and exposed the huge stretch of beach which was virtually empty. Patches of water on the sand reflected the orange and pink glow in the afternoon sky and the sea was an inky black. It had taken Alexander an age to paddle out, but that had been a great way to get warm. There had been a brisk wind blowing across the beach when he set out but sitting on his board now, in full winter kit, he felt toasty. And stoked. This was his new favourite surf spot by far. Looking back towards the land he could see the assorted houses, lights already twinkling along the curve of the bay. To the left, the bulge of Carn Lusow framed the cemetery overlooking the sea below and standing on its own, nearby, was the surfer's dream house, with its own steps winding through the cliffs to the rocky beach.

Two years ago, Alexander couldn't have imagined being quite so blessed as he was now. All those months of agony with his broken ankle and the utter frustration of not even being able to walk along the beach, let alone stand on a surf board. The terrible tragedy of lovely, loyal Buddha being run over right outside his house, leaving him totally bereft. And the final knife into his chest of that stupid, clueless judge's ruling. He had never felt so low. But look at him now! He was a perfect example of the resilience and fortitude of the human spirit. He couldn't imagine a better place to be surfing, looking out over a beautiful bay, with his own home nestling in the hills nearby, watching over him. It was a modest dwelling. He had no need for vast acreage which he had no time or interest in maintaining. But it was very high spec, with its own infinity pool and a fantastic roof terrace with the best views, arguably, in the world. And he should know, in his time having seen some incredible ones in some of the most heavenly holiday destinations. Locals referred to his home as *The White House*, but the name Alexander had carved in slate, by the electronic gates opening onto his driveway, was *The Retreat*. So often these days he felt in a state of bliss, as if he was permanently on retreat. Clemmie Service had done him a favour after all. Far from the court case being bad for business, it only served to increase interest in Zen Psyonics and of course, more people than not, wanted to get the pure, original version of it. From him, the creator.

There was no line-up today. Anyone that had been out earlier had long gone, making their way home for tea. So Alexander had the sea all to himself. He felt serene and peaceful in the water and was ready for his last wave of the day, the perfect one that he could see would be on him in less than a minute. He turned his board and felt the sea beneath him come alive. The roar of the wave grew louder and he only needed to make a few powerful strokes before he popped up and was carried along on the face of it, feeling the freezing water spray his face. He was no longer that little boy enjoying the sea alongside his father and his refrain had changed. It was not simply the waves he had conquered. He felt as if he was king of the world.

ACKNOWLEDGEMENTS

Thanks to everyone who read and commented on early drafts: Martin Callaghan, John Cromby, Biza Stenfert Kroese, Conor McMullin and Monica Priest. Special thanks to George Callaghan, my reader and discussant the whole way through, and Nelson Priest for helping negotiate the plot jams. Thanks to my wonderful friends in the Midlands Psychology Group (www.midpsy.uk) for keeping me going at desperate times, and to Paul Moloney, the true founder of Zen Psyonics, for better or for worse. Thanks to James Osborn, my wonderful clinical supervisor, whose ideas and wisdom feature in this book, and who also helped me survive the NHS for as long as possible. And to Ben Donner at Egalitarian Publishing and Craig Newnes, possibly the most extraordinary, audacious, maverick editor a writer could hope to meet.

Read more books from Egalitarian Publishing

www.egalitarianpublishing.com

Psychobabble and Snake Oil
by Henry Bladon and Marcel Herms

This book is a collection of poems about mental health in collaboration with the artwork of Dutch artist Marcel Herms. The collection seeks to highlight the hyperbole that has always existed in psychiatry. It also looks at the nature of suffering and offers thoughts and reflections on a number of experiences.

Cats, Water & Concrete
by Ruth and Ken Snowden

This collection of poetry, prose and illustrations is about lots of things, but mainly about living and working. It is also about the intriguing lives of cats.

Withdrawal from Prescribed Psychotropic Drugs
by Peter Lehmann & Craig Newnes (eds)

This volume presents a collaboration of users and survivors of psychiatry (ex-patients), professionals, researchers, lawyers, and academics around the world committed to helping people understand the potential harm (including drug dependence) that prescribed psychotropic drugs can cause and how to safely reduce or stop taking them.

Psychomusicology
by Cemil Egili & Craig Newnes (eds)

Via a selection of musical perspectives, theory and personal stories this edited collection demonstrates how music in its varying forms and styles, and the myriad of intersecting ways in which we engage with it, can have great therapeutic value and catharsis, in our lives.

La Bergerie
by Craig Newnes

La Bergerie, set in the stunning back drop of the Aude, Corbieres, tells a compelling cross-generational tale of love and war. As the stories of diverse characters intertwine, the plot moves between the horrors of the concentration camps of the 1940s through to modern day life and loves. We get to know Izaak, Rebecca, Clara, Michel, Alex and Kate and travel with them over several decades. A novel that is both heart-warming and devastating.

The Journal of Critical Psychology, Counselling and Psychotherapy
by Egalitarian Publishing

The Journal of Critical Psychology, Counselling and Psychotherapy (JCPCP), is a peer-reviewed journal which values personal experience above professional boundaries and doctrinal jargon. It provides a forum for ideas, experience and views of people working in the psychological world and those who use psychotherapy or receive psychiatric services. The journal encourages a critical, reflexive view of psychology and counselling and is a constant challenge to orthodoxy.

Our contributors reflect on their work and experiences in therapy, in relationships and in institutions. The journal embraces philosophical, radical and scientific perspectives in its analysis of psychological, psychiatric and psychotherapeutic systems. With a following wind, it will sometimes make you laugh out loud.

BV - #0072 - 230125 - C0 - 197/132/16 - PB - 9781838063641 - Matt Lamination